ENDURANCE TEST

Amanda Hall

ENDURANCE TEST

Published by Lulu.com

ISBN 978-0-557-29689-7

First Edition

To

Falko and Lorna Schilling

ACKNOWLEDGMENTS

The author wishes to acknowledge Editor Christine Yurick. The first chapter of ENDURANCE TEST appeared in the Winter 2008 issue of *Think Journal*.

ENDURANCE TEST

A wounded deer leaps highest,
I've heard the hunter tell...
—Emily Dickinson

1

One foot slammed down on the pavement, sending painful shock waves up a tightened calf. The other foot moved up, out and ahead of the other, making contact with the pavement and jarring the heel.

His willpower dissolved into the forward motion of his thighs. The hard masses of muscle burned, fulfilling their purpose. He did not command the tight stretches of flesh. His flesh moved as if obeying its own hardened will. The tendons, the veins, the bones and the skin—they carried him forward over the pavement—past houses, automobiles, neighbors and kids—past the demanding day behind him, the twelve hours he had spent in cardiovascular rehabilitation training with recovering heart attack victims—past the endless steps and inhalations, the gulps of water and sweaty towels—past the rhythmic slap of a jumping rope and the feet which learned to skip in time with the slap.

He ran along the familiar New England road, casting it all behind him. The treads of his sneakers made brief contact with the pavement and bounced away, pausing just long enough to gain traction and spring forward in a flight over earth.

His flight was the renunciation of disease. He felt—in his pulse which beat with forceful regularity, in his measured breaths rising and falling in time with his feet, in the simultaneous tension and release of his organs operating at optimal capacity—the very thing he tried to wrest from his patients: the euphoria of health.

It was a potent drug. Thomas Rivard was an addict. Though he had gone through the motions with his clients all day, though he had spent twelve hours walking, lifting, stretching and measuring food, he could not get enough. He needed that one last adrenaline rush before quitting. Even before meeting his wife, even before taking a nap or a meal, he laced up his sneakers and flew down the road.

As he raced forward, fragments of his day's labor chased the edges of his subconscious like a pursuer.

"Dr. Rivard, I can't stretch any further. I've never been able to touch my toes."

"Yes, yes you can. Never say never. We'll work up to it. Before you know it, you'll have your palms planted flat on the floor."

"No way!"

"Way."—

"Dr. Rivard, I'm confused about carbs. Everyone says they're the devil."

"Carbohydrates are not the devil. Everybody needs complex carbs. It's energy food."

"So I'm not going to hell if I eat mashed potatoes?"

"God, no! If that were the case, I'd be there with you. I love potatoes. Just keep your diet balanced."—

"I'm not going to lie, Dr. Rivard. I'm a couch potato. I'm here because my wife sent me. I *hate* jogging."

"We'll go through the motions together. Trust me: you'll be addicted to fitness in no time."

Thomas Rivard's feet carried him along a route he had traveled hundreds of times, over many years. The route had become so familiar, the houses and signposts so steady and fixed in his brain, he was largely unaware of his setting; he only noticed sights which differed from the ordinary.

He quickly spotted a man up ahead. From a distance, Rivard could tell the man was raking leaves. The awkward, uncertain movements of the man with the rake indicated a body unused to physical labor.

A gigantic body stood in the middle of the yard, fixed like a statue of Buddha. The man's right forearm shot out, pitching the wooden tines of the rake toward the ground with a stab. His massive arm was the only part moving, as if it functioned independently of the rest of his body. The ineffective jerk was the motion of one who wishes to resist motion; he dragged the fingers of the rake back over the earth in one long scratching stretch. The unsteady pressure of his arm did nothing but rip and tatter the leaves. Wide swathes of torn brown fragments marked the evidence of his exertion.

Rivard came up quickly on the man. It was his neighbor Stanley Humphries. The owner of the local hardware store had lived on the same street for nearly thirty years.

Rivard ran by and nodded at the man. When Stanley noticed Rivard he stopped moving and leaned against his rake. The wooden fingers bent, nearly breaking. Too winded to speak, he waved at Rivard. His pudgy face emitted a kind and friendly grin.

The pavement ended. Rivard continued running down the sunless road. The soles of his shoes pounded the smooth hard surface of compacted dirt. The dirt road was frozen. Brittle leaves stuck to the sides of the road, fixed to the ground with an adhesive of frost. Rivard could see the autumn chill, he could not feel it. His blood raced quickly through his veins, bringing warmth to the very tips of his fingers and toes. He could feel his pulse throb in the center of his gut; his ears roared with hot currents of blood. Rivard quickened his pace, welcoming the rush.

The sights of decay were all around him. He looked at the sharp grey lances of bare tree limbs, braced in a lonely duel with the November twilight sky. He looked at the brown quilt of fragile leaves covering the earth, the season's glorious reds and yellows faded and eaten by dust. He heard the call of a lonely crow, summoning the coming of night.

He saw and heard these things, he saw and heard the oncoming death of the warmer season, and blasted past it, feeling a desire to spend his last ounce of energy in a battle with death—not to battle the oncoming winter, he knew that winter was inevitable—but something much greater: to resist succumbing to winter, to death and inactivity—to make his own body an organ of movement and action, and to instill in his clients the joy of vibrant life.

Rivard looked up at the crow sitting motionless on the gnarled branch of a leafless tree. The bird was silent and still, a black patch against an ever darkening sky. Suddenly, as though before his eye, Rivard saw an Italian man with deep black hair, even blacker eyes, and a huge appetite for fattening food.

The case of Leonard Torro had never ceased to bother Rivard. He had tried his hardest to change the man's course, and lost. No amount of medical counseling could alter the fate of one who chose not to hear.

"Lenny, you have got to do something about your eating habits. I don't want to hear about ER again. So much can be prevented with the proper lifestyle habits. Read me your latest food diary entry."

"Breakfast. 8:30 A.M. Coffee with cream and sugar. Extra cream. Two croissants, warmed with butter. Three sausage links, three eggs over. Fruit cup, extra sugar.

"Lunch. 10:45 A.M. Roast beef grinder with provolone, lettuce, tomato, onions and extra mayo, oil and vinegar. Salt and vinegar potato chips, large sweetened iced tea, extra sugar. Peanut butter cook—"

"Lenny, Lenny—this is exactly what I warned you against. Where are your fruits and vegetables?"

"I had some melon and pineapple, with breakfast."

"That's great, that's a great start, but I want you to go further. Try doing something here. I'm not asking you to cut out fats and protein altogether. Every human body needs fat. Instead—invert your portions. Instead of eating three-quarters fat, one-quarter lean, change your diet so that you are taking in three-quarters fruits and vegetables, one-quarter protein and fat. You need to lower your cholesterol."

"I don't know . . . Ma does a lot of the cooking. She likes to watch us eat."

"Lenny, it's your life we're talking about here. Your blood pressure and cholesterol are very high. So is your BMI. Let's do everything we can to prolong your life. The surgeons pulled you out of death once. Let's avoid going *back* to the hospital."

Rivard looked away from the crow, shaking his head. Six months after that meeting with Leonard Torro, the man had died of a massive heart attack at his mother's kitchen table.

It had been a hard lesson for Rivard at the time, and he had never quite come to grips with the realization: there is no help for those who do not care to be well. No one can force health on another. No one can force another to take his health seriously, or to treat it as a value.

This was something Rivard had grappled with, and failed to understand. He had asked himself: Why don't people take care of themselves? Don't they know how important it is, to be in proper health? Why do they treat their bodies as if they can sustain any form of abuse, as if their bodies have no special requirements, and can be subjected to any type of treatment?

After Leonard Torro's death, and an endless

succession of such questions, Rivard had gone to visit his mentor, the great heart scientist, Professor Richard Dunn.

Professor Dunn had guided Rivard through medical school. He had led the swearing of the Hippocratic Oath upon Rivard's commencement. He was ancient, accomplished and highly revered. It was said that no one knew more about the human heart than Professor Richard Dunn.

Rivard entered the Professor's office, unleashing his frustration: "I have tossed and turned in bed for months, struggling to understand. What is it *they* don't understand? Their heart is a priceless organ, and it can't take repeated abuse. How can they live with themselves, knowing what kind of pressure they're putting on their hearts?"

The Professor let out a weary chuckle, when he saw the pain in Rivard's face; the crease between the pupil's eyebrows indicated a fruitless attempt to untangle the complexities of human behavior.

"Thomas, it's the hardest part of medicine, and hits you like a hammer when you finally learn: some people simply don't want to live."

Rivard stood still, letting the words of his mentor wash over his body, flooding his ears. He was struck dumb.

Not want to live? Why would anyone who doesn't want to live seek out a doctor?

The question resounded like an echo in Rivard's brain, as he ran into the evening. He did not have an answer, and was too tired to think of one now. He filed the question away, to be pondered later.

The road had grown dark; night had fallen. Objects appeared like shadows, black shapes without definite form or color. Rivard had reached the end of his route.

He pulled a stopwatch from his pocket. He held it lightly in his right hand, while using two fingers of his left hand to locate his pulse. He found the steady throb; it beat with forceful regularity under the pads of his fingers.

He started the clock. He counted the pulse beats until the face had reached ten seconds. He quickly drew the mental calculation:

Twenty beats. Twenty multiplied by six is . . . one hundred twenty. Perfectly within my range. Perfect target heart rate.

On a normal evening, Rivard would have raced home, running back over the nine miles he had traveled in a joyful sprint for Constance. Tonight, he felt like delaying his joy.

He knew that she would be cooking something wonderful; he could picture her leaning against the kitchen countertop with a novel, looking up and catching the pan just before it boiled over. Dark brown wisps of hair would have fallen from her headband and onto her face, as she used the palms of her hands to roll meatballs. He could picture Constance and her habits so clearly: he could picture the slender curve of the back of her neck, arched forward over her reading; he could picture the way she absently fingered the stem of a wooden utensil, simultaneously running the pad of her thumb around the bowl of the spoon.

He liked to watch her when she thought no one was looking. Even in these moments, perhaps all the more in these moments, Constance was sensual. He had never known someone who could make cooking look erotic.

Rivard smiled to himself, as he set off on a brisk walk for home. Constance would be there—the slender, lovely woman of his life would be there. She would open up to him like a flood, and they would talk of their day late into the evening.

The autumn night was still. In the cold clear southern sky Orion had risen. Rivard left the country and headed back into town. The stars faded as the village lights twinkled.

Houses became regular. Cheerful porch lights beat back the night. Rivard could see the vague outline of Stanley Humphries, raking his yard up ahead. He could hear the dry scratching sound of the rake's tines pulling leaves.

It was hard to tell in the darkness, but suddenly something did not look right. Rivard squinted at the figure. He relaxed his eyeballs, letting his pupils dilate against night.

He looked down at his feet, then back at the scene. He trained his ears for sounds of movement, and heard nothing.

The moment Rivard broke into a run, the

gigantic figure collapsed. Rivard heard the weight of the body plunge into the leaves.

He sprinted forward, unconscious of dropping his stopwatch. He reached Stanley Humphries and fell down to his knees. He took a quick survey of the situation.

The man had fallen onto his side. The wooden rake had bent and broken beneath him. Rivard grimaced when he saw that several of the tines had been forced into Stanley's abdomen upon impact with the ground. He knew better than to remove them.

He called out in a loud, clear voice: "Stanley, can you hear me?"

Rivard waited for several seconds; there was no answer.

"Stanley, give me a sign that you hear me."

There was no reply.

Rivard looked for signs of breathing. He watched Stanley's chest. The normal rise and fall was absent.

He positioned his ear close to Stanley's open mouth. He could hear nothing; he did not feel a shallow jet of breath.

Rivard did not waste time. With a physician's precise, disciplined movements, he rolled Stanley's body off of the rake and onto his back.

He took Stanley's head in both hands. He gently pushed back on the forehead with one hand, and lifted Stanley's chin with the other. The loose, flabby skin of Stanley's skull was clammy and covered with sweat. In the dim light, Rivard saw the man's face as a pale patch of ghostly blue.

Rivard inhaled deeply, before placing his mouth over Stanley's mouth. He pinched Stanley's nostrils shut and exhaled steadily for two seconds.

Rivard did not have an abundance of extra breath. He gave what little breath he had. There was no question in Rivard's mind about his ability to perform CPR after running his route; the rescue function was automatic, completely involuntary. From some untapped storeroom of energy in Rivard's system, he drew reserves for the time when it was needed most. This ability to keep moving after hours of physical activity, to soar through fatigue with a pure burst of muscle and sweat, had earned Rivard a special nickname: everyone at the hospital called Rivard "Endurance." It was understood that the rehabilitation coach would never give up. He would never stop trying, when he knew life was on the line.

This mania had seized him now. There was no world beyond the man beneath him; there was no function, motive or goal beyond saving that man's life.

Rivard heard the cry of some woman on the porch; he heard the sharp slap of the screen door, and a steady stream of hysterical utterances. These sounds might have come from some other universe; they were as insignificant to him in this moment as if they had. His eyes, ears and hands were incapable of registering anything but the stimulus before him.

Rivard administered another rescue breath, and

watched for signs of circulation. There was no breathing, coughing or gasp.

Without a second's hesitation, Rivard unbuttoned Stanley's coat. He placed two stacked hands on Stanley's lower breastbone, locked his elbows, and gave thirty forceful compressions, using his body weight to effect the jump.

Stanley Humphries was a large man. Rivard was strong, and skilled, but hindered by a massive layer of fat. Rivard continued the procedure, undaunted; he continued the procedure past the point of broken ribs.

"You're going to kill him!"

The woman had emerged from the house. She had called paramedics and rushed outside in time to hear the revolting crack of her husband's ribs. She looked at Rivard hunched over Stanley, sweat pouring from his brow. She heard him grunting as he pushed on Stanley's chest:

"Blood—move! Blood—move!"

The woman was horrified: "What are you doing?!"

Rivard did not answer. He did not look up from his task. He continued the compressions, grunting his chant: "Blood—move! Blood—move!"

The woman was not used to being ignored. Mrs. Heloise Humphries was the wife of a prominent local businessman. She attended all the civic functions, and organized the Sunday afternoon socials. She was used to being adored.

Rivard's fierce concentration drove her to fury.

"Aren't you going to answer me?" She crossed her arms and tapped her foot, waiting.

Rivard did not acknowledge her presence.

"Are you sure you know what you're doing? I think you're hurting Stanley more than helping him."

Rivard took Stanley's head in his hands, placed his mouth over Stanley's mouth, and breathed out slowly. He waited for signs of life.

Stanley Humphries did not move.

Haggard, shaking, Rivard began the cycle again.

"Shouldn't you be wearing a face guard or something? God knows what diseases you're giving my husband. Do you put your mouth on everybody?"

Rivard's body was giving out. He ignored the telltale ache. He kept pressing, feeling that he would rather die than let this man fail.

"I am not fond of your obstinate attitude, Thomas. I'm not! Don't you know that I have to be comforted, in times of stress? Don't you know that I'm a victim? I can't stand the stress of this—I can't!"

Heloise began crying hysterically, sobbing into her hands.

The sound of her sobs was drowned out by the wail of an ambulance siren.

Heloise stopped crying, once no one could hear her. She watched the paramedic team descend from the van.

One of the paramedics stopped short, when he saw Rivard positioned over the victim. Bill Metcalf paused, watching Rivard struggle and grunt. He looked on in disbelief: when he had come on to his shift that evening, Rivard had just been leaving the rehabilitation ward next to the gymnasium. Bill knew that Rivard was pushing over twelve hours of intense physical exertion.

He rushed to the doctor.

"It's okay, Endurance. We've got it. We'll take over now."

Rivard looked up at Bill. Several moments passed before he recognized his friend. Unsmiling, Rivard stammered, "Seven, ten minutes tops. Watch out for the broken ribs. You'll have to page Dr. Singer. I'm through."

Bill Metcalf and his team went to work. Rivard was forgotten. He slumped over into the frozen grass.

From some far away place, the ranting of Heloise Humphries reached his ears.

"Be careful when you move him. My husband's got a bad back. My husband is allergic to penicillin. You're not going to give him penicillin, are you? That stuff will do him in."

"Don't worry, Ma'm," the voice of Bill said. "Just go back inside and get warm. We've got everything under control."

Rivard pressed his face close to the cold ground, liking the sting of the frost. It was a preferable sensation to the otherwise relentless grinding ache.

He stayed in that position for many moments, before heading home. He replayed the scene in his mind. He retraced his steps, thought over his reactions, judged his timing. He criticized his performance, evaluating its merits and flaws.

While the paramedics lifted Stanley Humphries's warm body into the ambulance, Rivard's lay like a cold limp fish on the grass. It was the spent body of a perfectionist, the body of a man who would never give up on life.

2

Bill Metcalf stood before the large grey doors at the end of the hall. He placed his hands on the cold metal bar, depressing the lever. The cool cement blocks and dim lighting of the corridor gave way to an open space of light and energy.

The bright lights of the fitness center radiated from the ceiling like miniature suns. The air in the room was warm and highly charged, as though it were infused with the sun's glowing yellow rays. Stacks of freshly laundered towels, which looked and smelled as though they might have come from an airing on the clothesline, covered the tables near the wall. A giant wall-sized mirror caught the room's reflection; it sparkled and glistened like the pristine surface of an untouched lake.

Bill absorbed the light and energy pulsing throughout the room. The exhaustion in his muscles was replaced with a liberating feeling of ease. Within moments, the gloom and dank moisture of the cold November night had seeped from the pores of his body. A sense of all-pervading sunlight blotted out the evening's gloom.

It was four o'clock in the morning. There was no sunlight to be found. The bright light and radiance emanated from fluorescent bulbs positioned in the ceiling. The energy which permeated the air came from the man in charge of the room.

Bill watched Thomas Rivard's reflection in the polished wall of glass. Rivard was poised for a disciplined flight; he sat braced against the weights of a leg press. With a winged glide, the solid cylinders of his calves and thighs tucked themselves into giant upside-down V's and collapsed into I's. The bottoms of his feet marked the abrupt edge of the sweep; his toes accented the movement, looking like dots for the I's.

Bill waved at Rivard's reflection. Rivard caught sight of Bill's giant arc in the glowing sheet of glass. He nodded at the reflection of Bill. The two men smiled at each other's likeness in the glass.

Rivard adjusted his legs and leaped from the machine. "It's about time you got here! We need to celebrate!"

Rivard clasped Bill's hand; he gave it a warm and hearty shake. Bill felt a current of the same palpable energy that filled the fitness center flow from hand to hand. The energy was concentrated in Rivard's palm; it seemed to originate from a source within his chest. The visible current traveled down his arm, animating his fingers and wrist.

Bill clasped Rivard's hand tightly, as though receiving a transfusion. A night of stressful rescue calls had ended in fatigue. With Rivard's energetic handshake, Bill felt the first invigorating rays of a brand new dawning day.

Rivard's high spirits were contagious. Bill nearly forgot the reason that he came. He was tempted to say Yes to Rivard's invitation for an early morning workout. He was tempted to throw down his bag, and throw away the concerns he had brought with him into the room.

The concerns resurfaced when Bill's eyes stopped on the equipment in the middle of the room. He said, "Tom, how long have you been here?"

"I don't know. Where else would I be?"

"Do you know what time it is?"

Rivard clutched at his wrist. He shrugged. "Sometime after two?"

"It's four o'clock in the morning."

Rivard heard Bill's answer. He did not hear Bill's agitated tone. He gathered a small stack of towels and said, "I came in early. I couldn't sleep. How could I possibly sleep, after the evening I had with Humphries?"

Speaking of the incident was like flicking on a switch.

Rivard threw down the towels. He gripped Bill's shoulders, giving them a forceful squeeze. "We did it! Goddamn it Bill, the procedure worked! If we can save a fat slob like Stan Humphries, there's nothing we can't do! I don't think I'll ever sleep again."

The flash was brief, but Bill caught it. It glinted like a blade. Bill saw that thing in Rivard's eyes that always made him feel unnerved. He blurted, "That's what I wanted to talk to you about."

Rivard noticed Bill's irregular jerk. It was something like an involuntary spasm of protest. He looked closely at his friend. "What are you talking about?"

"I came to talk about last night. It's about Stan Humphries—"

"Of course." Rivard turned back to his work, his confidence swelling. "Don't let anyone tell you there's nothing to be done. I won't believe it for a second. There's always a way. What we proved last night—between you, me and the surgeons—Billy, we can win. There's no reason for anyone to die young."

Rivard looked at Bill. Bill stood listening, not offering a response. Rivard asked, "What's wrong?" Several moments passed in silence. Anxiously, Rivard said, "Don't tell me Stanley Humphries died."

"No. Stanley Humphries didn't die. He's alive. In fact, he's doing great. He's doing better than anyone had a right to expect."

"You sound perturbed."

"No."

"You look upset at the news. Would you rather Stan had died?"

"Of course not!"

"Bill, what's the matter? You should be elated. You should be floating on a cloud. You are a success. Your team succeeded. There's a lot of power in resuscitating life."

"I'd call it luck."

Rivard let out a laugh. "Luck? What we pulled off took skill. There was nothing lucky about it. Your attitude is all wrong, and strange, coming from an EMT. We did nothing less than turn back the hands of the clock, or wind it up again, one."

"That's what I came to talk about. I'll be blunt, Tom." Bill paused. He exhaled slowly. "What's with the superhero act? Are you on drugs?"

Rivard laughed. It was a flat, unnatural sound. "Am I—am I on drugs?"

"I'm serious."

"What on Earth would make you think such a thing?"

"A bunch of the guys have been talking about it. They think you're taking speed. Mrs. Humphries said you acted like a madman last night. Something about repeating a freaky chant."

"What?" Rivard's mouth dropped open.

Bill began talking. Once he started he could not stop.

"You get hardly any sleep. We're in the business, Tom. There's no way anyone can maintain your hours without an upper—something stronger than caffeine. You work out like a maniac. Someone always sees you running. You spend all day in here, then work yourself into a frenzy out on the street. I've known you for a long time. You've always had endurance. I think you're taking fitness too seriously. I think it's become an obsession."

Rivard closed his mouth. His hands were hanging at his sides.

"There's help, Tom, if you need it. An addiction support group meets in the Sayers Conference Room on Thursdays."

Rivard looked closely at Bill's face. He looked at Bill's frowning mouth. Bill's lips were lines of parchment, colorless and dry. It looked as though the pressure of speaking had drained them of their juice. Rivard looked at the lines gathered between Bill's eyebrows and the lines streaking from the corners of his eyes. Bill's whole face was a collection of lines. Whether evidence of exhaustion, or worry, Rivard could not begin to tell.

"It's okay, Tom." Bill's voice was quiet and gentle; he used a tone reserved for children. "I've seen it happen to doctors. Admitting you have a problem is the first step. There are people who can help. There's nothing to be ashamed of. Addiction can be treated."

Rivard watched the lines on Bill's face extend downward and contract with the motions of his mouth. Bill suddenly looked old, far older than his years. Rivard decided that the lines were a combination of exhaustion and unchecked strain.

"The guys don't know I came here. You don't have to worry about rumors or talk. No one will know. The programs stress anonymity."

Rivard looked at Bill's face. He looked at Bill's face, but wasn't seeing it anymore. He was seeing a parade of faces from his childhood, a parade of disapproving faces marked with stern lines and chronic strain.

He saw the white, sun-deprived face of his kindergarten teacher glaring down at the gymnasium floor: "Thomas, you are too hyperactive. Stop running around on your toes. Turn down that energy, before you hurt someone else, or trip."

He saw the pinched, agitated face of the barber—a face marked with fans of broken blood vessels and veins: "Mrs. Rivard, will your son ever stop talking? We've got a regular old motor mouth here."

He saw the belligerent, angry faces of his peers on the athletic field, twisted in jealous contempt: "Look at Tommy, jumping up and down! He's excited like a girl, gonna wet his pants. What are you high on, freak?"

"I'm high on life."

Rivard started at the sound of his own voice. He did not realize he had spoken the answer out loud. He had never known that there was a question that required an answer, until just now. The voices condemning his energy and enthusiasm had been buried under years.

Rivard looked at Bill, incredulity lowering the steady line of his brow. The full meaning of Bill's accusation suddenly became clear.

Bill looked at Rivard, concern clouding the tired planes of his face. He said, "I'm not trying to pry into your business. I just want you to play safe. Do some thinking about going to the meeting."

Bill turned to leave the room. Rivard watched Bill's back, slightly bent as though shouldering a burden. He felt like shouting: You want *me* to be safe? You look at my ambition and drive as something to be fixed? Goddamn you people! What's so threatening about energy?

Rivard leaned over onto the table. He was

overcome with a sudden weakness. A word and a face blotted out all the other objects in the room: Constance.

Rivard felt an overwhelming desire to be with his wife.

He hastily gathered his belongings, carelessly throwing his items toward a battered canvas bag. He did not know what items he was clutching, holding for a brief second and tossing in the bag. The items were just things, objects that passed through his hands, unseen and instantly forgotten. His mind was incapable of thinking about wrist watches and sweaty neon bands. His brain had reduced itself to the awareness of a single object, a single person, whose approving glance Rivard suddenly needed like the injection of a drug.

He fled the room, not conscious of what he was fleeing. He headed for the hospital cafeteria, sure of what was there.

Rivard watched Constance carry a breakfast tray across the cafeteria. His eyes followed the swish of her long blue cotton skirt. Swirls of steam rose from thick cobalt coffee mugs she balanced with her hands.

The vague movement of bodies surrounding her figure dissolved into the fog of his peripheral vision. Her face reduced all the other faces in the room to a collection of featureless ovals and anonymous orbs. The ovals did not exist. The only thing in existence was the woman walking toward him. As she approached his table, Rivard gazed at the stunning figure of his wife.

Constance Rivard had the petite body of a

gymnast. She had a gymnast's tight, agitated frame. Her limbs were resilient lengths of bowstring pulled just beyond the point of tension, positioned for release; her limbs moved with the measured assurance that is an athlete's incomparable ease.

Her gait was efficient, but fluid; her body performed a walking function, but garnished it with grace. The grace was in the effortless flow of motion. One could almost trace the current of energy originating in her abdomen, traveling outward and propelling her limbs. Each purposeful, evenly spaced step was a tightly controlled outflow of her animating energy. Each step she took looked like the opening step of a gymnast's perfected routine.

Rivard's face was frozen in an expression that was half smile, half overbearing gloat. As he looked at his wife, his face became like that of a child on Christmas Day, staring at a coveted toy. His eyes were filled with the same rapturous, possessive glaze as a boy with a gun or a train; they moved slowly over the coveted object and seemed to say two things simultaneously: This is mine. I want to try it out.

Two eyes met Rivard's and held them from across the cafeteria. The eyes were a stunning shade of ocean violet, punishing in their clarity. The clarity worked two ways: as clear as still water, the eyes revealed everything contained in their depths; as brilliant as sun on sea, they captured everything touched by their gaze.

The violet eyes looked at Rivard's eyes. They

communicated to Rivard that they understood his message. They directly sent one of their own: Do you like what you see? It's yours to try it out.

Rivard's mouth was set in a thin straight line. His teeth were clenched tight. He did not notice his tense jawbone or moist palms; he did not notice his veins throbbing forcefully in his temples and wrists. The whole of Rivard's body had melted away into the background; it had become an insignificant prop, a superfluous item which a change of lighting fades away for the change of a scene. The only part of Rivard's body still held in the soft lighting of the moment was his eyes. His eyes followed Constance walking toward him. Her body was set in the spotlight, the stunning starlet of his private scene. Rivard felt the present moment as a dramatic pause that merged into the past, becoming one with it. His wife looked at him in exactly the same way she had looked at him seven autumns ago . . . .

He felt it in every cell and fiber of his body. The thirty-second chin-up ripped a fissure through his gut. His body was supported by the steel of his jaw and the cables of his wrists.

He slowly raised his body to the level of the bar. His fingers melded to the rust-coated iron. He pulled his lower body up with his arms as though delivering it from the bowels of a precipice.

His muscle and his mind fused for the thirty-second lift. The twining rope of his muscle constricted his bones. The tension released hours of pent-up frustration.

Stressed out, sweat it out. That is what his father always said. *Sweat is safer than fist fights or sex, better for a case of the nerves*. Rivard ground his molars and tightened the cords of his neck.

He felt the weight of his body on the surfaces of his inner arms. He paused, suddenly feeling that his arms were no match for his weight. He considered dropping to the floor. He thought of his clients and made himself rise.

He saw Ron Pratt's puffy, bloated face, breaking into a sweat at the slightest exertion. He saw the empty exercise mat at morning aerobics, the mat Ron was supposed to occupy on Mondays. It was Monday. Ron had called in sick, coughing into the mouthpiece of the phone and groaning with pain. It was a pitiful act. Rivard stiffened and did another chin-up.

He saw Mindy Parker's giant mottled thighs and the tiny feet which tripped in an attempt to move the excess weight. He saw her park in the handicapped space so she would not have to walk across the lot. Rivard shuddered and did another chin-up.

He saw Henry Murphy's duffel bag stuffed with fast-food wrappers and soda cans. He saw Henry licking his fingers while he sat in the car, his pudgy, eager hands dipping into a grease-stained hamburger bag. Rivard cringed and did another chin-up.

He gave himself a reason to complete each lift. His body became the solid affirmation of his goals. *I will get Pratt in shape*. Rivard rallied and lifted his weight. *I will get Parker to move*. Rivard told himself *Yes* and raised his chin to the bar. *I will get Murphy to like healthy food*. Rivard carried his weight up over his arms.

He directed the weight of his body at his knuckles and wrists. His affirmations were poised with his weight. His power gave way to helplessness, as he dropped from his peak and let himself hang. His body jerked and ripped at the sockets. Rivard relished the sickening burn in his armpits. The sensation echoed his emotional disgust.

What went wrong? Just where did I go wrong? The question seemed to arise from the burning ache in his pits. Why am I not getting through to them?

Rivard looked at his reflection in the glass along the wall. He watched his body hanging from the iron bar. He thought of a gibbon hanging from a tree. He thought of a gibbon powering itself along by the strength of its arms, propelling its body through a kingdom of branches and vines. He thought of a chimp.

Rivard suddenly remembered a chimp he had seen at the zoo as a child. He remembered his overwhelming feeling of horror and fright. The chimp had been mad at a throng of spectators. It had paced back and forth in its cage, hissing and hooting, making rude gestures with its long hairy arms. Rivard could still see the angry, stressed-out face. He could see the lips peeled back to reveal yellow stubs of teeth. He could hear the cry of distress which sounded like insane laughter. Rivard had run from the exhibit, sobbing. His mother found him white and huddled underneath a metal bench.

Rivard felt like the chimp was laughing at him now. He could see the yellow teeth protruding from huge pink gums, mocking him with incessant chatter:

What has it amounted to, your precious career? You're surrounded by a passel of fat slobs and pigs, people no better than swine. They don't think enough of themselves to pick up their feet. They were given a second chance at life, and they're not interested.

I know, Rivard answered, mentally addressing his beastly accuser. I know, and I can barely stand it. I didn't go into rehabilitation to watch people head down the path of self-destruction. I wanted to teach them to live.

You wanted to teach them to live, did you? You wanted to turn them into fitness machines? The truth is: they'd rather eat themselves into an early grave. Potato chips mean more to them than health.

I know it! Just where did I go wrong? My fitness regimen has the endorsement of eminent cardiologists. My heart therapy program has been showered with awards. It's been called revolutionary . . . brilliant! Yet I can't make it work! All the coaching in the world is doing no good. What is it I'm missing?

It's not something you're missing, Thomas Rivard. The problem is you're prone to control. The perfect regimen is useless, if people do not choose it. They have to want to follow the plan. You may be a brilliant doctor, you may be a rehabilitation god, but it means nothing without others' consent.

Damn their consent, I'm the expert! I know what's good for them. I've studied anatomy and physiology for years. I studied under Professor Richard Dunn! Why don't they listen to me? Don't they know their lives are at stake?

Thomas Rivard, you poor misguided man. What makes you think that matters?

We're talking about saving life!

You're talking about saving life.

Right! And?

Not everybody thinks it's worth saving.

"Damn that!" Rivard dropped to the floor. He came down square on his feet. A sharp pain jolted his legs and pulsed through his knees. He grimaced at the stinging sensation and the imaginary conversation that caused him to drop.

I can't stand that pessimistic attitude, Rivard thought to himself. I can't stand that defeatist tone. I just need to try harder, that's all, come at the issue from a different angle. Once they get the hang of it, they'll come around. I can *make* them value their health. I know I can. Life isn't fun without health. There's not much one can do without a heart.

A sudden thought blazed through his skull.

Is a life without health worth living—is it really even life at all?

Rivard grabbed a towel and pressed it to his face. He dismissed the question as soon as it rose. Grey areas were distasteful; they made him feel unclean.

Rivard liked the certainty of a world made up of black-and-white, yes-and-no answers. He did not like dwelling in ambiguity or questions which could be answered different ways.

He stood with the towel pressed to his forehead for many moments, letting his elevated heart rate slowly descend. He deliberately ordered his thoughts.

Life or death—that is the alternative. It is a simple fact of either-or.

Rivard licked his lips, tasting the salt that ran from his temples to his mouth. He liked the taste of his drying juice.

When they sign on with me, they know the score. It's do or die, end of story.

His thought was a finalizing punctuation mark. The issue was settled. His workout was through.

Rivard's body was bronze and slick with sweat. The damp cloth of his tee shirt stuck to his chest. He decided against a shower, liking the smell of his sweat.

Rivard left the fitness center and headed for the parking lot on the other side of the hospital grounds. He took a short cut through the Alzheimer's ward.

The smell of Pine Manor assaulted his nose. No matter how many times he had walked through the door—no matter how many times he had pressed the combination on the key pad that released the lock, opening a world without youth or memory—the odor hit him like a stagnant wave.

It was air like that of a morgue, still and laced with something heavy. The air was ripe with the revolting sweetness of living death.

Rivard walked down the corridor. He looked at the grey blotches on the orange-pink carpet and wondered why he had come this way. He looked at the autumn decorations arranged along the wall. The corn stalks, pumpkins and bouquets of silver-purple mums were intended as a touch of seasonal festivity, but looked wilted and cheerless, as if they knew their own futility in a place without light or hope. A black metal cat peeping from around a pumpkin would have looked playful on someone's front porch or yard. Here, it merely added to an aura of unending gloom.

Rivard looked at a poster hung on a resident's door. A little smiling ghost held up a sign that said, "Boo!"

Rivard shuddered at that kind of thing displayed in a home for adults. It was a patronizing slap in the face, a reminder that the child who had placed it on his father's door had become the adult, and his father the simple-minded child.

Rivard cringed and quickened his pace. After the day he had had, this place was too much. He wanted to exit the building and breathe in some fresher air.

From around a corner, Rivard heard the startling sound of a female's voice.

"I know you don't believe me, Mr. Stern, but a walk will do you good."

Rivard stopped. He was not sure he really heard the voice. It clashed with the decayed atmosphere of the room. It seemed to come from another universe.

"Ira, are you ready to go for your walk?"

"I'm not going anywhere with you!"

"And why is that?"

"You're one of the damned!"

Rivard checked a sudden burst of laughter. He stood in the hallway, listening to the voices coming from a nearby room. The conversation was intriguing. He wanted to hear it through.

"I said you're damned!"

"Oh, that's right. One of the damned. I nearly forgot. Thank you for reminding me."

"I'll tell you what's more, you Jezebel, the day of reckoning is almost here. Before long, the Judgment will be handed down. The Day of Judgment is almost here."

"Can you confirm the date? I'll mark it on my calendar."

"Blasphemous female! Cunning she-devil! You think I'm kidding, don't you? You think I'm speaking in fun?"

"No, I don't. I know you're serious. I take you for your word."

"And what about *the* Word, Jezebel? Do you accept the holy truth that is The Word?"

"Which Holy Word are you referring to, Ira? The Koran, or the Tao te Ching? Perhaps you are referring to the Torah or the Bhagavad-Gita?"

"I mean the Sacred, Holy Word of God!"

"Which God? Are you ready to go for your walk?"

"I'm not going anywhere with you, devil woman. You'll lead me straight into the Pits of Hell."

"Nope. Pits of Hell are not on the schedule this week. We're going to take a walk around the block. I think you'll like the autumn colors. The sugar maples are coming out in stunning shades of orange and red."

"Orange and red, eh? The color of fire! Fire and brimstone! I knew it. You are taking me to Satan's lair!"

"Not today, Ira. You could use a breath of fresh air. Sulphur and ash would only aggravate your asthma."

"No, don't touch me! It's an evil ploy of deceit! A beautiful woman is the tool of the devil. You're trying to lure me into a false sense of security, seduce me with your charm. It's not going to work. I've got your number: 666."

"That's not it. My telephone extension is 4220."

"Jezebel, liar! Leave me alone! I won't walk with the likes of you."

"Suit yourself. I'll see if Mr. Bentley wants to go for a walk. He always loves to go with me."

"No! He can't walk with you!"

"Why is that?"

"He can't!"

"How come?"

"He's . . . he's not feeling well. I think he's got the runs."

"He didn't have any trouble this morning."

"It just came over him. Just a little while ago.

He's in no shape to walk."

"Does that mean you'll take his place?"

"Yes! I mean, I guess I'll go."

"Excellent. Let me help you with your coat."

Rivard stood frozen in his place. He was suddenly self-conscious, acutely aware of the workout clothes stuck to his body, drenched with cold sweat. He cursed himself for stopping and listening in. What would the nurse think, when she rounded the corner? How would he explain himself? What reason could he give for eavesdropping? Why had he let himself get caught up in their private conversation?

Two words flashed across his brain, when the nurse rounded the corner.

That's why.

That is why he had broken his body into a state of solid granite: *To make myself capable of pleasing a female such as you.* That is why he had never settled for anything less than full mastery of his body, commanding every strand of muscle to obey: *To know that perfection is possible, to know and to honor a living standard of perfection such as you.* That is why he had dedicated his life to the cause of priceless health: *Because health is so much more than working organs or limbs, it's a type of joy, impossible to describe, a fusion of energy and passion, a way of living, it's written in your eyes.*

It was there, in the violet eyes looking back at him. It was in her rising chest and tense, nervous limbs: *Come to my aerobics class. Just come and stand before the class. Let them see what's possible. Let them see what I mean when I speak about the visible glow of health. Everything I've tried to convey to them, everything I've ever worshipped is summed up in your body.*

It was there, seven years later, as his wife placed a tray of steaming coffee on the table.

"Good morning."

"Hello, my love."

Rivard saw it without even looking down. Constance wrapped one hand around her coffee mug and placed the other, palm down, over the rising curl of steam. Smoke-colored wisps slipped between her fingers and vanished.

She smiled at him. She knew what he was thinking: *She always does that. Even in the middle of summer, she loves to feel the warmth against her palm.*

Rivard smiled back at his wife. The stress of being misunderstood dissolved. She did not have to say it. He knew what she was thinking: *He loves to pretend he isn't watching. He loves to feign indifference, but it's my hands that turn him on.*

She took his hand. She slowly uncurled his fingers one by one. She held his hand, palm down, over the steaming cobalt mug. She pressed her palm to the side of the mug and laced her fingers through his.

The pressure of her hand and the twisting coil of steam pocketed his hand in warmth. A tingle of pleasure glided up his arm. He closed his eyes. This was his wife's early morning way of making love.

It was her way with everything. Constance relished manual contact with her husband, even during routine daily tasks. The simplest activities were an occasion for giving and receiving pleasure. She did not know the meaning of drudgery. It was her disposition to turn breakfast in a hospital cafeteria into something sensual.

It was the special significance of touch. Constance knew the world with her hands, by feel, rather than sound or sight. Her hands never stopped exploring—a habit many people thought was rude. Sales clerks cringed when Constance whisked a crystal vase from a table and held it to the light. Furriers scowled when Constance decadently caressed a mink coat, gliding the sleeve along her neck and chin.

Rivard felt Constance's hands on his forearms. Her fingers expertly tugged at his hairs. His eyes still closed, Rivard thought that Constance must have had good parents. They must never have slapped her hand away from a fragile, toppling object, gasping, Don't touch! They must never have resented sticky fingers on new upholstery, or frowned at mud pie filling under fingernails.

As Constance traced the veins along his arms, a torturous shiver traveled up his back. Rivard breathed a silent Thank You to the people who had encouraged their daughter's curiosity, rather than dampened it. He was reaping the benefits of her uninhibited kinesthetic greed.

She was unconscious of using her hands. Her

behavior was habitual, instinctive. The pads of her fingers grazed the surfaces of objects and seemed to hold them, to own them, without applying any pressure. Her hands were her natural mode of perception. They were as talented as those of a person who saw the world in Braille. Rivard had often wondered whether Constance would suffer, if she became blind. A minor setback, he had concluded. As long as she had her hands, Constance would be fine.

Rivard opened his eyes when Constance drew her hands away from him. She ran her palms back over the polished surface of the tabletop and stopped at her mug. She wrapped both hands around the vessel of warm liquid. A smile of pleasure played across her lips.

Rivard tore his eyes away from Constance's hands and the sensual way she held her mug. He was suddenly aware that they were in the middle of a cafeteria. He wondered whether anyone had noticed; it seemed impossible that anyone could fail to notice a woman so openly sensual. The energy emanating from her body was powerful and potent as a drug. Feeling protective, Rivard cast a hasty glance around the room.

Two tables over sat a group of nurses. The women were dressed in brightly colored uniforms with busy floral prints. Their collective mood did not match the vivid shades meant to impart cheer to the sick. There was no cheer among the group.

One of the women jerked a spoonful of cereal toward her mouth, chewing mechanically; she did not appear to taste or savor the food that she ingested.

Another stabbed her fork into a pile of greasy home fries, looking down at her plate with a contemptuous sneer. Rivard could not see the faces of the other women, but he could tell by their posture they were resentful of an early morning out of bed.

Several janitors had just come off a night shift and slouched in a booth along the wall. They consumed an egg and sausage breakfast with the same indifferent motions with which they pushed a broom or slung a mop: it was all repetitive, monotonous motions. Whether eating, or wiping a table where others ate, their attitude was one of unchanging disinterest. Rivard could not tell that they had stopped working. They used a fork the same tired, apathetic way they used a dirty rag.

Rivard could not bear to look at the workers any longer. His eyes eagerly fell on his wife. Constance was eating fresh fruit with her fingers. Her lips and fingers were stained with bright red strawberry juice.

Rivard watched Constance peel green leaves back from the crown of a strawberry and nibble at the glossy tip. He pulled a purple grape from her bowl and popped it in his mouth. He rolled the grape around in his mouth before pulverizing the tiny ball of fleshy juice.

She did not want to talk. She was thoroughly enjoying her meal. With the unabashed eagerness of a young girl who has not been taught that women should peck at their food, Constance drew a handful of blackberries to her face and breathed in deeply. The berries were deposited onto a steaming bowl of oatmeal. Constance licked her fingers before picking up her spoon.

Rivard could not believe the contrast between Constance and the other people in the room. Eating was for them a thoroughly uninteresting activity, a duty, just something one was supposed to do: bite, chew, swallow. For Constance, nourishing her body was a happy form of pleasure. All her senses were stirred at the sights and smells of wholesome food. She was not bashful about eating with her fingers, or gushing over delicious smells. Like everything she did, Constance turned the ritual of eating into a source of pure physical pleasure. It was this whole-body approach to life, this near-animal physicality and sensuality, Rivard had fallen deeply in love with. As he sat at the breakfast table with his wife, savoring his food, Rivard savored the blissful span that had been their seven years of marriage . . . .

She did not know that her husband was watching. She did not know that he had forgotten and scorched two sets of grilled cheese sandwiches while standing at the picture window, distracted by the sight. She did not know that there was a person such as her husband; she had even forgotten herself. She was aware of nothing but the quiet stillness in her outstretched arm.

Constance stood still as a garden statue, booted feet planted firmly in a crusty bank of snow. One hand hung at her side, holding two fuzzy mittens. The pink cup of her bare palm was extended away from her body and raised up to the sky. The sprinkle of an offering coated her palm.

A group of plump, nervous chickadees danced on the branches of the nearest apple tree. Their tiny round bodies flitted and bobbed in the sun. Several birds descended to the feeder, scattering sunflower seeds over the frosty snow. They chirped and rose back up through the branches.

Constance waited in silent patience, her body an unmoving pole. The only indication of life was the healthy pink flush of her fingers and cheeks. Though the clear winter air stung her figure, she kept it still as ancient stone.

Her patience was rewarded when one brave chickadee broke away from the tree. It hovered in midair just over her palm, beating wings and tiny feet. Constance felt the bird before she saw it land. It flew back to the safety of the apple tree, leaving the fleeting sensation of its weightless scratch along her palm.

She gasped in surprise. A smile broke the lines of concentration streaked across her face. It was a sudden outpouring of rays, the spontaneous, delighted look of a young girl who has witnessed a miracle. The look vanished as Constance bit her bottom lip, silently willing the bird to return.

The chickadees chirped violently. Their tiny buzzing bodies formed an angry cloud. Plump feathered bodies rose and fell between the branches of the tree.

Constance resolutely held her pose. She lifted her hand slightly, making an attractive tray out of the shallow cup of her palm. The only discernable movement was the slight pull of her teeth on her lips.

Minutes passed. The birds hovered near the feeder, chastising one another with pretty chirps. A thick layer of sunflower seeds formed on the snow.

A tiny darting ball suddenly took to the sky. Invisible wings held the black and white bird in the air above her palm. Constance felt a weightless scratch and then it was gone.

Another bird flew away from the tree. It beat the air with lightning flaps, pecked at a seed on her hand, and returned to its open cage of twigs.

One by one, the nervous chickadees discovered the feeder. The look of surprised delight returned to Constance's face. Her eyes moved in an encouraging line from the tree, to the air, to her hand. The fingers of her hanging hand danced within her mitten.

A crimson flash diverted her attention. She broke her statue posture and looked over at the tree. A bright red flag blazed between the branches. A stunning male cardinal took the highest post as it alighted on the tree.

The remaining sunflower seeds made imprints on her palm, as she ground them in an excited fist. Ice crystals forming on the fibers of her woolen mittens melted in her hand. An exhilarating rush flooded the planes of her cheeks. She glanced at the large picture window on the front of the house, straining to see through the sun-flooded glass. Was Thomas watching? Had he seen the magnificent bird? Constance waved at the window, hoping to catch his attention.

She did not know that he was standing just behind the sun's reflection, safely out of sight. An afternoon glare had turned the window into a shining one-way mirror. He could watch his wife in privacy, with no possibility of discovery. All she could see was a rectangular sheet of light.

Constance turned away from the window. Thomas must still be in the kitchen, she thought. And he's missing the cardinal! She glanced up at the brilliant red bird and fought to catch her breath.

She was right. Thomas was not looking at the cardinal. His focus was elsewhere. He was looking at the beautiful flushed woman who was his wife.

Rivard's eyes rested on Constance's face, tilted back into the winter sun. Her eyes and chin were raised toward the cardinal. The flush of excitement had left her cheeks; it had been replaced by a warm quiet glow, barely visible. Rivard felt the radiance on her cheeks, even as he saw it. He felt the radiance on her face, for it was the very same radiance lighting up his own.

She is stunning by the way she is stunned, Rivard thought. A sight of nature's beauty nearly brings her to her knees. She forgets herself, she loses everything but vision . . . as she's as unself-conscious as a happy little child!

Rivard looked at the smooth ivory of Constance's forehead. The rich dark hair swept back with a ribbon curved under her chin. Her mouth was closed, but not set tight. The corners of her mouth and eyes were lifted points, held up to the cardinal.

Yes, Constance is a child, Rivard thought. She is definitely not an adult. Not if being an adult means walking down a pleasant summer street not seeing, head fixed on a pile of bills and unread mail. If being an adult means stumbling blindly from house to car to work, moving in a perpetual triangle with a zombie's set of eyes—if being an adult means missing the white cascade of spring blossoms and fragrance because wars and job security and gas prices need constant attention—if being an adult means ingesting a thirty-minute lunch on the freeway or in front of a computer without savoring or tasting the food—if being an adult means perceiving the world and not seeing it—Constance is truly a child.

Rivard's chest swelled, as he watched his wife watching the bird.

I've never met a person in love with their senses, he thought. The sight of her seeing is the most beautiful sight in the world.

He could hear her excited voice tinkling like chimes as she stamped through the door.

"I've never seen such a stunning shade of red. It had the most perfect little head I've ever seen. What is that little point of feathers called—a crest? I think he knew he had the nicest crest."

She threw her coat on a hook, cheerful and flushed. She bounded into the living room.

Rivard stood looking out the window. The look on his face surprised her. It caused her alarm.

"What's the matter? What are you looking at—oh!"

Before he could stop her, she had raced outside without her boots, coat or mittens. She tore for the feeder, her thin socks kicking up powdered clumps of snow.

Startled by the sudden commotion, the cat jumped, turning from its fallen prey. Constance was a streaking wind of flailing arms and bitter moans. Knowing it had been caught, the cat abandoned its prisoner. It did not fail to smile at Constance before it fled, whipping its tail several times in sly triumph.

She fell down to her knees. The snow under the feeder was the same violent color as the crimson bird. Hands shaking, blinded by tears, Constance scooped the mass of broken feathers in her hands. A large glazed eye rolled in a sea of red and dimmed.

She did not feel the winter chill on her unprotected body. She only felt heaving seizures of impotent rage. They began in her chest, behind her eyeballs; they jerked her tiny frame and make her teeth chatter. It was not the cold making her spasm. It was her anger at the mangled bird.

Goddamn Irene Clement! I've told that old woman to keep her cats indoors. Do we have to go through this every winter?

Constance cried out when the dying bird twitched in her hand. A broken, impotent wing flicked against her palm. The ugly movement filled her with disgust.

Such a magnificent bird! Only five minutes ago this bird was a jewel. Now it's an eyesore, a hideous, disjointed collection of bloody wounds!

Constance knelt in the snow, refusing to move. Her knees had stopped stinging, had stopped prickling, and began to feel rather warm. Only the bird felt cold. The bird was becoming a solid red brick in her palm.

Rivard felt a sudden wave of tenderness, looking out at his wife with head bowed in the snow. He had been glued to the window as she had raced outside in a broiling rage, fuming at the cat. He had watched with narrowed eyes as she had passionately scooped up the bird, cradling its remains, crying over lost beauty.

A perfect nurse, he thought. Constance feels the pain of even the smallest creature.

Rivard felt a stinging prick in the back of his eyes. The words that came to his mind were abrupt and sharp as the prick.

So sensitive! No one feels such pain over the death of birds.

He thought of his wife as she had looked ten minutes ago. He thought of her face, the glowing cheeks brighter than a happy girl's.

No one feels the kind of joy Constance does in spotting a pretty crimson bird.

He breathed in sharply. The sudden question left a fiery imprint on his skull: Does her great joy necessitate pain? Would she feel such pain but for an unbreached joy?

He stepped away from the window, hurrying to get his wife's coat. It was not only the winter chill he wanted to protect her from. He had grasped something violent, unthinkable because it was true: unhappy people are the ones immune to pain.

She sat at the kitchen table wrapped in blue flannel; a cup of tea steamed in her palms. Her winter-stung face had the spirited look of a little elf. There was no indication that she had ever been forlorn.

Rivard listened to Constance chatter. He relaxed, knew that his fear was unwarranted. Constance would bounce back from anything. She was too full of vigor to stay down for long.

"It was actually a marvelous leap. That old Maine Coon is quite a birder. They don't make hunters any better than cats."

Rivard broke out in a playful grin. "So now you're siding with the cat?"

"Absolutely! You know my sympathies are always with the predator." She shot him a knowing look. Her eyes were bright and restless.

"Con! You're not turned on by animal carnage? Do I have to worry about you developing a twisted fetish?" He pushed back his chair.

"I've never claimed to be anything but an animal," she said, gripping the arms of her chair. "Like all prey, I have a certain fascination with competent predation."

She saw a single vein throb in his temple. His jaw was set in a rigid square.

"There is something vital about animal nature. Vital and clean." She looked at her husband with undisguised greed. "No ambiguity in the animal kingdom, no complications. It all boils down to blood and bone."

He caught her with his stare. She fought to raise her eyes, but could not lift them from the floor. He had her pinned.

He had her up on the table before she could catch her breath. White dishes were swept aside, crashed to the floor. He tore the button at her collar; his mouth was brutal on her neck. Fingers splayed on his back, she threw her head back so far she thought her neck would snap.

Her head was held on her shoulders by a string, the string of bruises he left on her neck. Her head was light and felt like it would come off at any moment. She did not care, as long as he kept pressing at her neck.

His voice was hard, harder than the pressure of his mouth and hands. "There's nothing clean about what I'm going to do to you."

She moaned, gripping him tighter. Fine points of light stung the backs of her eyes. "I—don't—want—clean." She gasped and arched her back when his mouth tugged and sucked at her breasts. "I want to be your dirty bitch."

His breath was a snort and he held her tighter. His sensitive little snow angel—nothing but a dirty bitch! The happy, open-mouthed little girl who fed chickadees and smiled at a cardinal in the winter sun—the hurt child who flushed with rage at the stealthy murder by a neighbor's cat—the passionate woman who cried at nature, then bowed to it, bowed to the inevitability and necessity of the fact of life and death—this amazing creature was begging him to hurt her, to bite her, to treat her like a filthy whore.

He opened his eyes and looked down at her face. Her eyes were closed, her lips were drawn. Her cheeks glowed with a passionate blush. He saw the dark hair spilled over his arm as he held her head in his hands. It was the tumbled mane of an untamed beast. He twisted the hair in his fingers and drove his tongue into her mouth.

Her body was bent back under the pressure of his chest and mouth. His tongue was fire like a rigid iron brand. She felt the hard surface of the table strike her back; his blow was hard as the stained planks and less forgiving.

Her arms, legs and tongue stiffened at the brutal shock, then coiled and greedily writhed. Every cell in her body begged for him, needed him. Her need of his body was elemental as her need of food or air.

I can't stand it any longer!—her body screamed. I won't last another second if you don't—

Take over. Take over and take me out. Blind me, beat me, crush me into pulp. Make me froth, make me jerk, Oh Thomas make me—

Beat me! Beat me! Beat me! Beat me! Beat me!

Beat me!

She opened her eyes. She could tell by the pale slant of light it was late afternoon. Soft winter rays passed through the bedroom window, making yellow shapes along the floor. Just outside, the branches of a dead maple formed a giant stencil over the window. Light filtered through the stencil in acute angles and broken shards.

A triangle of winter light touched Rivard's bare abdomen where he lay on the bed. Constance touched the light with her chin, then pressed her cheek into the plane of his warm belly. A faint rumble of hunger rose to her ear.

"Our lunch is all over the kitchen floor," she said, her voice toneless and small.

"So were we," Rivard answered. His voice and his face were smooth and did not mock.

"Have I been sleeping long?"

"No."

"Did you sleep?"

"No."

"Talk, Tom. I like to feel your belly muscles move. I like the way your insides sound."

That's right, he thought. Women don't know what it's like to be inside a man. Men get women inside out.

"I'm sorry about your bird."

"I'm not."

"No?"

"Be sorry about what? Nature? Cats do that."

"Yes. Cats kill birds."

"And birds kill worms. No one feels sorry for worms."

Rivard laughed softly. He did not mention that he had seen her stoop to a steaming parking lot after a summer rain, removing worms to nearby grass.

"I'm sure a few softies out there care for worms."

She buried her smile in his belly. She knew that she was caught. Is there nothing about me he doesn't know? She knew there was not and she liked it that way. Well, nothing that mattered. He knew everything that mattered.

She shot up and looked him square in the face. "So what if I do rescue worms? So what if I'm soft? What's it to you?"

Rivard lounged on the bed, his body relaxed. "You are gorgeous when you are defensive."

She wrinkled her nose and clucked. Tom was such an awful kidder. He knew that she had nothing to defend. Not from him.

"And you, Mr. Dr. Rivard, are gorgeous when you are full of it." As she spoke the words she placed her finger on his lips, hushing him.

She smiled and leaped from the bed, all business. "I've got a plan, Tom. Your violent carnal behavior inspired me with the perfect approach."

Constance heard labored shuffling as Irene Clement hobbled to the door. A curtain was pulled back; a pale pinched face peered through the glass. A long chain of curses, uttered just loud enough so that Constance could hear them, filtered through the door. The door flung open. Constance smelled cat urine and the undisguised disgust of a bitter old maid.

"Connie, what do you want?"

"Hello, Irene! I just thought I'd stop by and bring you some cookies. It's a lovely afternoon for a visit."

The old woman sniffed. "Visit—bah! You've just come by to brag. I know all about you, little gold digger. You just want to show off your glitzy diamond ring."

Constance pretended not to have heard. The insults were unending and had been for years. Irene hated doctors; she begrudged them their wealth. Like any talk prompted by envy, Constance let it roll off her back.

"You'll like these cookies, Irene. They're shaped like cats."

A flicker of interest gleamed in her eye. Irene looked at the plate, then remembered who was standing at her door. "I don't want your treats. Think I can't afford my own? Think I'm poor and need help?"

"Not at all, Irene. I came to praise your cat."

The old woman nearly fell over. She had expected anything but that. Constance hated her old Maine Coon. It was always eating her birds. The subject was a heated neighborhood battle, a bitter, ongoing feud.

"I—unlike some people—can't afford to stand here with the door open, heating the yard. Come in, Connie, if you must."

Constance breezed into the old house, triumphant. As she set the plate of cookies on the table and took off her coat, she thought: I've been let into the house. That's victory number one. All I have to do is stick with the facts.

She looked at Irene's scowling face and a shock of clarity blazed through her skull.

The facts! Everything is so easy when we stop fighting nature, stop trying to resist.

Her heart beat with irregular thumps, as if keeping time with the words tumbling around in her brain.

Sometimes the best thing to do is admit the inevitable, surrender and take the hit. Isn't that the essence of Grace? What freedom when we do not struggle!

Her smile was brilliant and completely disarmed. She laid her cards out on the table: "Your cat is the most perfect feline specimen I've ever seen. I've never observed such consummate skill. He was on the cardinal before it could even—"

Irene let out a cry. She frantically groped for a chair. "Have you lost your mind?"

Constance guided the frail body into her chair. "Quite possibly. I've come to call a truce."

Irene's eyes shot to Constance's face. They were two dark points set deep within her skull.

"I have to be honest and admit a defeat. I can't even hope to compete. That perfect hunter you've got"—Constance saw an unchanged kitty litter box out of the corner of her eye—"is faster than a fox. He's got the whole neighborhood under his paw."

Constance waited for the stream of insults. She waited for the shrill voice to shout, Liar! She braced herself for the usual torrent of ridicule and scorn.

When it did not come, Constance looked closely at Irene's face. The old woman had an absent, dreamy look about her, as though she had forgotten Constance was there.

Constance cleared her throat and reached for a cookie. "I've changed my mind, Irene. That cat is a pest and it's mangling my birds. I'm going to call animal control and have it removed."

The woman's face was blank and unchanged. Constance saw the expression and began to feel alarmed. This was not the Irene Clement she loved to hate, the old neighbor who sneered at her entreaty to keep her cats indoors.

"Irene,"—Constance reached for her arm—"are you all right? Did I say something wrong?"

The sharp gleam in her eye returned, but there was a film over it, as though a light had dimmed.

"Oh, Connie, I'm really glad that you're here. You reminded me of something. Wait right here."

Constance sat in the kitchen for what seemed an eternity. She nervously nibbled the legs off a sugar cookie cat. She broke the head from its body and licked the icing face. She heard Irene coming and quickly devoured the cat's head. She longed for a cold glass of milk.

With obvious effort, Irene placed the heavy book down on the table. Her fingers shook as she fumbled with the sticky page.

"I haven't opened this book in so long, the pages are stuck. Connie, be a good girl and get them apart."

Constance slipped a slim finger between the pages of the old photo album. The ancient snapshots separated with a sickening rip.

A young boy in swimming shorts danced in the yard with a gushing hose. As he chased the photographer, his eyes twinkled with a mischievous spark.

"That's my boy, Connie, that's Peter."

Confused, Constance started to say, "I never knew you had a—" but did not finish. The look on Irene's face told her not to talk.

"Peter was twelve when he drowned in the gorge. They never found his body. He and his father went camping—it was their annual summer trip. They called it the He-Man trip—no women allowed.

"I sent my boy off with a package of hot dogs and insect repellent. He never came home. When the state police failed to recover his body, my husband shot himself. He blamed himself. I found his body in the cellar."

Constance went numb with shock. She fumbled

for something to say. Her cheeks burned with mortification. She had never had a clue.

Irene's voice was without emotion, untroubled and matter of fact. "I know what you're thinking: 'This explains her nasty behavior. This is why the old woman acts like a coot.' It is and it isn't. Death is not a bad thing. Not really. Did I grieve my heart out, did I feel like dying myself? Sure. That's normal. I lost my men.

"I'll tell you what though, Connie. This is what drove me mad. All the people saying, 'It happens for a reason. Everything happens for a reason. Trust there's a reason.' What reason? To bind me in a living hell? There are no reasons in nature. Life and death, coming and going—it just happens. It doesn't make sense. Life would be so much easier if we stopped fighting nature, stopped trying to resist—"

Constance gasped aloud. They were her own words. Not twenty minutes ago her mind had reached the very same conclusion.

"Ah!" Irene's voice was a peal of triumph. "So you think so, too? You understand what I mean?"

"Why else would I have praised your cat? I hate the mangy beast. Hating it is not going to change its nature—or—or bring back my bird."

Irene laughed with bitter amusement. She was beginning to enjoy the conversation. "I'm going to tell you this because I like you, Connie, and I only tell the truth to people I pretend to hate. I don't know whether it's to feel our own importance, or to pretend we have control. I don't know what makes humans want to be immortal. And I'm not one of those nut balls who refuses to go to the doctor, or condemns medicine, clamoring about God's will and Reasons. I hate Reasons. Nature doesn't care one way or the other. She's going to get you, sure as shit. What I'm trying to say is—and I say this because I know your husband, know that he's one of those maniacs out to beat death, like he can win the final race—live like there is no death. Milk the seconds for all they're worth. That's all life is, a string of seconds. If you waste even one second thinking about death, it's got you. The reaper's at your door. To the extent we think about prolonging life, we're not living it. And when death comes, we find he's been there all along."

Constance drew her hand to her chest. She felt the violent, troubled thump. Did Irene know? How did this woman know what to say? Why did it feel as though Irene could see through the skin of her chest, see right down to the muscle and its labored throb?

"You look like you've seen a ghost. Can I get you some milk to go with those cookies? Don't fret about your birds, I understand. From now on the cats will stay indoors."

When winter passed without incident, Rivard questioned Constance about her visit with Irene.

"What did you say to her? I haven't seen any sign of the cat. I thought that afternoon would be the start of World War Three."

Constance looked at her husband with a glimmer in her eye, the glimmer of one who knows more than she's going to tell. "Armistice," she said. "White flag. We've called a truce and made our peace."

Rivard did not know why he felt there was emphasis placed on the word "peace." Her voice had not changed. Her tone had stayed the same. Perhaps it's not her at all, he thought, but me. Perhaps I'm imagining the word had an echo.

Why this should be so he did not know. He did not know what made the word "peace" warm his ears. He knew only that it lingered like a gentle touch, like the soft, healing stroke of a woman's hands. "Peace" was balm on his compulsive brain.

He carried the word like a charm for several days, then forgot about it—until the spring day he accidentally crushed Cindy Beale.

The nutrition class met in the room adjacent to the gymnasium. Large bodies had squeezed themselves into chairs with attached table tops in order to hear the lecture. The sound of labored breathing and crinkling food packages competed with the speaker's voice.

"You will be relieved to hear I'm not asking you to give up sweets," Rivard said. "The goal is not to live on carrot sticks and watercress. That would not be healthy. Healthy eating is about a well-rounded diet, low in fat and cholesterol—not free of it. Proper protein will give you the right kinds of fat."

He asked the students to produce their food diaries. He gazed out at a sea of uncomfortable, perspiring faces. One woman looked alarmed.

"Cindy, do you have a question?"

All eyes turned to the woman with a bright red face.

"No," she said. Her voice was embarrassed and harsh.

"Do you have your diary with you?"

She looked away from Rivard. His eyes made her feel like she was being accused. It always happened when she sat in his class. Her nerves prevented her from speaking up. She managed a "No." Her voice barely left the folds of skin around her chin.

"How are you going to participate in the nutrition seminar without your food log?"

Rivard had not condemned; he had not sneered. He had simply asked the question. Cindy did not hear what he said. She heard: How are you going to get skinny?

Her eyes anxiously took in the room. Her bottom lip quivered with fright. Everyone was watching. She saw ridicule and laughter shoot from each face. They were mocking her.

She balled her hands into tiny fists. Her eyes closed, she mouthed the words her self-esteem coach had taught her to use: I am a whole, confident person. I do have a voice. My voice is great and free as a bird. My body is the holy chamber of my voice.

She repeated the words again. They were ready and soothing as a prayer. She had memorized an entire selection of such phrases to use in times of distress. Enrollment in Rivard's weight management program had driven her to a counselor. His mantra was a weapon against Rivard's advice.

"Cindy," Rivard said, "are you able to participate today?"

Her eyes still closed, Cindy saw the accepting face of her self-esteem coach. She heard his emphatic words: You are beautiful just the way you are. Don't ever let anyone tell you different. A large body is nothing to be ashamed of.

The words rose up from her belly, up like a fountain, up past her anxiety and fear. They poured forth from her lips, an ecstatic utterance: "A large body is nothing to be ashamed of."

There, she thought. I've got him. He can't bully me any more.

Rivard paused, his hand in the air. Powder from a piece of white chalk coated his fingers. He said, "A large body is nothing to be ashamed of. That's true."

Cindy grew angry. He doesn't really believe that, she thought. He's making fun of me.

"Large bodies are beautiful. We even—we can even look hot in lingerie!"

Her voice was a triumphant burst. She had slapped that arrogant know-it-all in the face.

The eyes in the room moved from Cindy to Rivard. The sound of snickering met the surprise on his face.

"O-kay. And?"

"And we even make good models. We have our own special type of beauty, a different kind." Her voice came out a violent gush. Hate and fear glittered in her eyes. Her fingers constricted into compact fists. "I'm tired of being told I'm not good enough. I'm tired of put-downs and insults. I'm tired of being discriminated against!"

Her eyes shot to Rivard's face. She waited for his angry burst. She was totally unprepared for what she saw.

Rivard had lowered his hand. His arms were loose and hanging at his sides. The only tension present in his body was the slight pressure of two fingers gripping the chalk.

It was the casual posture of his body that drove her to tears. She thought: How can Dr. Rivard be so heartless? How can he be so insensitive? Doesn't he know that I have feelings?

Tears of angry frustration poured down her face. His silence was maddening. She began to talk and hiccoughed. Her words came out an ugly croak: "You hate fat people!"

Rivard's eyes were large and staring into space. He seemed completely unaware of the people in the room. He did not appear to have heard Cindy.

Finally, he said, "Cindy, what makes you think I hate fat people?" His voice was inflectionless and low.

Rivard's tone silenced Cindy. She let out a belch. The room was hot and silent.

"Cindy," Rivard repeated, his voice lower than before, "what makes you think I hate fat people?"

"This class is anti-fat." The sentence came out a blurt. The other bodies in the room shifted in their chairs. No one knew what to do. The scene was embarrassing, but embarrassing in a satisfying way, like the sight of a fight breaking out in school.

Rivard said, “Of course this class is anti-fat.”

Cindy had expected a guilty refutation of her words. She had not expected agreement. She said, “I don’t mean anti-fat the way you do. I mean you want to change our bodies.”

“Of course I want to change your bodies.”

Cindy scowled. She was not getting anywhere. Why did he keep changing the meaning of her words?

She said, “You don’t like us the way we are. You think we’re not good enough.”

“You are never ‘good enough.’ One can always improve.”

Cindy gasped. His words were too much. She forgot that he was repeating her own statements. She said, “How dare you make a judgment about me—about any of us!”

She looked around the room for support. Heads were bowed, papers shuffled. There was not a single ally in the group.

She whirled to Rivard: “What makes you so high and mighty? Who do you think you are?”

Rivard nodded once, then walked over to the window. His eyes rested on a tiny patch of dirty snow.

“Cindy, let me ask you a question. Why did you sign up for this class?”

Cindy looked at Rivard’s back, bewildered. She thought: What’s that got to do with anything?

She said, "I—my doctor told me I needed to lose weight."

"He told you you needed to change?"

Cindy's face flushed purple. She felt like the question was a trick. "Not change—not change like there's anything wrong with me, with who I am. He doesn't think fat people are bad."

"But I do?" Rivard's jaw was a granite square as he tore his eyes from the window. "I think fat people are bad?"

Cindy's eyes welled up. The folds of skin around her chin began to quiver. She had never been more frightened.

Her mind groped for one of her familiar phrases. Through the anxiety and fear filling her brain, she heard the voice of her self-esteem coach: Many people fear large bodies because there is power in them. Let your body be a source of empowerment.

She got up from her chair. Her body quivered and shook. Though frightened, she knew what she had to do.

"Dr. Rivard, I've seen your wife. I know what turns you on. You're just a chauvinist who wants to turn us all into skinny bimbos like—"

"Say no more!" Her words were cut off and drowned in the roar.

Cindy's body seemed to visibly shrink. She knew that she had overstepped her bounds. A vein on Rivard's temple stood out and pulsed.

She watched the vein, happy she had angered

him. Her success gave her reckless confidence. She said, “I’m going to tell you something. You think you know so much. Well listen to this: I like cupcakes and cookies. I like lots of them. It’s my life, and if it makes me happy I’m going to eat them and eat them everyday. It’s my life, you hear?”

Rivard did not hear. His brain was reeling from the reference to his wife. Suddenly, the promise he had made to himself did not matter. An old habit, one that he had fought to correct, rose up and squashed his better judgment.

“It’s your life, is it? You want to carry on that way?” His eyes flashed with bitter derision.

“Eating these,” Cindy pulled a package of chocolate cupcakes from her bag, “makes me feel good. It makes me happy.”

“Happy?” Rivard spat the word. “What could you know about happy? You can barely stand on your own two feet.”

He might as well have pushed her over. Her body seemed to sway back and shrink.

Rivard looked at her large helpless body. A rush of satisfaction coursed through his veins. He felt the kind of pleasure a pet owner feels in striking his dog, the pleasure of lashing out at something weak.

He said, “Happiness is something reserved for people who can move.”

Cindy drew in her breath. Her mouth was sour as a pickle. She had gotten what she had asked for—she had angered Dr. Rivard—and now she did not know what to do.

She looked around at the class. Her soft cheeks burned. Her cheeks belonged to a miserable child who knows he has caused a scene. “I can move as good as anybody! I just like to eat!”

Rivard let out a chilling laugh. The people in the room wanted to leave. No one dared to move.

“You say happiness. Happiness! I’ve often wondered how anybody could confuse gluttony with quality of life.”

The tears flowed freely down her face. She was long past caring about dignity. Her voice came out in violent heaves.

“My life would not be fun without soda and sweets. I’m not going to listen to you fitness Nazis anymore. I’m sick of starving myself, and being told than I should want to starve. It’s my life, and my choice. My quality of life means lots of food.”

Rivard stopped. His face darkened. His voice was cold and sharp as a blade. “I have spent my entire life proving that is wrong. I will never, ever concede what you just said. The choice to kill yourself is not acceptable. It’s not ‘quality of life,’ it’s greed.”

“Who are you to say what is *my* quality of life? What makes you think you know?”

Rivard sighed. The anger had left his body. All that was left was exhaustion. His limbs and eyes were cold dead weights. “Humans can’t live without a heart. That’s science. That’s a scientific fact.”

Rivard looked out at the group. A vague

question rose in the air and hung:

Or is it love?

They had been hiking for several hours and he had told her everything and they had been quiet for some time when she said,

"Make peace with the fact that you won't always win."

She said it simply, without emotion, just the plain statement and nothing implied.

That word, Rivard thought, recalling something hidden, that word is one I've heard before, a word with special meaning.

He could not remember the context the day or the hour. He could not be certain she had said what he remembered hearing. All he knew was that her statement was more than the sum of her words. It was the clue to something he was missing.

For now, it was enough to hear the sound of her untroubled voice. It was enough to be silent while she removed his helmet and his armor and washed off his wounds. It was enough to surrender to a woman's healing wisdom.

Rivard grasped his wife's hand as they climbed up the trail. Her hand was small and warm and fit neatly in his fist. Rivard wondered how so much strength could fit in such a tiny body. She had strength enough for the both of them—unlimited heart.

Rivard wrapped his fingers around his wife's wrist and drew her close. With the pads of his fingers he felt her wildly thumping pulse.

"What are you doing?" Constance said, laughing. "Giving me a checkup?"

"Yes. You are a rare specimen and need to be examined."

"Only if you catch me!"

She broke away from Rivard and was in the woods before he could speak. She fled into the brush, a pretty deer, an agile deer determined to get caught.

The moist spring earth was soft beneath her feet. She dodged slimy roots, decaying tree trunks and moss-coated rocks. She held her hands in front of her body, ineffectually grasping at sapling branches and twigs, pushing them out of her way. She raced past sharp switches that slapped her face and scratched her cheeks.

She laughed as she streaked through the trees. She knew that Rivard was a better runner—much faster with better endurance—but his body was large and he would not be as nimble. She could hear his body catching up with her, crashing through the trees.

She made zigzag patterns through a stand of soft maple trees. Young leaves of red and green uncurled like tiny fetuses. All around, shoots were uncurling, unfolding, exposing their soft bellies to the cool air and warm sun of spring.

Constance looked up at the rays of light pouring through the leaves. Green growth, rich dark fans of green stretched up and out toward bright uncompromised light. She felt as though she and Rivard were brighter than the light, more intense and more insistent. She felt her heart in her throat and raced harder, not caring if it burst.

Rivard was closer to her now, he had gained ground, but she thought that she could still outrun him. She took sloppy, reckless steps. Her feet sank into the soft red-brown decay of the forest floor, and bits of rotten logs sprayed up on her legs.

Her arms and legs were scratched. Red blood oozed from the cuts and scrapes she did not feel. Her arms and legs were numb with motion—numb to the rocks crumbling beneath her feet, numb to the branches lashing at her arms—she did not feel anything but the pull to keep going, the pull to make her husband run.

She was in a part of the woods she did not know. The trim hardwood trees that lined the edge of the trail had given way to old giants, huge sprawling trees with twining branches and rotten cores. This part of the woods was dark—very little light filtered to the forest floor.

Constance tore forward, unconscious of her surroundings. Something impelled her forward—she did not know what it was. Something was summoning her, like thoughts she fought to push away.

Thomas! Come and find me. Come and get me before it's too late.

Her mind raced as fast as her body. The thoughts kept coming, kept springing into her head with the same rapid pace as her heart.

Make peace with the fact that you won't always win.

They were her own words. She had said them

and she knew they were true. Now she did not want them to be true.

You don't have control, my love. You will never have control over this. There is so much you don't know, so much that would kill you if you knew.

She could not hear him behind her. All she could hear was the hot rush of blood in her ears, which sounded like water. All she could feel was the wild irregular thump of her heart. It felt like the ancient beat of raging falls.

But I can't tell you. Not now. Not until our time is through. And we have much more to go. And it's going to be pure, untainted time. Not time clouded by death, time with the end hanging over. We're going to live each second like it's the last on earth—

Then there was no earth beneath her feet. She had slipped, somewhere up above, from some high point she was descending. She felt the absence of ground beneath her feet, an occasional slap against her arm, like something streaking up, and there was the edge of a crag, a few tiny spruce trees clinging to exposed ledge.

She focused her eyes on the spruce trees. They looked so small and helpless on the edge of the cliff, they almost looked comical. Constance laughed as she fell into the water. She was not horrified, or frightened for herself. She felt sorry for the scraggly trees.

Rivard made it to the edge of the cliff in time to see his wife hit the surface of the water. His first instinct was to jump in after her. With every ounce of strength he possessed he stopped his body. He quickly surveyed the space between himself and the water. How could he get to her without breaking his neck?

It took enormous discipline for Rivard to tear his eyes from the water where Constance had gone in. Terror and desperation tore at his heart. How deep was the water below? Had Constance struck a rock?

He could not keep his eyes from the spot. He began the decent down the nearly vertical hillside with the edges of his feet thrust into the rocky earth and his hands grasping at flimsy trees. Sections of loose gravel shifted under his feet as the eroding hillside threatened to give way beneath him. He half-wished for a landslide, as it would hurry his decent.

She had not surfaced. The water below boiled; Rivard feared hidden rocks. The pressure behind his eyes nearly blinded him as he scanned the churning water for signs of his wife. His wild eyeballs nearly popped.

Where is she? Please don't let me be too late!

A patch of gravel shifted beneath his feet. Rivard lost his footing and began to slide. He grasped at exposed roots. Dirt and tiny pebbles were forced under his fingernails and cuticles as he clawed at the ground, but the grade was just too steep. He could not stop himself. He let himself go.

The roar of the falls was deafening. Rivard's eyes were blinded by a high wall of mist. A sick numb feeling had paralyzed his body so that he did not feel his own gashes and cuts. The sinking realization that he had lost Constance made his own body a superfluous fact to be thrown aside and dealt with later.

A bright blue flash of color leaped out at his eyes. Wedged between the rocks was—his wife's sweater! Constance had grown warm, had tied the cardigan around her waist as they had climbed up the trail. Now it was stuck between rocks. The bright blue color which had looked so cheerful just a few hours ago now looked like a funeral shroud.

Rivard's throat tightened. He suffocated on a sob. He plunged into the raging water, struggling with all his might to run through to the other side. The water swirled around him, holding him back as with powerful arms. It never occurred to Rivard to try to swim. He kept walking, pulling his body through the liquid barrier, determined but not frantic, for what did it matter now?

One thought beat against his skull like a club: I could have held her back. I could have held on to her wrist.

The water was deep, deeper than he had suspected. It flowed over his chest and circled his neck and he was nowhere near the other side. It took a great deal of strength for Rivard to swallow. The water constricted the tight cords of his neck. It seemed like a vice suddenly squeezing the breath from his body.

The mono-thought continued to beat at his brain: I could have held her back. I could have held on to her wrist.

Rivard's eyes did not leave the blue sweater as

the water came up over his chin and he was forced to swim. His eyes were staring at the object but seeing Constance and her pretty face.

Two violet eyes flashed laughter and a reckless joy. She had said: What are you doing? Giving me a checkup? Her eyes had said: I like it when you squeeze my wrist.

And he had let it go! He had let go of her wrist and sent her to die!

Suddenly Rivard hated himself. A passion stronger than any he had ever known consumed his body and blurred his vision. He felt something he had never felt before: an overwhelming desire to die.

The feeling was so strong it was surreal. It was surreal because it violated every instinct and motive he had ever possessed.

Rivard reached the rocks. He pressed his face into the tattered sweater. The sharp rock edges which had torn the sweater stabbed his face. He did not stop pressing his cheek to the rock, he pressed harder. His mind had renounced his body. His mind wanted to cause his body pain.

It was suddenly as though he were split in two. He began to dash his skull against the rock and end it forever. At the same time, he felt shock at a completely foreign state.

Water rushed into Rivard's open mouth, choking him. Mucus ran from his nose and he was forced to breathe through his mouth. He coughed, half-drowned by the water filling his lungs. He fought to raise his head so that he could slam it down.

His head was suspended over the rock. He knew that it would only take one swift, decisive blow. He wanted it. He had never wanted anything more than he now wanted to end his life.

He opened his eyes. He looked at the blue fibers stretched over the rock. He saw a bull's-eye, swimming in and out of focus, a target point on which to dash his head with a crack.

A voice whispered something to him. Some thought rose up through his insanity and flooded his brain. Rivard listened.

So now you want to die? Just this morning you laughed at Cindy Beale. You told her it was greed to want to die.

Rivard looked at the sweater. It was twisted and deformed, plastered to the jutting rock like a sneering face. He clawed at the face with his fingernails, screaming a reply in his brain.

It *is* greed to want to die, what I said was true. But not the way I meant it then. Death is greed to those who have something to live for, those who have something precious and irreplaceable and unrepeatable—and lost!

The water swirled around the sweater and it seemed to Rivard that the face had changed its expression and was laughing at him—laughing at him for not seeing the obvious.

You mean to say that life is only worth living for selfish reasons? And that those same selfish reasons could make a person want to die?

Yes! No! I don't know what evil thing you're trying to get me to say. All I know is that I'm sick and I'm doomed—I let the woman I love run into the woods and die!

The water suddenly shifted and the face gave a wink. Crazed and delirious, Rivard heard the voice of some ugly little imp, goading him on:

Go ahead, dash your head against that rock. It'll be all over the papers: Thomas Rivard, Suicide. Thomas Rivard, alias Endurance; Doctor, Fitness Coach, Taker of the Hippocratic Oath: Committer of Suicide. Ha! Some healer you made. At the first sign of misfortune you do violence to your oath.

Rivard screamed. He clawed at the sweater until there was nothing left but stray fibers which glistened against the rock like mermaid hair and washed away. Where his fingernails had been, raw pulp oozed like sausage and his fingertips were stubs of ground meat. He watched the strands of mermaid hair twist around the rocks and get lost. He thought that he had almost lost the only thing that mattered more to him than Constance: his fidelity to the Hippocratic Oath.

Though he was in shock, though the raging spring water was ice cold and quickly freezing his body, Rivard reaffirmed the words which were the psalm of his religion: "I will neither give a deadly drug to anybody who asked for it, nor will I make a suggestion to this effect . . . In purity and holiness I will guard my life and my art."

A calm feeling entered his brain. His body shook violently, his nerves spasmed in protest to the unendurable cold, but his mind was serene. His mind was soothed by the knowledge that it would protect and respect his body, as it was bound to protect and respect every human body. No matter what happened, no matter what unforeseen circumstance placed in his way, this much was true: Thomas Rivard would never—could never—knowingly end a life, his own or another. Life at any cost was a graven absolute.

He crawled up onto the rock, some kind of half-formed creature emerged from the sea, some kind of being only partway through its evolution. Rivard gasped like one forced to breathe air after developing in fluid; it was a violent, wholly unconscious transition. He clutched the wet rock with the desperation of an infant.

The mist rose around his shivering body. The horror of what he had nearly accomplished suddenly seemed insignificant, completely unimportant and trite. What did it really matter, if he were alive or dead? What good was his body without his appendages?—for losing Constance was like losing his legs and arms.

Rivard felt dead. He felt dead and wondered whether feeling dead was not actually the same thing as being dead. His body was hard, laid out prone on the rock, but it was not the hardness of strength; it was the hardness of rigor mortis. He looked down at his hands and clenched them as if clenching a sudden thought: Is a life stripped of *life*—of the things that make life worth living—not the same as death? Is death the cessation of life, or is it the cessation of feeling *alive*?

His brain screamed in protest to the question—screamed, fought it—and lost. Another part of him, the gut part of him that he had always pushed down and ignored, silenced and shunned, fed him something secret, something primal and forbidden: Was it life he was sworn to protect and defend, or the quality of feeling alive? Was there a difference?

Rivard was sick. He did not know whether to run for help or search for her body alone.

Her body! Rivard remembered the day he had seen her body naked for the very first time. They had been hiking. Constance was hot and sticky. She had mentioned a bath. Rivard had taken her to a secret swimming hole. Her clothes had fallen to the rock and her lean white body in the water had looked like a minnow. When she had emerged, she had pulled her hair over one shoulder to wring it out.

Rivard smiled to himself, a delirious, half-crazed smile. Across the water, standing in the mist with her hair hanging over one shoulder, was Constance. She smiled and waved.

Rivard burst out laughing.

He spoke out loud and his voice was drowned in the roar of the falls. "So now I'm seeing ghosts. Now I'm seeing lifelike apparitions. What do you want, Siren? Have you come to lead me to my grave? Have you come to seduce me under the water with a bewitching tune?"

He watched in amusement as Constance shook her head and bit her bottom lip.

I'm crazy, he thought. I'm having a hallucination. Constance bites her lip in just that way when she's deep in concentration.

Rivard slipped on the rock as he rose up on his feet. He caught himself and began to dance. He danced on the wet rock like an insane elf. His voice was high and mean like an elf with a hex.

"I've lost my mind and I don't care. Nothing matters now, not even my underwear!"

He began to pull the drenched clothes from his body. He balled up the sopping garments and flung them into the mist. He turned to see if the apparition was watching.

Constance was studying him and imitating his movements. Her wet clothes formed a rainbow that arched up over the mist and disappeared.

"Oh, let me see if I can get that pot o' gold at the end of the rainbow," Rivard said with glee. "I'll be rich and it won't matter that I see visions of the dead."

He was back in the water and moving through it with the fearless certainty of a dog. His mind had gone and his body had taken over, as if his body were in control and instinctively knew what to do.

Constance was naked and laughing and beckoning to him. He paddled toward her, tongue hanging from his mouth like a big dumb Newfoundland, eyes without whites like a big protective dog.

Then there was the moment he could not feel her hands on his arms, because his body had gone numb. He could not hear her whisper "Were you worried about me?" because he knew there was nothing to worry about ever again, the horrible unthinkable thing that he had almost done would never threaten him again because Constance was life itself and his professional promise was one with the life of this woman. The two were linked in some religious way—his vow to protect life and this woman who was the symbol of life, a human life, a life of unbreached joy.

Rivard did not put these feelings into conscious words. He was in a state of relieved shock which made him oblivious to the existence of words. As he and Constance walked home together and he was leaning on her like an old man there was this thing that his gut knew but his brain did not:

It *was* life he was sworn to protect and defend, and life is the quality of being *alive*.

They had been sitting in the cafeteria for some time. Their plates were empty and their mugs had stopped steaming. Their napkins, thrown haphazardly on the table, looked like fallen gulls.

Rivard spoke first and the tone of his voice contained the things he did not have to say: "There's nothing better than a good breakfast. You work till six?"

"Yes." Constance smiled in answer to the message contained in the tone of his voice: *It's not the hunger of my stomach that brings me here, it's the hunger of my eyes.*

She found his hands and her eyes were bright and anxious. The sun was beginning to rise, daylight was streaming through the windows, and she was too excited to remain in her seat.

She popped up, a pretty jack-in-the-box, a bouncing girl propelled by springs. Rivard saw dishes rise, the cheerful flash of a wink, and a blue skirt swishing around snappy legs.

He laughed and reached for his mug. He was in such high spirits, his mood was so much like the breaking morning and Constance's purposeful snap, that all the slouching janitors and scowling nurses and concerned colleagues disappeared. Constance had waved her wand and made them all go up in smoke.

He looked at the sun and the words that came to his mind were an affirmation and a salute: You're right, Billy. I am on drugs. I am on a perpetual high. And you have no clue what you're missing. You and Mrs. Humphries and the whole world with its suspicions and resentments and accusations and doubts—you are denying yourself something that I will never feel ashamed of and never dream of giving up. Why don't you want it, too? Why are you living on a plodding treadmill, when you could run totally free? What is stopping you? What is stopping you from chasing this thing? What is stopping you from chasing this fleeting thing called life?

3

"Don't touch that! Get your hands off—don't you dare! Stable boys have no business meddling with the objects of the Queen."

"Stable boy, eh? That's the thanks I get for trying to save your hide? You covet those fancy jewels and it's the devil meddling with your soul. Greed will send you straight into the Pits of Hell, mark my words."

"Devil—ha! It's not the devil eyeing our fortunes, it's that crafty thief of a nurse. I know she's got her paws all over our loot."

Three Pine Manor residents—Dorothy Wheeler, Ira Stern and Agnes Lunk—turned to the director of the Alzheimer's ward: they turned to Constance Rivard.

Constance was sitting at her desk, busy with paperwork. She heard the comment but did not look up.

Ira shook his head. His heavily lined face settled into a scowl. He spoke to no one in particular: "I'm surrounded by she-devils. This one"—he jerked his arm toward Dorothy—"has diamonds and rubies flashing in her eyes. That one"—his arm was thrust at Agnes—"is constantly adding up her piles of hundred-dollar bills." Ira picked up the Bible that never left his side. He held it over his head with both hands, then stretched it in the direction of Constance. "And that creature—Jezebel!—she is the worst of all. That one has been trying to lure me into a life of sin!"

"Stable boys are always trying to have affairs," Dorothy said. "It's quite all right, as long as it does not affect or taint the saintly virtue of the Queen."

"You're about the furthest living thing from a saint," Ira replied.

"Or a queen." Agnes eyed Dorothy's royal scepter—an old marching band baton studded with enormous rhinestones. "All that stuff is counterfeit. It wasn't mined, it was mass produced. No queen has fraudulent treasure."

Dorothy looked down at the costume jewelry which was her pride. Twelve beaded necklaces, left over from a Mardi gras celebration, hung around her neck. Her lavender sweat shirt was covered with an assortment of old cameos and large faux jewels. Gaudy rings, purchased in the supermarket entryway, were stacked halfway up her fingers. Her favorite part was the large plastic orchid—the bright pink and purple corsage—that fit around her wrist.

Dorothy gazed at her jewels, not the slightest bit offended. "It is normal for the peasantry to resent and envy royalty," she said, using her most magnanimous voice. "The nobility are aware of this and, in their great benevolence and generosity, are able to overlook the petty squabbling of the people." She tried to stand tall and swayed on a mismatched pair of high heels.

"Who are you calling a peasant?" Agnes sniffed, shifting in her chair. "I've got more loot stashed away than King Tut. I've got stacks of bills lining the mattress I sleep on."

"It is not money that makes one royalty," Dorothy replied, "but family lineage."

"Neither of which matter when you are talking about the Kingdom of God." Ira's wrinkles deepened. He looked like a grumpy old Shar-Pei. "All this talk over money and jewels is sinful. I'm going to tell you both the tale of Mammon. It just might save your souls from—"

"Save us from what? Dragons and sorcerers and ogres and ghouls? Oh, stable boy, do save us from these dangers—rescue the kingdom and I will be so grateful for your valiant conduct that I will—I will dub you a knight!"

Dorothy teetered on her mismatched heels as she waved her marching band baton and adjusted the ermine stoles draped around her neck. She made sure the little weasel face was not hidden beneath her purple feather boa.

"No one ever became a knight by getting hit with rhinestones," Agnes said. "What you need is metal, something with weight. We need a sword of precious metal."

"I'll take no part in this blasphemous game," Ira said. "I am not a knight from some fairy tale—I am a dedicated soldier of God!"

Agnes began to sing "Onward, Christian Soldiers" at the top of her lungs.

Dorothy marched around the room, keeping time with her fancy baton.

Pleased with the selection, Ira snapped his

fingers and bounced the Bible on his knees.

Constance heard the commotion and looked up from her work. She looked up just in time to see Dorothy sway back a little too far on her ill-fitted heels—

She was in the room before disaster. She led Dorothy to her dress-up trunk. "I think we do have a sword," Constance said. "It came with the old pirate costume. Help me look for it, Dorothy. We also need to find you a nice pair of flats."

"Queens do not wear flat shoes. Whoever heard of a Queen in flat shoes? Queens do not wear flat shoes."

"No, queens do not wear flat shoes," Constance said, rifling through the contents of the trunk. "But goddesses do." She held up a pair of sandals on two slender fingers.

Dorothy's eyes grew large and glittered like sequins. Two arms dotted with liver spots reached out for the shoes.

"Silver nail polish would look stunning with these sandals, Dorothy. If you want, I can get it out for when the podiatrist comes." Constance smiled at Agnes. "Would you like a pair of sandals, too? You and Dorothy can both have goddess feet."

Ira's voice came out a sudden roar: "Just what are you up to, Jezebel? Undoing all the good work I've done in educating these two? What is this devil-talk about goddesses? There is only One True God!"

"Moneybags was talking to me," Agnes said,

scowling at Ira. She turned to Constance. "I do want sandals—*gold* sandals, with gold nail polish to match." She narrowed her eyes. "You'd know all about gold, now wouldn't you?"

Constance reached into the pocket of her sweater and produced some change: one quarter, two nickels and four grubby pennies. "That's it, Agnes. I'm worth a whopping thirty-nine cents."

"That's very clever, Moneybags. Pretend poverty, when you are secretly pilfering loot. You don't think I notice, do you? You don't think I know that you're ripping me off? I've got you for an exact amount. I count my fortune every night."

"I knew it! I knew it!" Ira pointed to Agnes with a finger like a hook. "I knew you were one of those tabloid astrologers!"

"She said 'count my fortune,' not 'tell my fortune'." Dorothy pushed up the tiara that was slipping down her face. "But I really wish she had. I'm dying to know what is the ultimate fate of my kingdom."

"You leave fate to God, sinner. Your fate is in His hands."

"Right now your fate is in my hands," Constance said, rising to her feet. Come into the kitchen with me while I prepare your lunch."

Constance hummed to herself as she diced celery and onions. The Pine Manor finches accompanied her with periodic "cheeps." The autumn day was unusually warm and a pleasant breeze came through the open window.

The residents had been quiet for some time, when Agnes's eyes narrowed into watchful slits.

"What are you putting into that tuna salad, Moneybags?"

"Mayonnaise, onions, a little salt and pepper."

"That's not what I mean."

"I know you don't like celery, Agnes. I'm not putting any celery in yours."

"What else are you putting in my tuna?"

"A little TLC."

Agnes let out a contemptuous snort. "I know you are a thief and now I've caught you in a lie. What are you using today, Moneybags? Is it rat poison, like usual? Or are you going to use cyanide and finish me off quick?"

"I don't have access to cyanide, Agnes." Constance's laugh was benevolent and bright. "And it's not my policy to poison the people under my care."

The copper kettle whistled and Constance stopped to fix their tea. She did not have to ask: Ira took his black, Dorothy used milk and sugar. Agnes liked to squeeze her sweetener from the sticky honey bear that "guarded" her seat.

She knew their preferences as well as she knew her own. She catered to their wishes with the fastidiousness of a butler: a side of extra mayo for Ira—he put mayonnaise on everything, even peanut butter and jelly, and Constance made sure that it was "the *real* thing, not Miracle Whip"—a full place setting for Dorothy complete with shrimp fork, salad fork, dinner fork, butter knife, teaspoon, soup spoon, water glass, wine glass, champagne flute, coffee cup, saucer and an elegant cloth napkin, "for royalty could expect to dine with no less"—and disposable flatware with salt, pepper, relish, mustard and ketchup packets wrapped in plastic for Agnes, who was taking all the necessary precautions, as she was convinced that Constance was poisoning her food.

Tuna salad sandwiches were placed on the table. Agnes pulled back the top slice of bread to examine the contents. Ira reached out and slapped her hand.

"Don't touch your food, we haven't said Grace!"

"Don't touch me, you old monk! There's no need to say a prayer over this food, it's going to send me straight to the grave."

"All the more reason to say a prayer: one last chance to repent for the sins of your wretched soul!"

"I'm not the one who needs a prayer," Agnes said, using her plastic fork to poke at a pickle. "You'd better pray for that murderous thief standing at the kitchen sink."

Constance laughed, her hands immersed in soapy water. "Don't you dare say a prayer for me. I won't accept it."

Ira gasped. Agnes dropped her fork. Only Dorothy seemed unaffected. She was daintily cutting the crust from her bread.

"What do you mean—you won't accept it?" Ira looked at Constance with eyes narrowed into lines.

Constance dried her hands and stood with her back to the sink. "I mean," she said, eyes alive and twinkling, "that a prayer is a waste of breath where I'm concerned. I *make* my fortune."

"Everyone needs prayer." Ira said it with a voice that was tired and small.

"Not me." Constance and her voice were pretty as a chirp. "How is your lunch?"

Agnes and Ira were confused and turned to their food. Dorothy set down her fork and spoke as though on cue. "This meal," she said, dabbing the corners of her mouth, "is one of the most delicious I've ever had. Thank you, scullery maid, for so honorably serving the Queen. Good food is one of life's simple pleasures."

"Hallelujah!" Constance said, laughing. "Hallelujah, Amen!"

They did not know why she laughed. They did not know that she was laughing in delight, in abandon, in simple human joy at the completely unexpected.

Dorothy Wheeler had slowly chewed her food, carefully swallowing every bite. The last morsel left on her plate, the last morsel she popped in her mouth with the eagerness of a child anticipating a treat, was the pickle. She, who used her silverware with the polished elegance of a noble lady, grabbed the dill pickle chip with crooked fingers and stuffed it in her puckered mouth.

Constance laughed, because she loved the sour tang of dill pickles. Like Dorothy, Constance always saved the pickle.

Pine Manor was quiet, in the usual way of a nursing home in the afternoon: the residents had settled down for naps. Constance was combing Dorothy's hair, still damp from the shower. Dorothy broke the peace with her characteristic chatter.

"Yes, dear, you are still my very best lady in waiting. All the other girls tug and yank at the knots in my hair. And you know how tender my scalp can be . . . ."

Constance smiled down at the crown of her head. The medication had taken most of her hair; it had turned thick silver locks into pale grey wisps, as thin as bands of cirrus clouds. Nonetheless, Dorothy retained a high level of vanity about it all, and requested that Constance pin her hair in a bun at the nape of her neck.

"I have positively wrung my hands about the quality of household servants these days. Why is it so difficult to find respectable maids? Thank goodness I have you. To think, a Queen with only one decent maid."

Constance gently passed the comb over Dorothy's scalp, treating it with all the delicacy and softness of an infant's scalp. She took special care around Dorothy's ears, making sure not to scratch them or upset the large clip-on earrings that dangled from the lobes.

"It is such a hard life, being a Queen. Being a Queen is much harder than you might think." Dorothy twisted in her seat to look up at Constance. "Is your life difficult, dear? You're pretty so the answer must be yes.

Life is always more difficult for pretty gals."

Constance laughed at the word "gals." Sometimes Dorothy forgot that she was a queen and lapsed into the common banter of her era.

"The only thing that makes life difficult," Constance said, "is knowing that it's going to end."

The film that normally clouded Dorothy's eyes suddenly cleared. Constance was looking into the face of a total stranger.

"Do you think about that often?" Dorothy snapped the question in a manner of true authority that made her royalty routine seem like a bluff.

"I—well, no, not at all. I made that promise to myself." Constance looked into the sharp crystal eyes of a judge. "When life stops, it's over, that's it. The second that the living stops and the questioning sets in—that answers the question."

Dorothy's voice was another snap: "And what is the question?"

The next span of seconds seemed to move—not according to time—but according to the irregular beat of her heart. Dorothy clutched onto her wrist, the old fingers were pressed down over her pulse, and Constance could not believe such strength could come from the hand of that woman. It forbade her to hold anything back.

Constance said, "When living stops, when living stops but organs have the nerve to keep pumping, keep on pushing blood and air—what would you call it?"

Dorothy's eyes were probes and her fingers

constricted Constance's wrist. She waited for Constance to finish, her body still as stone, only her fingers coiling like tiny serpents around the point of her pulse.

Constance said, "I'd call it living death."

"And the question? What about the question?" Dorothy's voice was touched by hysteria.

"Can living death be called a life?"

A sound rose up from Dorothy's gut. Constance was not sure whether it was a grunt or a growl.

What Dorothy said next made Constance think that it had been a growl.

"And what would you do with us old timers, love? Would you give us all a fatal shot?"

"Of course not!"

Dorothy laughed and the sound made Constance shiver. "I would!"

Constance did not know what to say.

Dorothy had not released her wrist. Constance felt her flesh bruising under the pressure of the serpent fingers.

"You're a smart girl," Dorothy said. "But it's not a brain that gives you the opinion you're afraid of, the opinion you're afraid to say out loud, even around a kook like me—it's a heart."

Constance felt her pulse begin to race. She knew what was coming.

"You know it, don't you?" Dorothy looked right at Constance, right through her. "You know why we're all in here: fear. It's fear. No one with any courage lets their brain turn into mush." Dorothy loosened the grip of her fingers around Constance's wrist. "Senility is the suicide of cowards."

Dorothy stood up and walked over to her bed. She sat with her legs hanging over one side. Wrapped in a white bathrobe, she looked as fragile as a doll.

"All of us in here—we all copped out." Dorothy waited for Constance to say something. Constance was silent. She knew that the thing to do was hear the woman out. Dorothy continued. "Insanity is easy. It's a whole lot easier than taking a bottle of pills or aiming a gun. It's also a whole lot less dignified."

Constance was shaking. She had trouble holding up her head. She wanted to run from the room, but her strongest quality kept her from leaving: Constance was, above all else, unfailingly humane. She knew that Dorothy needed an audience. Though she might live for many years, this was Dorothy's final moment.

"Do you know what killed Ira Stern? Do you know what made him stop living, and turn into a babbling mystic? He backed over his grandson with a riding lawnmower—and the little tot lived. They held his body together with a blanket and brought him to the hospital—in time to find out he'd never walk, never make love—the lawnmower blades mangled his genitals. He'd be eliminating in a rubber bag for the rest of his life. How's that for happy news? You've condemned your grandson to the loveless life of a freak. Or worse, some pseudo-marriage based on pity. But guess what? Ira Stern was too chicken to pull the trigger and now he's hanging on in here. He lost everything, his life is worth nothing, *by his own admission*, and those damned organs—what was it you said?—they have the nerve to keep pumping, keep on pushing blood and air."

Constance felt nothing but a blinding beat behind her eyes. The rest of her body was empty and light. It was as though she were withstanding a severe beating and, simultaneously, receiving a pat on the back.

"What about Agnes Lunk?" Dorothy said. "What drove her to a state of living death? What incident ended her life?" Constance shook her head. "Did you ever stop to wonder, what is the origin of Agnes's obsession with poison? I'll bet it won't surprise you to find out that Agnes deliberately poisoned her only son's wife. The reason? Agnes was convinced that June—that was the name of the wife—was not worthy of her son, something about 'poor white trash.' I guess he didn't think so because they found him in the garage on a noose. Not only did Agnes lose her soul, by committing murder—her actions also resulted in the loss of her son, that son being everything. And though she lost everything, those pesky organs still continue to function as though there is some human life there to sustain. I think you and I would question whether that is true or false."

Dorothy gave Constance a conspiratorial wink. Constance felt a chill, even while her palms were oozing sweat.

"And what about me? What is the nature of my insanity? It's not as interesting as the others, certainly not as scandalous and dark." Dorothy's eyes drilled into Constance's face. "I'm dying. Just run your finger down the list and pick a disease. Every one of them involves a long, ugly, drawn-out death. Nothing quick and easy. No—I got stuck with death by molasses."

Dorothy suddenly seemed tired, and she stopped to catch her breath. Her eyes did not tire or cloud; they poked at Constance like cattle prods.

"Do you know how badly I want to end all this—all the hair loss and bed wetting and needles and gout? I hate it. Life isn't fun anymore, and if I had half of your courage or heart, Constance Rivard, I would end it this second."

Constance's jaw fell open, literally fell, and she was incapable of believing that she heard the words correctly.

"Don't look so shocked, my delicate lady in waiting. Senile types still have eyes and ears." Dorothy smiled, and Constance knew that she was nearing the point of her speech.

"One thing that we have plenty of time for in a nursing home is thinking. I've been doing a lot of heavy thinking." Dorothy's hair was slightly damp and she adjusted the collar of her robe around her neck. "The way I see it, there are two responses one can give to Mother Nature—one human, the other not."

She slowly closed and opened her eyes in preparation for what she was about to say.

"When nature takes your greatest values—when nature takes away your husband or your wife or your health or your kids—you've got to ask yourself a question: Is life without those values bearable? Is it really even life at all? If the answer is No, if life without your values is unbearable, truly unbearable, then the only thing to do is get rid of it. One can literally get rid of it, or end it, which is the human way of doing things—the uncompromised way—or one can go nuts by default. Going nuts is not a choice—it's the abdication of making the ultimate choice."

Dorothy was looking at Constance and the sadness of ages was etched in the lines of her face. Her smile was even sadder as she said, "I didn't have the courage to make the human choice."

She laid down on the bed. Her body was wrapped in the robe and looked small, smaller every second, as if it were quickly disappearing. Constance thought her body would suddenly shrink out of sight.

The film returned to Dorothy's eyes. Constance knew that she had witnessed the end.

"Bring my scepter, maid," Dorothy said. "You know I never sleep without my royal jewels."

Constance had lived with it for several weeks, had lived with it like one lives with a deep wound and now the wound was only on the surface and even that was healing. She had forgotten the initial gash, forgotten the initial pain. She had forgotten the pain of hearing another speak the contents of her soul. She had sorted through the contents of her soul—discarded what she did not like, tucked away the rest. She knew that she would have to take it out again soon—she did not know when, whether it was close or fairly far—she knew only that it loomed ahead, a milepost set off in the distance.

But today was not the day for thinking of the future or even of the past because the clouds were high and white in a clear blue sky that suggested autumn's peak, not November. The peak had come and gone, fall's brilliant red climax had given way to the greys and browns that preface winter—but a hint of autumn's fire remained in the color of the light: the sun was a gold-bronze glint of precious metal.

Constance saw the polished metal light in the delicate, paper-thin outlines of leaves. The season had degraded their surfaces, they had been swept and battered by cold weather, dry air and dust, but the glorious light was transforming brown into bronze, and the leaves looked like gilded cups.

Constance stood knee-deep in fallen leaves. The sound of her metal rake was a brief scratch and a twang, tines dragged over earth and an abrupt lift that ended with vibration. Her feet crunched through the thick layer, her bent elbows pumped back and forth, and the sun warmed the crown of her head to a halo of chestnut.

Her nephew looked away from the woodpile and over at Constance. "It's leaning pretty far to one side. What do you want me to do?"

Constance looked at the wall of stacked wood

she had asked him to build. It curved in several places, like a back with scoliosis. A dangerous lean threatened the integrity of the spine.

His eyes moved from his aunt to the pile and back to his aunt. A frown of self-loathing clouded his face.

"I never get things right," Ethan said. "I'm just no good at this stuff. I always mess things up!"

He was pouting and sorry for himself and Constance did not speak to the rotten habit her younger sister coddled and encouraged.

"There's nothing wrong with that pile," Constance said. "Let me show you a trick."

His eyes were slanted and defensive. He watched his aunt through suspicious slits.

She picked up a piece of hard maple. Bits of shaggy moss sloughed off the bark and stuck to the suede of her oversized gloves.

He smiled at the funny hollow knock, as she struck the protruding piece of wood into line with the others. Several more knocks and the surface was flush.

She turned around. His smile vanished but not quickly enough. She saw that he had forgotten to pout.

"That didn't fix my pile and my pile still stinks," he whined.

"And?" Constance looked directly at Ethan with eyes that were merry and bright.

"I don't want to do this anymore! I'm no good at it and I hate doing things I'm no good at. My mom would never make me do this. I always have to come here and do things I don't want to—"

"You don't have to stack wood." The words abruptly cut him off.

Ethan stopped. He blinked several times and looked away at the trees. Constance said it again. This time her voice was firm but sounded soft. "You don't have to stack wood, Ethan." His eyes shot to her face and bounced back to the trees. "I only want your help if you are willing to give it. There is no coercion here."

His eyes widened slightly, as if in disbelief. This was not something he was accustomed to hearing. He thought of his mother, and how different she was from her sister. His mother always said: You're going to do it whether you like it or not!

He shrugged his shoulders and scowled at unfamiliar talk. He forced the words out through the space in his teeth. "No, I'll do it. It's fine, I don't care."

"Why would I want the help of someone who doesn't care?"

There was no hint of sarcasm and Ethan stared at his aunt in complete disbelief. Constance noticed his surprise and rephrased the question: "What fun is working with a grump?"

Ethan's face turned red and he kicked at the ground. Constance said, "Go ahead and do what you want, Ethan. I'll finish the yard by myself."

She grabbed the rake leaning against a tree. Ethan heard the harsh scratch of the rake's tines dragging leaves. He watched her for awhile in sulky silence. He realized that he had been forgotten and it began to bother him. He did not like standing on the periphery.

Slowly and quietly, like a sneaking child, Ethan stooped to the ground and picked up a small chunk of wood. He placed it on top of the stack, trying not to make a sound. He waited for Constance to notice and say something. She continued to rake so he went on with the wood.

Constance switched the rake from one hand to the other. The feeling had begun in her chest when they had started working; it had moved out to her hands. She wiggled her fingers in her glove, hoping to shake off the numbness. It always came on suddenly, but never lasted long. Constance bit her lip and thought: Just breathe, it'll go away. It always goes away.

Ethan noticed the grimace and assumed it was directed at him. Acutely self-conscious, he reddened and threw down the wood.

She concentrated on even breathing. She spoke through breaths that felt like gasps. "You are a good helper, Ethan. I'm really glad you want to work."

It's subsiding, she thought. My fingers are prickling. Just a few more minutes. I can ride it out.

Ethan was suspicious of the compliment because her body was stiff and the words did not match the expression on her face. It seemed to him she was suffering.

"You don't have to lie, Aunt Connie. I know you don't need me—my work is no good."

She did not open her eyes when she smiled.

"You're wrong, Ethan. I do need you."

It was the tone of her voice—simple, benevolent and strong—that made him know she spoke the truth.

His chest was too full for words. He did not want to spoil the feeling by speaking. He picked up a chunk of cherry and quietly studied the bark.

After several minutes, her face was smooth and clear. Turned up to the sun, it had the quiet, infinitely thankful look of a nun engaged in prayer. In her moment of desperation, Constance had whispered, "Please, please, I'll do anything, just make it go away." When the danger had passed, when the worst of it was over, Constance forgot all about the appeal that she had made.

The pair continued to work. Ethan decided that being needed was better than being pitied. He cheerfully stacked the remainder of the wood, gathering little shards and slivers for kindling. Constance raked up the rest of the leaves—and would have raked the leaves from every yard in the area—she was glad the spell had passed and she could move. Constance felt that work was bliss, for work meant the rigorous use of arm and leg muscles that did what they needed to do.

Constance looked around the yard and said, "We're finished except for one thing."

"What's that?" Ethan brushed a spider from his shoulder and watched it scurry beneath a piece of hanging bark.

"A bonfire." His eyes leaped to her face. "Do you want to go with me to get the permit?"

"Yeah!" His leather work gloves were two severed hands suddenly flying through the air.

Constance laughed. "All right, Ethan. You take the navigator spot. Just let me run inside and grab a drink."

She stood over the bathroom sink, drawing handfuls of ice cold water to her face. She liked the painful sting because she could feel it. She looked down at her hands. She waved her fingers under the stream of water. She smiled at the uncomfortable pinch.

Pain is a good thing, she thought to herself. The body is not functioning correctly if there is no pain.

She went outside to meet Ethan. Pain of another kind flooded her chest. That's normal, too, she told herself, trying to forget it. The heart is not functioning correctly if there is no response.

The feelings did not last. Ethan had discarded his habitual pout and turned into an enthusiastic young man. The change was delightful and Constance became as excited about a campfire as he was.

"Can we get hot dogs and marshmallows?" he said.

"Of course. I'll show you how to whittle down the perfect sticks."

The owner of the general store smiled at the happy twosome as they stamped through the door.

"Well, if it isn't Connie Rivard!" He pronounced her last name "Riverd," like "herd" without the "H."

Constance smiled at the man. "Hello, Burt.

What have you been up to lately?"

"Oh, just minding the business, which means minding everybody else's business. Hey, haven't seen you in a while. Do you have time to talk?"

The look on his face said: No kids allowed. Ethan headed off in the direction of the candy and chips.

Burt watched Ethan disappear. "Man, he's growing. How's your younger sister?"

Constance did not like small talk, but directing a nursing home had endowed her with infinite patience. She said, "Corinne is fine," hoping he would get to the point.

Burt seemed to sense her anxiety. His voice changed abruptly as he said, "How is Dr. Rivard?"

Her eyes searched his eyes for some sign or a clue. She did not know where the conversation was headed. "Tom is well, Burt." A note of impatience crept into her voice.

"Listen, Connie, I like you. You know I like you and Tom both a lot. I want to give you a heads up on something."

"What is it?" Constance was tired of the build-up and her voice came out a snap.

"Have you talked with Bill Metcalf?"

"No."

"Mrs. Humphries?"

"No."

"How about any of the guys in the Moose?"

"Burt, just tell me what it is!" She could not

bear another second of the lame small-town drama.

"Good. I'm glad I got to you before they did." He waited for her to prompt him on. When she did not beg him to continue, Burt felt the secret press at the back of his throat and he blurted, "They think your husband's strung on speed."

Constance burst out laughing.

Burt looked like a hurt puppy whose master refused to throw the stick.

"What's the matter, Burt? I'm taking your news so well, you should be pleased."

"Connie, this is serious." His face had the strained look that accompanies a bout of constipation.

"No, it isn't serious. It's rumor. I don't pay attention to rumor."

Burt's face changed. It was no longer strained, it was annoyed. Constance knew that Burt was disgusted because she had not become indignant.

He tried again. "I've seen it happen to a few doctors over the years. Stress of the job, pressure to keep long hours, competition with colleagues. Are you *sure* your husband's not on crank?"

Constance laughed. It was a loud, obnoxious sound that made everyone in the store turn and stare.

She was so happy that the terrifying numbness had gone away—she was buoyant and carefree and nothing mattered but the fact that she had a body that worked and hands that could feel—she was incapable of anything but generosity. Constance felt an unlimited benevolence toward every other human being in the world, even the town gossip.

Her voice was light and effortless as she said, “Listen, Burt, I know I can trust you, so try to keep it under wraps, okay? My husband is addicted to endorphins. He has been for years. All the running and the sweating, the endurance training and iron weights—it’s all about reaching an opiate high. Tom lives to flood his brain with tranquilizers.”

Constance had no idea that Burt Lancaster had no idea what endorphins were. She had no idea that the man had never finished school or taken science. She did not suspect that, as soon as she and Ethan left the general store with a paper sack full of campfire provisions and a permission granted by the local fire marshal, Burt Lancaster called Stanley Humphries and asked to speak with his wife.

Constance knew nothing about their breathless conversation:

“You were right, Heloise. By God, you were right. His own wife said as much. She said, ‘amph’—‘amph’—oh what’s that big long word that stands for speed?”

“Amphetamines?”

“That’s it! She said that, and something about opium.”

“Opium!”

“Yes! It’s worse than we thought. It’s worse than all the old boys suspected.”

“Oh, Burt, I’m so glad you found this out. I knew there was something strange about that man.”

“Thank heavens Stan wasn’t hurt. Incidentally, how is old Stan getting on?”

“Fine, just fine. He’s actually better than he’s been in years. I just thank the good Lord above he wasn’t hurt by that drug-crazed maniac, the night that he collapsed. Stanley is a very strong man, to come out untouched by that madman’s abuse.”

“We’ll make sure no one is abused by that quack again, Heloise. We can’t afford another close call. There’s no telling what might have happened if you weren’t there at the scene.”

“I know it. Times sure have changed.”

“Yes. Yes they have. It’s pretty unsettling when the man you’ve got to watch out for is the doctor.”

Constance and Ethan were unaware of the store owner’s conversation. They were unaware of anything but the gold-rimmed sun of a late fall afternoon. The small car zipped along the winding road and seemed to move through a world that was still and gilded. Constance looked out over the harvested fields—she looked at the bleached stalks of left-over hay—and for the length of a moment, the world was held in a frame of sepia. Gold-slanted, flooded by light, a burnished antique still life filled the window.

Constance knew it by the vague sensation in her bones—she did not put it into words, there were no words for the thing she felt—only a vague sensation that reached down to her marrow. She felt it when she looked at the solitary hay wagon, old boards warped and bowed, great gaps between the slats where sunlight streamed in brilliant orange bands—she felt it when she saw the wagon's crazy pitch, a wheel with busted spokes collapsing, buckling under the weight of the season's last impatient load, and orange sunlight breaking through like axles.

Constance looked out over the field. The view was tinged with something infinite and final. Her chest was filled with longing, and it was not the usual longing felt toward day's end—it was not the bittersweet stirring peculiar to dusk—it was longing of a type she had not felt for years. Constance looked out over the sundrenched earth and felt like she was hearing tolling bells.

Her mind recalled what had previously given her the feeling and she quickly looked at Ethan. He was staring out the window, a faint, slightly absent smile on his face, lost in private thoughts.

Constance never interrupted thinking. She never talked to people with books, or disturbed a look of contemplation. She always granted quiet to the workings of the mind. An unnatural dread had replaced her native inclinations and her voice came out shaking: "It's a beautiful afternoon, don't you think?"

Constance knew that Ethan sensed something because he did not answer, just turned to her and stared. She repeated the words; this time her question was a statement. She said, "It's a beautiful afternoon," as though trying to convince herself that the only thing of importance was the weather.

Perplexed but not alarmed, Ethan turned back to

the window. Constance looked at the late sun on his hair, she saw the light brown like spun gold, then turned and trained her eyes on the yellow lines in the road.

That day, that day the sun was orange flame.

Thoughts leaped to her mind like the curves in the road. She jerked the steering wheel, not so much in time with the curves as with her racing thoughts.

The sun was orange, brighter than noontime sun. The sun was nearly down, and it looked like it would mint the earth in solid gold.

She slapped down her visor to shield her eyes from the glare. Her eyes narrowed into protective slits. It was not the light she was trying to avoid; it was the sudden flashback.

Constance watched the hitter through narrowed slits. Her eyes were closed against the sun, her vision lessened by a lowered screen of lashes. She kept the hitter within sight. Uncle Ed was known to hit the ball out past the trees.

There was Ed's ceremonial thump, the dust rising up around the wooden bat as it slammed down on the plate. There was one quick hoist, a tense anticipatory twirl, and a wild swing that wrenched his back. Uncle Ed was a good hitter, but her father was an even better pitcher.

Constance smirked. She loved to watch her father strike him out.

Ed took his time moving back into position. He kicked at the ground, raising some dust. He spat into the cloud and watched it settle. A little of the vigor had gone from the hoist—it was slower, more consciously directed—but the lazy twirl had turned into a cyclone. Ed was gearing up to hit the ball beyond the trees.

From the outfield, her father was a distant pillar. He stood with both arms hanging at his sides. The baseball looked like a tiny globe rotated by long fingers. His body snapped into action and the ball became a planet held by rays—then a planet spinning through space, a celestial body warmed by the sun on its fixed destination—as a space casualty disappearing into the black hole of the catcher's glove.

A group of relatives cheered. The planet had been caught; it had not gone spinning into another universe. Constance breathed out quickly, her relief an ugly snort: she would not have to search for the ball in the woods.

The stakes were high and everybody knew it. A strikeout meant the defeat of invincible Uncle Ed. A strikeout meant his brother Jonathan would become victor of the Dannonworth clan. The umpire called a time-out. The players moved in for consultation.

Constance watched her family members walk across the field. The sun was low in the sky, everything was orange. She knew that they wanted her to come in—the other outfielders were trotting across the grass, her father was waving, motioning with an arm like a crook—but she did not move.

Suddenly, everyone she loved was far away.

It was not a question of distance. Something

else had come between her and the other people. She watched the late sun glint off of wrist watches—she watched the slanted light gild excited faces and bare arms with pushed-up sleeves—and the world seemed to come to a stop. The world was solid and precious in the way that far off things are very dear: distance and low sun cast her view in solid gold.

She stood off in the field, away from her family—she heard the tinkling of laughter and the wild shriek of her unruly cousin Pearl. The smell of roasted hot dogs lingered on the air and Constance felt, rather than thought of, Indian summer.

She had not removed her glove. Her body was still except for the slight movement of her fingers. She was testing them. She knew better than to move too quickly, that always caused a cramp and aching pain—but slow, deliberate undulations, like the waving arms of a tranquil anemone, always seemed to do the trick.

She had not told anyone. She had never spoken of the funny sensation that began in her chest and numbed her fingers. It frightened her and she tried to ignore it. She always hoped each time would be the last.

More than the primitive terror, Constance hated the hot rush of embarrassment that accompanied a spell. She told herself that she should not feel that way, that she had done nothing wrong and there was nothing to be ashamed of—but the embarrassment never failed to flood her face. She was terrified the redness would give away her secret.

She knew that her family could not see her face

from across the field. She gave them a casual wave, letting them know she would remain where she was until the end of the at bat. Distance meant privacy, as well as isolation, and Constance wanted privacy in which to nurse her hand.

They might think I'm stiff, she thought. They might think I look sore but they will think nothing of it. The games have gone on for hours and who wouldn't be a little stiff? Constance smiled at an even better reason: she had carried Pearl piggyback all around the park. If anyone said anything to her she would just mention the squirming kicks of little Pearl.

She removed the battered leather glove and looked down at her hands. They looked completely normal: long, slender fingers with cuticles like crescent moons. She flipped them over: palms like cups of seashell pink, wrists with rivulets of blue. Constance stared at her hands and half-wished for some mark or a bruise. A bruise would indicate *something*, it would give her the help of a visual clue. The absence of any deformity was terrifying: a transparent malady is preferable to inexplicable bad news.

Constance pressed her palms together and did what she always did when the numbness passed and her fingers could feel: she buried it.

The players were moving back into position. Ed was at the plate. Jonathan trotted to the mound. Her sister Corinne had taken charge of rambunctious little Pearl, who was shouting, "Hit it, Daddy! Hit that ball out of this world!"

Constance watched the little girl twist and hop and a smile broke out on her face. She saw Corinne, ever suspicious of anyone having a good time, hush and chastise Pearl. She laughed when little Pearl, too independent to listen to Corinne, squirmed from her grasp and viciously slapped her away. Pearl ran to get a view of the infield and began to dance and hop.

The little girl's antics were contagious and Constance felt her spirits soar. The bad thing had passed and there was nothing to worry about. There was nothing to worry about but the outcome of Uncle Ed's at bat.

Each body was riveted with tension. The outfielders had pairs of hawk eyes with long talons ready to seize the flying ball. The basemen were standing on high alert, ready to spring like agile cheetahs. The catcher was crouching in wait behind his glove.

A breathless stillness fell over the field. For several moments no one moved. Late sunlight gave the scene a timeless quality and Constance felt like she was standing in a yellowed photograph, a moment caught and held. Everyone was silent, there was no sound except for one: a Saturday evening service had commenced. They all heard the steady mourn of tolling bells.

There was the sudden crumpling of her father's body, a collective gasp as his limbs unwound and flung the sphere. There was a set of arms merged into a single line of force that was the bat. There was the "Crack!"

then the arc, then an object held up in space by anxious eyes.

Head thrown back, glove raised and ready, Constance willed the ball into her hand. Piece of cake, she thought. I've made this catch a thousand times.

Something went wrong.

They all looked on, and no one could believe it: the ball fell and bounced two feet from her outstretched hand.

Constance collapsed and landed right next to it.

She tore her eyes from the yellow lines on the road. She looked over at Ethan. He was glued to the window, mesmerized by the landscape flinging by.

She looked back at the road and fought to overcome the nausea that liquefied her gut. Why did she always feel sick at the thought? Why did the mere suggestion of dependence turn her stomach into mush?

She knew that she could not relive the memory. Not now, not while she was driving. The thought of that horrible twenty-four hour period was enough to make her lose composure.

For some reason, as a result of some force she could not control, she recalled the memory:

"Just tell me if I've put too much on your spoon."

Margaret Dannonworth carefully scraped the milk running down her daughter's chin.

"I don't want any."

"Connie. You have to eat."

"No, I don't."

"You have to eat if you want to live. You want to live, don't you?"

"Not in this condition."

"I will hear none of that, Constance Dannonworth. The doctor said it's only temporary."

"That isn't all he said! He said it might come back again."

Margaret threw her daughter a look.

"That is not the proper attitude. It is not a Christian attitude."

Constance jerked her head from her mother's advancing spoon and said, "I am not a Christian."

The spoon rattled to the floor.

"Of course you are a Christian! A Christian must be grateful when he is asked to bear a cross."

If Constance had been able to move, she would have fled the house and never come back. Instead, she said, "Grateful for immobility and pain? Why would God make his children suffer? Why would God ask his children to like it? Is God trying to manufacture a world of little masochists?"

"Constance Dannonworth!"

Margaret Dannonworth was so enraged she bit her lip. She hated the taste of blood and she took her anger out on Constance: "Shut that filthy mouth! I can't believe you are capable of saying such things! Don't you know how special this is? To be martyred like a holy saint?"

Constance could not feel her arms or her legs

but she felt the blood within her veins turn cold. A terror like ice, a terror far worse than any she had experienced pricked at her spine and filled her bones. Her teeth chattered as she said, “You don’t really mean that, do you?”

Margaret’s face softened when she saw the look on her daughter’s face. “Of course I didn’t mean that, honey.” Constance was relieved to the point of tears. She heard her mother add, “I *know* you feel nothing but great devotion and strive to emulate the saints.”

Every cell of her body called out to her, Escape! She did not care if she had to crawl; she did not care if she had to travel on her hands and knees. She was going to get out of there, and fast.

With a gigantic effort, Constance focused on lifting herself out of the seat. She bit her lip and ground her molars. She strained as hard as she could and managed to get . . . nowhere. The full realization hit her like a fist: she could not move herself and any attempt at it was futile. Angry tears of protest rolled down her cheeks.

Her mother clucked several times and reached for some tissues. “It’s okay, honey. I know you are stressed out. Tough times always test our faith.”

“It’s not that!” Constance spat the words from a face that was red and inflamed. Her mother tried to get her to blow her nose into a tissue and Constance refused. She did not want help from her mother, from anybody; she would rather let the phlegm run down her face.

The more Constance struggled, the more her mother fussed and cooed. Her mother's behavior was worse than her inability to move, so she stopped trying.

She managed to choke down the rest of her food. She was beginning to feel a little better until she realized she had to use the bathroom. The indignity of help with the toilet was more than she could bear. Constance felt like dying. Dying was preferable to that kind of coarse humiliation.

She dealt with it because she did not have a choice.

She told herself that she would never, ever allow herself to be without a choice.

They were flying over a winding country road. The car was in a race with dying light and Constance felt insistent and slightly mean. She knew that Ethan was a good kid—she knew that he would have been a great kid if she had raised him instead of Corinne—and she said what she said out of protest to her sister's coddling.

"We've got one more thing to do before our fire."

Though Ethan was in his early adolescence, the late sun softened his features and made him look like a boy. "What is it?"

The steering wheel turned abruptly and the little car veered off of the main road and onto dirt. Thick woods lined one side of the road. A gigantic field spread off to their left.

Constance's face was set like a mask and Ethan

could not interpret her expression. Her voice was easily readable; it held nothing but derision. She said, "I'm going to teach you how to drive."

Most thirteen-year-old boys would have shouted and jumped at the chance. Ethan shouted, but his reaction was the kind that would have been approved by Mom. It was Corinne who suddenly spoke with a shriek.

"I can't do that! I'm not old enough and I don't know how!"

"I'm going to teach you how."

"No, you're not! I'm not old enough and you can't make me! What makes you think I want to drive this car?!"

"Don't you want to be competent and independent?"

Ethan's face crumpled into a grimace. "What's sex got to do with it?"

Constance laughed and her laughter broke the tension. "Not impotent, Ethan—competent! I wouldn't think you'd want to be impotent!"

Ethan's face turned several shades of red. He looked down at his lap and his voice was a sheepish plea. "You'd really, you'd really let me drive Aunt Connie?"

"Of course." Her voice was easy as a gust of wind. She realized that Ethan's baby act did not go all the way down. She suspected that it was just put on for the benefit of his mother.

Her complete confidence in his ability was a

shock. Ethan's mouth fell open and he stuttered a meager "Thank you." He barely heard her say, "Thank you for what? You don't need me to tell you that you're able."

The car was alone in a vast expanse of field. Constance and Ethan had switched places, and there had been no need to adjust the seat: the petite woman and the thirteen-year-old were nearly the same size.

Ethan clutched the steering wheel, then wrenched his hands away as though he had touched something hot. "I don't want to do this. Can I have my seat back?"

Constance linked her hands behind her head and stretched her legs as though she were lounging. "I've just made myself comfortable," she said. "I never give up a comfy seat."

The infant expression came over Ethan's face. His voice was a frightened whine. "I can't do it, Aunt Connie. I'm not big enough and I—I don't want to get in trouble."

Constance had closed her eyes as though settling in for a nap. She did not open them or alter the tone of her voice. "Get in trouble with who? Who's here to see?"

"God will see."

Constance chuckled. "I don't think God has qualms about under-aged driving."

Ethan was not convinced. He tried again. "It's not really that, Aunt Connie. I'm scared. I'm scared I'll do something wrong."

Constance lazily opened and closed her eyes. Her attitude was casual, and totally unconcerned. “We are in the middle of a barren field. There are no parked cars to dent, no old ladies with shopping carts to watch out for.”

“But what about the car?” Ethan said. “What if I do something to the car?”

“Such as?”

“What if I pull the wrong lever!”

“Ethan, this car is an automatic. It does all the work for you.”

“What do you mean?”

“I mean driving it is effortless. There is really nothing to it.”

Constance opened her eyes and looked at Ethan. His body was quivering and small. Constance suddenly felt intolerant and resentful: she had never liked weakness of any kind; she detested the newborn puppy helplessness his mother failed to wean.

She spoke as much to her sister as to her sister’s son. “Trust me, Ethan: you’ll like yourself better if you do this.”

The appeal surprised him. Ethan jumped. His young mind scrambled to figure it out.

What does she mean, I’ll like myself better? What’s that got to do with it? He stretched his toes toward the break pedal and gave it a tap. It’s almost as if she knows I . . . how does Aunt Connie know I hate myself when I’m scared?

He grabbed the steering wheel with both hands,

as if in self-defense. He looked at his aunt with eyes too large for his face. "Aunt Connie, if I do this, will God stop loving me?"

"What do you mean?"

"Mom said God loves people who are meek. If I drive this car it'll be doing something brave and God might not love me anymore."

Ethan stopped. Constance knew he was not finished.

She said, "And?"

"I'd rather love myself!"

Constance laughed and turned the key in the ignition. The guilt on Ethan's face melted into a smile of uninhibited joy.

As the little car jerked around the field, Ethan thought that he had a new favorite person. He thought he loved Aunt Connie even more than he loved his Uncle Tom.

They were both flushed and excited when they traded places and finally set off for home.

"You are a natural, Ethan. Soon you'll be tearing up the race track, surrounded by groupies."

Ethan's proud grin matched the satisfaction in his voice. "Did I really get it up to twenty-five?"

"You were going thirty."

The approval in her voice was like a badge pinned on his chest. Ethan sat on the edge of the passenger seat and looked straight out the windshield. His gaze never once veered off to the scenery. His eyes were focused on the road.

Constance did not have to look over at Ethan to know that his body was tense and alert, that his hands were balled into fists, that his fists were making indents in his thighs. She did not have to see the expression on his face—pupils like new moons, lips pressed into a set of rigid lines—to know that he was not seeing a strip of pavement leading to her house. Constance knew that Ethan was following the road, not as a child follows the pathway home, but as an adolescent follows the open stretch into his future.

They reached the crest of a hill. Rays of evening sunlight glinted off the hood, sending bands of gold in all directions. Momentarily suspended in space, the car was caught in the day's final wink, a flash of light more brilliant than morning.

When Constance and Ethan regained their eyesight, the sun was gone and they were headed down the hill. The roar of wind in the open windows was deafening; the rush of cold air sent their hair flying in violent whirls; their breath was wrenched away and left at the top. Constance looked at Ethan, then back at the plummeting road. The world was racing toward them—the world was streaking toward their windshield as quickly as they were flying down to meet it—and Constance felt it hit when her stomach dropped.

The grade steepened to a pitch. The car was catching up to the trees that jumped to meet it, the wooden posts that flung themselves up the side of the road. The posts turned into lines of rail and Constance was aware of the gorge that cut the hill off to the right.

The spreading hardwood trees that had populated the edges of the fields were gone. The hill was dominated by stark triangles of grey and green, sharp spears of crowded spruce with crowns like lances thrust into the sky.

Ethan's body barely touched the seat. Very carefully, without taking his eyes from the road, he unbuckled his seatbelt and eased the belt around his shoulders, careful not to let it snap. He did not want the buckle to strike the window; he knew the clack would give him away.

Constance looked straight ahead and did not mention that she knew what he had done. She did not say to Ethan that he should fasten his seatbelt and sit back in his seat. She would have had to shout over the roar of air. She would have had to pretend that she was sitting back in her own.

It was suddenly as if she were on a course hurdling toward a finish line. Each foot closer to the end the grade was steeper and she picked up speed. The car was a zooming shuttle taking her and Ethan to some fixed destination—it zipped past trees like poles marking her place at the edge of the cliff—and Constance felt herself flying, her body moving so fast her mind could not register the pace or think of keeping up.

She saw the curve ahead. She did not recognize the curve by sight, or even by the pull of memory. She recognized the curve by the sudden wrenching in her gut.

Her hands grasped the steering wheel, two skeleton hands with fingers frozen into bony fists. Her body was concentrated in her grip on the wheel, the memory of skidding out of control on a patch of ice embedded in her hands.

They were going too fast. Constance knew their speed was too great to safely navigate the curve. She reached out to tap the break.

Something went wrong.

She reached out again. Foot and pedal did not meet. She reached out one more time, consciously directing her foot to the break. She did not find the pedal. White with terror, Constance suddenly realized she could not feel her feet.

She wiggled her toes in her boot. There were no toes; there was no shoe.

She tore her eyes from the road and glanced down at her feet. Two boots on the floorboard, inches from the break pedal, did not rise to meet it.

She looked up, her glance a streak of panic. The curve was approaching at the unchecked speed of the car. A sharp turn to the left would bring them to the safety of the bottom of the hill. To the right, a twisted guardrail, corroded and eaten by salt, served as a thin barrier between the car and the edge of the gorge.

A sudden thought broke through her panic. The hand break! Two large tears sprang to the corners of her eyes when she realized all she had to do was pull the break.

She directed her hand to the emergency lever.

Her hands were stuck to the steering wheel and would not move. She tried to lift one finger from where it coiled around the wheel. Like tiny anacondas, her fingers had wound around an object and frozen in their grip. She told her hand to move—she willed it, then begged it to move. Her face became the same white color as her knuckles when she realized she could not feel her fingers.

"Ethan!" She did her best to calm the panic in her voice. "Ethan, I need you to listen very carefully to what I tell you and not get scared."

It was too late. A note of hysteria had crept into her voice. Ethan's body stiffened to a rigid form like a corpse.

"We are in trouble. I need you to help us out. You must do what I tell you and not argue. Do you understand?"

The boy was too stunned to speak.

"I have lost the use of my arms and legs. You will have to stop the car before we get to the curve."

He looked at the curve. Beyond the curve was sky, the end of earth marked by ancient spruce trees standing like sentinels. The sky was some way off but getting close. Ethan's face seemed to fall and gather at his mouth.

"We have some time. Don't worry and be brave. You will have to pull the break." She jerked her head toward the lever between their seats. "You must push that red button and pull up on the lever at the same time. Can you do it?"

A tiny voice breathed, “Yes.”

“Do it, Ethan. Do it now.”

He looked at the sky flying toward them. Timid hands reached out for the break.

“Don’t be shy, Ethan. Be decisive and do it.”

His face was in his mouth, two flapping lips over a chin like crumpled paper. A sound eked out between the lips; it was a squeak: “I—I can’t get it! I think it’s stuck!”

“Make sure you are pressing and pulling at the same time.”

“I am!”

Constance watched Ethan pull at the lever with both hands, frightened mouse sounds coming from his mouth. Constance knew their time was almost up.

“Ethan. Stop what you’re doing and push the regular break.”

“But you’re in the—”

“Don’t argue. Crawl over my lap and get to the break. You know which one it is—the one on the left.”

“I don’t want to touch your—”

“Ethan! This car is going way too fast. The old guard rail will never hold. You have to stop the car and you’ve got to do it now!”

He scrambled over the hand break and onto her lap. Constance felt his body quivering like a rodent. She hated the fear more than she hated her paralysis. The thing Constance hated most in the world was fright.

“Which one do I press?” His feet shot to the floor like crazy probes.

The car pitched forward as Ethan stomped on the accelerator.

"The side you write with, Ethan! Press the side you write with!"

His foot crashed down on the brake. At the same moment they began to hit the curve.

"The wheel! Turn the wheel, Ethan! Drag it toward your writing hand!"

The car struck a patch of gravel the same moment Ethan wrenched the wheel. Three sounds rose and smacked the sky: the scream like a young girl and the screech of shredding tires were not as loud as the silence that followed and hung over space.

4

"I would trade places with you if I could."

She moved her head in a slow arc over the pillow. She looked at him for several moments before she said, quietly and with no emotion, "No."

"My father used to say that to us when we were kids. When one of us had chicken pox or flu, he'd say, 'I'd give anything for it to be me.' He couldn't stand to watch children suffer. I think my father would have taken the world's suffering on his back."

There was a sudden metallic glint in her eyes—it was not the steely flash of anger; it was the scorching burn of heated brands. She said, "You will not."

"Will not what?"

"Take up any suffering."

He looked into her eyes and did not see what he expected: there was no plea for him to share her pain.

He smiled. He said, "My job is not to take up suffering, my job is to relieve it."

She smiled, and he was glad, but something nagged at him. He thought that she was smiling at something other than his words.

He tried again: "I'm not a monk."

There it was. She did not smile at the joke. She smiled at some private thought of her own.

He thought that he could draw her out. He said, "I do get the feeling you're laughing at me. Is it because

I really do live an ascetic existence?"

The metal gleam took over her eyes. There was a steely edge in her voice: "You are the furthest thing from a monk."

He wondered why there was no laughter in her voice.

"Come on. You know I live like a friar. Never a morning spent in bed. The strictest abstinence when it comes to alcohol and rich food. A fitness regimen more disciplined than—"

"Thomas, stop!" Her face was turning green.

"Oh God, Con, I'm sorry. I wasn't trying to upset you."

Her face relaxed. "It's okay." She leaned back on the pillow. "You're definitely not a monk. I think you fail the lust part."

He laughed and his laugh was a burst of relief. *This* was the Constance he knew and loved. He ran with it: "A little too lusty for the monastery? They do tend to frown upon an exuberant lust for life."

The secret smile lifted the corners of her mouth. Rivard did not care that she was not smiling at his joke. Whatever it was that amused her, Rivard was glad to have created a distraction.

He looked down at his wife, her small body like a fragile doll. She was tiny to begin with. Injury and trauma made her look like she would shrink out of sight. Rivard feared to touch her. He felt that even a finger's pressure would make her disappear.

"You don't have to look at me that way," she

said. "I'm not made out of glass." Her voice was full of maternal tenderness. "Perhaps you are the one in need of a nurse."

Rivard shook his head. Even though he knew Constance was metal-tough—in many ways the stronger of the two of them—he could not help feeling protective of the wife who was no larger than a girl.

"It's okay, Tom. Really. I want you to touch me."

His face was set into a grid of masculine lines. The corners of his mouth turned down as one large hand reached out and touched her cheek. It was the way he always reached for her. Rivard never touched Constance in a way that was not serious.

She closed her eyes, comforted by the sensation of his hand. Rivard felt her cheek in his palm, and a sudden, stinging prick behind his eyes. Her little body had sustained so much. Her little body would be so long in recovering, and Ethan hardly got a scratch. The prick turned into tears.

I would take your pain, if I could. If I could take your pain and put it onto myself, I would do it in a second.

He gently stroked the skin of her cheek. He thought of what he told her: My job is not to take up suffering, my job is to relieve it. He ran the pad of a finger over her eyelashes. He thought of his answer:

Where you are concerned, my love, I would take it all. I would gladly heap your pain upon myself, if it meant that you'd feel better.

As if she knew what he was thinking, Constance smiled and opened her eyes. She saw the tears in his eyes and moisture sprang to her own. She tilted her head slightly, to look him full in the face. There was a wordless message in the glimmer in her eyes:

People with your love of life are not born to take up suffering. You were made to fight suffering, Thomas. Your own as well as other peoples'.

He removed his hand from her face, as if startled by some sudden thought. He looked at the wall, then back at her eyes for a clue.

Constance looked at Rivard with eyes that were impossible to read. They danced with a funny light Rivard was certain carried mischief. He said, "What are you up to, little imp?"

"Do I look like an imp? I'm feeling far closer to a slug."

A rush of tenderness softened his voice: "Oh my God, Constance, you make a gorgeous slug. With eyes so bright and alive, the state of your body doesn't matter. One doesn't notice it at all."

He was so happy to share the news with her, so sure that she would be delighted to know the truth—that her sparkling eyes contained the life that was missing from her limbs—that the energy and vitality coming from her face was enough to diminish any sign of infirmity—that her reaction completely threw him off. When her face fell, Rivard was mortified and stunned.

"Did I say something wrong?"

His voice had the effect of an alarm, jolting her from a dream. She had been staring off into space; she had been looking past the world at some new thought, some foreign consideration. Rivard's words cast light on a puzzle piece she did not know was missing.

She said: "Do you mean—do you mean there's life enough just in my eyes?"

"Of course!" Rivard's spirits returned when he realized Constance had not understood. "All the energy in the world is coming from your face. It wouldn't matter if you never walked again, it wouldn't matter if you were permanently crippled—your spirit is impossible to dim!"

Constance screamed. Rivard cursed himself and continued to talk.

"I know it isn't nice to talk about crippled arms and legs. I only mentioned it because your condition is temporary and you're going to be able to use your arms and legs again soon. But the truth is,"—Rivard's face was beaming and triumphant—"it wouldn't matter if you couldn't use your arms and legs ever again. Everything I love about you—everything I've tried to teach to people, to cultivate and instill in them, is coming from your eyes. Your face is unquestionably alive!"

Constance was too upset to scream. She was not angry at her husband—how could she be angry at someone for pointing out the truth?—she was angry at herself for not realizing that he would only need her eyes.

If everything he loves about me—her rabid mind thought—if everything he loves about me is in the parts that are left, why would he ever agree to their extinction?

Constance ground her teeth. And if what Tom loves about me is still there, if it is enough and in existence, shouldn't I want to hang on to it as well? She bit her bottom lip, fired at the question. But I don't! I don't want it part way. I want it all or I want nothing. What he considers all is not what I do. Besides, what he loves best about me is my—

"Hands!" Her voice was a shriek.

Rivard looked at his wife with mounting concern, when he saw the twist of anguish on her face. "What about hands?"

"It *would* matter if I could never use my arms and legs. Don't pretend that it wouldn't. It's easy to say that when you think it's not the case. I know you, and I know us. You wouldn't love me without hands."

Constance waited for a reply. Rivard was staring, looking right through her. He did not seem to have heard the last two sentences.

He said, "What do you mean, 'when you think it's not the case'?"

"You said it yourself"—the quotation came out an exasperated whirl—"I only mentioned it because your condition is temporary."

Rivard's face was frozen in the unseeing expression. He was not seeing Constance. He was not seeing the room. Rivard was seeing a string of words seared across his brain: *It's easy to say that when you think it's not the case.*

He could see the words, but he could not see the meaning. When he spoke, his voice was flat and dead as a drum. "What's not the case?"

The hysterical edge was gone. Her head was laid back on the pillow and she suddenly looked weary, as if she had tired of the matter. Her eyes rolled in spent circles when she repeated his words.

"You're going to be able to use your arms and legs again soon."

Rivard's voice came out a drumbeat: "You're going to be able to use your arms and legs again soon."

"Right," Constance said. "That's what you said."

The beat picked up in pace. "Once you get over these injuries—it'll take some physical therapy—but you know the best coach in the world—we'll get your limbs back into shape, even stronger than before. You'd be surprised how resilient human appendages are."

"There is no injury."

"In a couple of months, you'll be good as new. You'll bounce back in no time. You're too stubborn and determined to be stopped by any accident."

"This isn't a result of the accident."

"It's really amazing—the way the human body bounces back. The body can recover from all types of severe trauma. I knew—"

"I haven't suffered any trauma!"

Rivard looked at his wife like a mute. She

repeated herself slowly, trying to get past the stare. "I have not sustained any injuries."

His face was blank. There was no reaction, only the absent look of a person who is deaf and dumb.

She tried again. "This isn't because of the accident."

He did not reply. His face did not register a response.

"Thomas, say something. I need you to understand."

His mouth was opened slightly and a word came out like a prayer: "Ethan."

She smiled, thinking he had understood.

Rivard said, "You took it all for him. My God . . . you don't even consider it a cost . . . ."

Her head flew from the pillow. He had not understood at all! He thought that she had shielded Ethan with her body, protected him from the impact. He thought that she was denying her injuries as the insignificant cost of a necessary sacrifice.

"Tom! Don't you get it! Ethan didn't get a scratch!"

A dreamy look softened his face. A faint smile raised the corners of his mouth. "The perfect nurse," he said. "Always sparing pain."

"I didn't spare anyone! Ethan was the one driving! If anything had happened, his body would have gone flying over the wheel!"

"Can't even admit that what she did was brave."

"He was sitting between me and the wheel." Her

voice was desperate, a plea. “I made him operate the pedals when he couldn’t pull the break. Tom!”—her eyes flashed with a hard metallic glint—“if anything, I put him at risk!”

These words had the effect of a gong. An ugly note resonated in the air. Rivard was roused from his peace, suddenly conscious of his wife. “What are you saying?”

“Does it make sense that this would happen to me while Ethan went untouched?”

“I thought you were protecting—”

“There was no time to think of that. We did what we had to do to stop the car.”

Constance could see his brain working in the lines on his face. Rivard always scowled when he was confused.

“Ethan is fine—not because of any action on your part—but because the crash was not that bad?”

“Yes.”

“I thought the car was totaled.”

“It was.”

“How in the hell—”

Rivard looked down at his wife’s body where it lay on the bed. A thin lilac blanket covered arms and legs as rigid as a doll’s. The blanket was tucked under Constance’s chin and the light purple color intensified the violet of her eyes.

“You weren’t hurt in the crash?”

She shook her head.

“None of this happened in the car?”

"No."

Rivard picked up a chair and brought it to the side of the bed. He sat down and, with a silence more telling than words, waited for her to talk.

"Corinne doesn't know," she said. "All she knows is that neither of us were injured."

Rivard's eyes shot to her face with an expression of hurt and confusion. She had never seen his eyes look so startled or large. She began to regret her approach.

"It's too late to start from the beginning," she said. "I guess I'll have to start at the end." Her chuckle was weak and unconvincing. She gave Rivard a questioning glance, hoping he would pick up the hint. His face was grave and unforgiving.

"We were coming down Nightmare Mountain. You know that really sharp curve that swings to the left? That's when it happened." She paused and watched his face for familiar signs. His face was drawn into stiff lines like nails. "It's not the first time it's happened." The nails in his face became spikes. "It's not the first time I've felt the numbness. It's the second time I've been crippled by it."

Constance saw the look on his face and could not go on. She saw two large, bewildered eyes; she saw a slump cave proud shoulders and a limp helplessness take over masculine hands. She thought that her husband looked more like a child than an adult, and she knew that she had been the cause. She forced herself to speak over mounting fear.

"Do you remember that time you said you could not understand how sick people refuse to see a doctor? I do. I mean, I don't understand it, it doesn't make sense, but I know the feeling. For the longest time, I shut it out and hoped that it would go away."

She knew her husband was like an injured child, she hated what she was doing, but she did not stop. She had to do this thing she had known was coming, had tried not to think about through all their years.

"I think there's something good about ignoring illness. I think it says something good about humans: we want to be healthy and strong. Almost like we can wipe the illness out by an act of our will."

With each word she spoke, Rivard's body grew smaller. It looked like his body was caving in.

"It really doesn't make sense. I have this horrible symptom and I ignore it, pretend that it will go away. Reason tells me to get real, to shape up and go to a doctor. Some other part of me blots it out, pretends that it isn't happening. It's completely irrational. A lot of it's fear."

She paused for a moment, suddenly aware of how desperately she wanted to use her hands. She wanted to touch her husband, to stroke him. She wanted to comfort him, even while she was inflicting pain. She could not reach out to him; that fact justified the speech and any cruelty.

"It always went away after a while. The numbness always started as a funny feeling in my chest—I can't describe it. It was not a pinch or an ache. It was just a change. I knew that something was different, not working the way it was supposed to. The next thing I knew, I couldn't use my hands."

Constance saw Rivard curl his hands into fists. He slowly opened them, as if testing his fingers to see if they worked. A faint smile softened her face. That was the first thing she did after the numbness went away. She always tested her fingers.

"We're just alike, love." It was the tone of her voice that made him look up. His fingers stopped moving and stiffened. He looked like a guilty child who had been caught.

"It's okay, Tom. I do the same thing." Her face grew dark, as she added, "I would do it if I could."

Rivard looked at her and his face was like a dog's face: attentive in spite of being afraid. He was incapable of removing himself from the source of the hurt. In any conflict between loyalty and self-preservation, loyalty won. No matter what Constance chose to do to him, no matter what harsh things she said, he had to hear them. Loyalty to Constance was an unquestioned absolute.

"There is a reason I've never told any of this before."

A light came into his eyes, a faint light of hope.

"I chose to ignore it. I made the conscious, deliberate effort to forget it and blot it out."

The light in his eyes disappeared.

Constance noticed, and corrected herself. "I was

not feeding some delusion. I was not pretending that the problem didn't exist. I thought about it only to the extent that it was necessary."

Rivard cleared his throat. "What is the problem?"

"I have Rivard's disease."

The walls collapsed. Rivard was suddenly standing in a large open chamber. The words reverberated around the walls, bouncing back and forth in a ceaseless echo: I have Rivard's disease, have Rivard's disease, Rivard's disease, disease.

The hospital bed stood alone in the middle of the room. He walked toward it. It took one million footsteps to get to the bed. The blankets were pulled up high and he leaned over to get a closer look.

He closed his eyes and bent for a kiss. He smelled something funny and opened his eyes. The princess was a hag! She smacked her toothless mouth and strands of saliva stretched between her lips. Glassy eyeballs screwed into points trained at his face and he heard the shift of a bedpan. He tried to scream and nothing came out.

"Are you all right?" The walls sprang back into place and the real bed reappeared. Rivard looked over at Constance.

"I must be going insane," he said. "I thought I heard you say, 'I have Rivard's disease'."

"I did. I do."

The walls fell down and he was standing by the bed in the hall. The hag was spitting in his face: "Come closer, Tommy! Come give an old sick woman a kiss."

Rivard screamed. There was the sound of hurried footsteps in the hallway and the door to the room flung open.

"Dr. Rivard, is she okay? What happened? I heard the scream."

Rivard just looked at the nurse. He could not speak. Constance was the only one able to talk.

"Everything's fine, Millie. You can come by in a little while to change my pan."

The nurse bowed her head and left the room.

Rivard sat looking after her, as though she had not been fully real.

Constance said, "Tom. Are you all right?"

There was no answer. She tried again: "Are you okay?"

He looked at her as if seeing her for the first time. "No. I'm not okay. I must be losing my mind. I keep hearing something about 'Rivard's disease'."

"You heard correctly."

"What?"

"You were not hearing things."

"I heard something." He glanced off as if trying to remember what it was. She pulled him back with the insistence in her voice.

"What I'm trying to say is that you aren't imagining things."

"You did say 'Rivard's disease'?"

"Yes."

"I didn't make that up?"

"No."

"That's not what I wanted to hear."

His face was as long as his body. He was standing now, backing away from her.

"You aren't glad to hear you're not insane?"

"No." He was looking at her with frightened eyes, his back against the door. "I prefer insanity to this."

She did not like that her husband had moved away from her, was looking at her like she had a disease. The pain was acute because she did have a disease.

"I'm not contagious," she said defensively.

"I'd say what you've got is damned contagious to have my name."

"Oh that," she said, realizing what had bothered him. "Professor Dunn named the disease."

The blow stuck him at once and he fell to the floor.

He was looking up at the ceiling. The ceiling had become a screen. Rivard watched the people on the ceiling like players in a movie.

The lecture hall was packed. A controversial Supreme Court decision had fired up the nation, and everyone was eager to hear the opinions of medical experts. The foremost cardiologist in the country was about to address a standing-room-only crowd.

A small bent man with a shock of white hair rose to the podium. He moved so slowly—his steps were so measured, his climb so stiff and deliberate—the crowd was simmering into an impatient froth. It seemed that he would never take his place.

They knew he was ready to begin when they saw the crown of white hair flying in all directions. Two hands as gnarled as burls gripped the sides of the lectern. Serene blue eyes looked out at the audience and it was some time before he spoke.

"I'm afraid what I'm going to say will come off as a disappointment," he said. "No doubt many of you are anxious to learn my opinion of the Supreme Court's decision." He paused. Heads bobbed in agreement. "The fact is I have no opinion."

An audible gasp went up into the air. Professor Dunn chuckled in the manner of one who is used to making waves.

"I did not come here so that you could take notes on my views and spout them at the next dinner party. It is not my job to fill university students' heads with a batch of dogma, ready-made."

Soft laughter bounced around the auditorium. Professor Dunn's fingers were wrapped around the sides of the lectern like hooks.

"It is not my job to indoctrinate. My job is to get you to think. Today, I want you to think about the purpose of medicine."

The house did not make a sound. Silence replaced the usual shuffling of papers and stray cough. When Professor Dunn spoke, the audience listened.

"I have been roundly criticized for leaving the narrow confines of cardiology and venturing into the realm of medical ethics. There are those of my association who believe I am doing something blasphemous. Combine the realms of philosophy and science? Scandalous. It would do little good to tell them that the entire field of medicine is a definitive answer to a philosophical question. The answer is: Yes. The question is: Should we prolong life?

"The question seems silly, I know. The answer, self-evident. The fact that these seem silly and self-evident is proof of the fact that the premise underlying them is beyond dispute. The question, Should we prolong life? presupposes the fact that we have a choice. It would be meaningless to ask ourselves whether we *should* prolong life, if there were no possibility that we could do so. Medicine presupposes the fact that we have a choice and are capable of acting on it. We can help life along—or not. We can choose life—or let it go by default. Medicine recognizes that we have this choice, and comes down resoundingly on the side of furthering life. Medicine says: Life is good and worth saving."

Professor Dunn reached for a glass of water and drank the entire contents without stopping. A water stain darkened the front of his shirt.

"Let me point out something. We are talking about choosing to help and protect life, as opposed to the choice to do nothing. We are not talking about avoiding the inflicting of harm. Medicine is the *active* furtherance of life, as opposed to a passive letting chips fall where they may. Medicine does not say: Do I help or do I harm? Doing nothing is doing harm. The *deliberate* inflicting of harm to the body is out of the scope of medicine, this discussion—the entire realm of human endeavor."

Rivard lay sprawled on the floor, watching the ceiling. Constance could not move to the side of the bed to look at him; she was frightened and calling for him, begging him to get up, but he was riveted to the screen. The memory was passing in front of his eyes as though he were living it.

"There's a lot of nonsense these days about discrimination," Professor Dunn said. "Whites are discriminating against blacks, heterosexuals are discriminating against homosexuals, the able-bodied are picking on the disabled." The strands of his unruly white hair shot out from his face like exclamation points, punctuating his remark. "Let me say, in response to this nonsense: I am a chief discriminator. I proudly discriminate against heart disease."

The applause began as a hesitant set of hands and ended in thunderous clapping. Professor Dunn's face became grave.

"Medicine is inherently discriminatory," he said. "Medicine necessarily privileges health over disease. Disease is the enemy, as far as medicine is concerned. If life is the goal—if health and life are inextricably linked—disease is the enemy to be stamped upon, nullified, obliterated and rooted out. In the name of life, medicine declares war on disease."

Rivard saw Professor Dunn on the ceiling. He

saw the heavily lined face scowling when he spoke of disease. He felt the scowl was directed at him; Professor Dunn had given his name to a disease.

"Tom!" Constance's shrill scream came over the side of the bed. "Tom, where are you? If you can, get up!"

Rivard tried to obey the command. He tried to move his legs but could not raise his body from the floor.

"I'm frightened, Tom! Can you hear me?" Constance's voice was getting louder. "Can you hear me? Can you hear me?"

Rivard heard the question. He could clearly decipher the words and her voice. He knew that she wanted a reply—he wanted to say something, but all he could do was look at Professor Dunn scowling at him, hear the old voice say: In the name of life, medicine declares war on disease.

She was suddenly crying for the nurse. She screamed for Millie. Rivard heard the sound of hurried footsteps in the corridor, and saw a red face glaring down at him.

"You're blocking my view," he said. "I can't see Professor Dunn."

"Who's Professor Dunn?" Millie turned to look at Constance. "Why is Dr. Rivard on the floor?"

"Please help him into the chair," Constance said, her voice full of agitation. "Tom had trouble dealing with the news." She wished that she had not called the nurse. Now that she knew Tom was conscious, she wanted the nurse to leave them alone.

"You're in no shape for this kind of excitement," Millie said to Constance, helping Rivard off the floor. "And you"—she cast a searing glance at Rivard—"have no business frightening your wife. What happened to the Endurance we all know and love?"

Something about the word "Endurance" made him feel sick. Haven't I suffered enough?—he thought. Am I some kind of martyr? Why have they given me a name that sounds like a cross?

"He's all right," Constance said, hoping to get rid of the nurse. "I think what we both need now is a little privacy." The tone of her voice was unmistakable.

Millie sniffed. She was noticeably offended. "I'll come back in a little while to change your pan." She stood in the doorway and added, a little defensively, "I only come when I'm called."

Constance breathed a loud sigh as soon as Millie shut the door. She closed eyes that were filled with resentment. She wanted nothing more than to blot the whole thing out of existence.

Rivard was the first to speak. His voice was toneless. "What is this thing Professor Dunn has dedicated to me?" Constance did not answer. He said angrily, "He christened it with an interesting name."

Constance's voice was lost in terror. She was suddenly afraid of her husband. She was terrified of what he would do when he found out.

"You—you know Professor Dunn?"

Rivard laughed and her skull went numb with

fright. He said, "Do I—do I know Professor Dunn?" Rivard laughed for a long time. He was thoroughly amused by something and Constance was frightened because she did not know what it was.

She asked, "How do you know Professor Dunn?"

Rivard's laughter abruptly ceased. His voice was cold as a blade: "Richard Dunn taught me everything I know about the human heart."

Constance was struck to the quick. Her brain scrambled to make sense of his remark. "You mean, you know him personally?"

The chilling laugh filled the room. Rivard looked greatly amused. His voice was filled with sarcasm as he said, "I told you I studied under the best, Con. I received the best medical training in the world. What else would lend such legitimacy to my ventures as a cardiopulmonary coach?"

He watched her face contract with shock. He laughed and said, "You never read the blurb on the back of my book? 'A four-star fitness regimen, from the expert in cardiovascular rehabilitation therapy. Take it from one privileged to be his mentor—Professor Richard Dunn'."

Her voice sounded faint, like it was coming from a great distance. "I never knew. All these years, through all the appointments, he never mentioned it. Maybe . . . perhaps he didn't make the connection."

"Did you speak of me?"

"Incessantly."

"Then he knew. He goddamn well knew." Rivard was in a state of quiet anger. The anger passed into silent rage when he realized he had been deceived.

He said, "How long has this been—no, wait. What exactly is going on?"

He looked at her with eyes so hard and sharp, Constance knew better than to lie. She said, "I've been seeing Dunn for four years. Those times I went to see my parents? It was him."

Rivard shot up from his chair. "You've been sick for four years?"

"Ten."

"Ten what?"

"I've had this thing for ten years. The symptoms go back further. My doctor had heard of some obscure sickness. Something so rare it had not been named. He recommended Dunn."

"And Richard Dunn had the privilege of naming the disease. He had the good taste to give it my name."

"It wasn't him, Tom." Constance was upset that he was not taking it the right way. "I'm the first official case. That's how these things work."

His shoulders hunched like a startled cat. "How these things work? How they work? Tell me Constance, how do these things work?"

She closed her eyes against the angry barbs. She knew his anger was justified. She knew it would not last, that he would calm down once the whole truth came out. She waited patiently, knowing it was temporary.

"Could you please inform me how this works?" Rivard's body was leaning menacingly over the bed. "I am ignorant and in need of higher wisdom."

"I know how this must sound," Constance began, trying to pacify him. "You'll feel better once you hear—"

He did not let her finish. "Once I hear what? That my wife and trusted mentor are plotting against me?"

"Plotting against you?"

"What else would you call being stabbed in the back?"

Her head churned and reeled. It was not how she had envisioned breaking the news. Constance thought: This is not at all how this was supposed to go. This was supposed to come out different!

Her voice came out a desperate gush: "Please, Tom. Don't make it sound that way. That wasn't it at all. No one was trying to hurt you. I—I was trying to spare you pain."

He suddenly remembered the words he had used: The perfect nurse. Always sparing pain. He stiffened because he did not want to be spared. He said, "Tell me what I was to be spared."

He could hear her draw in a breath. The breath came out an inconceivable string of words: "I have lost my arms and legs."

Several moments passed. When he spoke, the question was innocent as a child's or a fool's. "Lost them? Where did they go?"

Her defective heart swelled and nearly burst. Whenever Tom was hurt he became literal. She said through a sob, "It's a defect of the heart. I don't have normal circulation. My heart did something to my limbs."

She paused and waited for him to say something. He did not respond, or even appear to see her face. He looked like he was lost in a distant vision.

Come to my aerobics class. Just come and stand before the class. Let them see what's possible. Let them see what I mean when I speak about the visible glow of health.

"The way Professor Dunn explained it, my heart is not a normal size."

Everything I've tried to convey to them, everything I've ever worshipped is summed up in your body.

"My heart outgrew my body. My body could not keep up. My heart and my body do not go together."

Rivard was jolted by the force of his sob. He wanted to scream: They do go together! Your body contains all the proud strength of your limitless heart! Instead, he said, "Your heart has become enlarged?"

"Yes. No. It's always been like that."

"Is there a buildup of fluid?"

"No—"

She stopped talking because she was choking. She was crying for herself; she was crying for him. She was crying for the grown man who was weeping like a boy.

He dropped to his knees beside her bed. He took her thin arm from under the blanket and kissed it over and over again, pressing his cheeks and his tears into her skin.

“Whatever you need, whatever Professor Dunn says we should do we will do.”

She could not breathe. The reality of what she was about to do prevented her from drawing air.

“You were right, Constance. Of course you would have gone to him. I would have been shocked if you hadn’t. Don’t mind me, I’m just stunned. I’m mean because I’m worried. I take back everything I said. I’m just glad to finally know the truth because now I can help with the treatment.”

She thought her heart stopped. She wished it had.

Rivard spoke with lips pressed to the white skin of her arm. “I love you, Constance. Don’t you see that none of this matters? You didn’t have to fear telling me any of this. You didn’t have to keep it in the dark. I love you because you are strong and brave and can overcome anything. This thing will not slow you down and we will not give up.”

She tried to wrench her arm from his grasp. She felt revulsion, not at Rivard, not at his words, but the fact that she was powerless to welcome or resist them. She could not return his embrace. She could not push him away. In a very real sense, she had no ability to act on her own volition.

He said, "You are strong, so strong Constance." He raised his hand to touch her cheek.

It was involuntary. Impelled by frustration at impotence, goaded on by madness at her paralyzed state, Constance raised the only part of her body that would move: she lunged forward and snapped at his hand with her teeth.

Stunned, Rivard did not pull back. She took advantage of his shock, sinking her teeth into the flesh beneath his thumb. She felt the skin burst, and tasted the salt of his blood.

She threw her head back on the pillow, exhausted and spent. Rivard did not say a word; his surprise had given way to an almost animal understanding, and he moved back into the chair, soundlessly sucking at the wound on his hand.

Constance did not feel fear. She had *done* something; she had exercised the only form of will that was left to her: the ability to inflict harm. She still had that one last choice and she was going to cling to it no matter what. Until she could not do it anymore, Constance was determined to act on her will.

She did not apologize. She did not attempt to explain or justify her action. She was beyond the point of caring whether Thomas understood. When the reality of her situation overrode anybody's feelings about it—when the fact that she could not move got in the way of grieving with her husband, lamenting the loss of her arms and her legs—when she could neither embrace him nor flail her arms in angry frustration—she knew that it was time.

Constance thought that any hardship was bearable if explosive action were possible—if the body could vent. None of this would be so bad, she thought, if I could kick a tree or punch the wall. If there were some way that I could act out my frustration. But I can't. I can't wrestle the anxiety away. I can't run; I can't lift; I can't sweat. I have no outlet to show that I hate this. I can't even hit or beat myself . . . I have no means to end it.

She looked at her husband and knew that the time had come. When she spoke, her voice was calm, almost serene. Her face was peaceful and untroubled.

"Professor Dunn has been researching my condition for many years."

Rivard looked at his wife with a questioning glance. He wondered at her change in tone.

"The best cardiologist in the world has been on the case."

Rivard's brows began to rise.

"I have taken every measure, precaution and recommendation he's given."

Rivard's eyebrows were two arches suspended over his face. The arches quivered slightly, as if waiting for the word to drop.

"I've followed his advice to the letter. I've done everything that he's told me."

The arches fell back into place. Rivard's face settled with the conclusion drawn from her statement: She's been in good hands. She's listened. She'll come through with flying colors.

"What happened to me in the car was unavoidable."

Rivard grimaced. He did not like the word "unavoidable." It sounded too much like fate. Rivard believed that people made their fate.

"I did everything Richard Dunn said. I did it knowing—he said it too—that the symptoms would stop coming and going. At a certain point, they would not go away. Paralysis was inevitable."

Dunn said that?—Rivard thought. Why would Dunn have called paralysis inevitable? What would make him give up on a cure and let nature take over? Since when does Dunn concede defeat?

Constance saw confusion in the creases on his brow. She attempted to clarify: "Inevitable insofar as the defect is concerned. My heart and limbs cannot coexist."

"So what about a different heart? Why did Dunn let it go this far?"

"By the time I got to Dunn, it—he said it was already too late."

He did not want to shout or raise his voice. She was lying peacefully and he did not want to disturb her. Instead of screaming the words, he suppressed them, and they echoed around in his brain: Too late! What kind of incompetent doctor would claim that it's too late? It's never too late to try, it's never, ever too late!

"Constance, this is all new to me, and I'm struggling to understand. If I sound mean it's because

I'm stunned. Do not take it personally. I need to know something. What would make Professor Dunn give up?"

Her face crumpled and she bit her lip. She looked about to cry. After several moments she regained the untroubled expression. With a calm voice she said, "A transplant was his initial recommendation."

Rivard could not contain himself: "I thought you said you'd followed his advice!"

Constance was unaffected by his tone. "I followed the advice of Richard Dunn, after the establishment of certain terms."

"What terms?"

"That he would not speak of a different heart."

Rivard had to catch himself, before he fell out of his chair. "You're telling me you refused a transplant! You refused to consider the idea?"

Her voice was even. The steadiness was forced. "Do you know how tired I am of the whole affair? I'm not going to live with a strange heart and I'm not going to live without my limbs."

"What do you mean?"

"My arms and legs have to come off. It's scheduled for Thursday."

Rivard's voice came out of two unmoving lips: "Without a new heart, your limbs will die. The rest of you will die if the limbs don't come off. New heart, same limbs. You won't consider a heart."

She blurted, rather than spoke the words: "New

heart, different person!"

"Constance, you don't believe that mumbo gumbo, do you? That stuff about losing your soul is superstitious myth."

Rivard could not believe it. He felt like he was in a hospital room with Henry Murphy or Cindy Beale. Why in the world doesn't Constance want to be well?—he thought. Why is she resisting treatment? What made her shun the advice of someone who could help? What had happened to Professor Dunn?

Rivard heard Dunn's voice in his ear: Medicine is the *active* furtherance of life, as opposed to a passive letting chips fall where they may. Medicine does not say: Do I help or do I harm? Doing nothing is doing harm.

Rivard shot up from his chair. He began to pace the length of the room. He spoke out loud, as if Constance were not there.

"Why didn't he force her to go through with it? Why would he allow an act of self-destruction? I thought he, more than anybody, had the power to persuade."

Constance was small beneath the lilac blanket, nearly invisible. Rivard continued to pace and mutter as though she were out of sight.

"If anyone could convince her of the necessity of treatment—he could! He is not one to embrace passivity, and not one to tolerate it in a patient. Richard Dunn is the greatest advocate of aggressive medicine in the world. Why would he allow my wife to make an insane decision?"

"Insane decision?" Rivard jumped when a voice came from beneath the lilac blanket. He had forgotten she was there. "Could you please tell me how to be sane in this situation? I'm sure you know exactly how I feel."

Rivard looked at her childlike figure and his heart bleed. Because he loved her, he clung to his truth. "If I were you, I'd fight it! I'd beat Rivard's disease into the ground. I would not sit back and let it swallow me." His voice softened. "You're not one to let anything keep you down."

She motioned to his punctured hand with her chin. "I know it."

He looked down at his hand. Her bite marks had left a jagged crescent moon. He suddenly felt proud of the wound; he realized it was her strong and valiant effort to do exactly what he wanted her to do.

"*I'm* not giving in to anything," Constance said.

Rivard's spirits began to rise. He knew that he must have misunderstood. Constance would never surrender to defeat. And Professor Dunn would never let her.

"I *am* fighting for myself and my world."

Rivard's chest swelled with love and pride. What a fool he had been to think that Constance would ever give in! What a fool he had been to think she did not love her life!

"I am not capable of forgetting my interests or acting in a self-destructive manner. I reject the religious nonsense my parents tried to shove down my throat. I am not a martyr, and I will not take on the role of sacrificial saint."

Rivard felt like crying, his relief was so great.

"That is why I will repeat what I said earlier: I'm not going to live with a strange heart and I'm not going to live without my limbs."

Standing tears suddenly froze in his eyes. "You said the surgery is scheduled for Thursday. You're not going through with it?"

"No."

"So you've changed your mind about a transplant? I'm so glad to hear that. I was—"

"Tom, I haven't changed my mind about the transplant."

His face fell from his skull to the floor. A skeleton head addressed her. "Do you realize what you're saying? I don't think it's coming out right."

"It is."

"You said you're not going to let them take your limbs."

"I'm not."

"But you said you're not going to consider a transplant."

"I'm not."

The dark circles under Rivard's eyes looked like the empty sockets of a skull. He forced the words out through a set of clenched teeth. "It seems to me it's got to be one or the other. Neither means you won't survive." The hollow-eyed skull snapped the question at her face: “Unless one can live with Rivard’s disease?”

“I can’t.”

“Neither can I.”

The husband and wife were silent: neither wanted to take that next crucial step.

“Connie, what are you saying?”

Her words were a statement, not a plea: “I need your help.”

He gave a brusque, hasty response. “If Richard Dunn could not convince you or come up with a plan, what makes you think I could?”

The tone of her voice sent shivers down his spine. “I’m not asking for help with the disease. I’m asking to be rid of it.”

“If the foremost heart expert in the world couldn’t—Constance, what do you mean?” Rivard’s veins were rivulets of ice.

“I want you to make it stop.”

The world stopped. There was no world. None that he could recognize.

“I’ve been given an impossible choice. I’m making the choice not to decide. I’m opting out.”

The world began again. It was not right. It was wobbling off its axis—not spinning out of control—teetering clumsily like a drunk.

“I’m not going to spend the rest of my days as a torso on pegs. I’m not going to live with a thing in my chest that isn’t my heart. I’m not going to choose the lesser of two evils and hate each waking moment. Suffering is not an alternative and I will not live in a subhuman state."

The world was wobbling in wide slow circles, throwing everything off balance. The planet was not whirling. It was sent adrift.

Rivard felt he was the last man on earth, standing at some deserted outpost. His entire field of vision was filled with desolation, a barren landscape void of anything but dust.

Her voice filled the abandoned world: "I made this decision ten years ago, before I even met you. I made the decision and then forced it from my mind."

Rivard stood at the outpost, feet planted firmly on the ground. Something fluttered and caught his attention. He looked up and saw a brightly colored flag.

"I need your help. I know what I'm asking. I don't expect you to approve. I need you to understand."

There was no person such as Constance. He had never had a wife. There were no people, no attachments, nothing that was dear. He was standing in an atomistic world in which the link between past, present and future had been severed. His only connection to anything was the message on the flag.

"That was the reason I never told you," Constance said. "I told myself that it would be all or nothing. Where you and I are concerned, I had to have it all."

Rivard heard her say "all," and stood at his outpost in the abandoned world, looking at nothing. He had nothing. There was nothing left of who he had been—he could not even remember what it felt like to *have*. She said that she wanted it all. She did have it. She had taken everything.

"The secret was necessary, because—if I had even told you—our entire marriage would have been a countdown to death."

Rivard was dead. She had wanted life and the cost was within her means. She merely sacrificed her husband. Seven years meant more to her than the rest of his life.

"Don't you see, Tom? Do you see why I did it? Ours was a blissful span, something that can never be taken away from us, something we wouldn't have had—"

"You took it." He was seeing a desolate stretch covered in dust.

"I took, I took—*what!?*"

"Everything. My life."

"Your life? I gave us life! I gave us seven uncompromised years."

"I'd say they're compromised. It was all a fraud." He saw her crushed face and said, "It will never be what it was. It's gone."

"It would be gone if my life were to continue."

"You must think I'm pretty small."

"Small?"

"Shallow. Whatever. You must be totally blind to think that I'd love you any less."

"It's not about you, it's about me! *I* couldn't live with it! I can't and I won't. Your wanting me to stick it out is irrelevant."

"My feelings mean nothing to you?"

"They mean everything! You are too full of life to be chained to a marriage of pity. I'm not going to let that happen to you, to us. That would be taking what we had."

He tried to remember what it was that they had. All he could see was the empty dusty world. The only thing remaining was the fluttering outpost flag.

"I'm not going to stand by and watch you die, Constance. I'm not going to do nothing. Your life means more to me than avoiding discomfort."

The voice that rose up from the blanket gave him chills. "It isn't 'nothing' that I'm asking of you, Thomas."

He spoke hastily, trying to blot out her awful tone. "Yes, please let me do something. Let me try. I'll give up coaching. I'll go back into research. You know I've kept up my connections—"

"I'm not going to be passive about this thing."

"Good."

The small rigid body did not belong to his wife. It was a demon's voice that came out of it: "I want you to administer a drug to make me die."

Thomas Rivard had never given much thought to good and evil. He had always associated the good with his profession—he had always believed that the good was that which furthered life, and conversely, that which threatened it was evil. He had never questioned these truths; they seemed completely self-evident. As a doctor, he had always regarded himself as a champion of the good. As the husband of an energetic nurse, he thought his marriage was a moral code engraved in stone.

That is why, when he looked at the thing on the bed that asked him to cause death—its own—he knew that he was looking at a monster.

He knew that his assessment was correct when Richard Dunn's words echoed in his ear: The *deliberate* inflicting of harm to the body is out of the scope of medicine, this discussion—the entire realm of human endeavor.

Rivard cringed when another blasphemy came out of the demon's mouth: "I want you to administer a drug to make my heart stop."

He could not believe what he was hearing. The words violated every motive and goal, every action he had taken. Each day of his life had been a struggle to keep hearts beating. Now, he was being asked to bring one to a stop.

It was not his mind that recoiled from the request. It was the part of him to which medicine was a religion. He had carried his truth to classrooms full of disbelievers and hypocrites—he had borne insults and condemnations while spreading the holy word—but he had brushed it aside as inconsequential. Nothing mattered but furthering life—which meant stopping anything that hindered it: *anything*.

He heard the words from his adversary which made him certain he was engaged in a dire crusade.

"I'm asking you to make a mercy killing."

The only thing I will kill, Rivard thought, is that idea. He heard the words like a drumbeat signaling battle: Death is the enemy to be squashed, to be rejected, to be squelched. To take life—and assist death? Never! To turn against the very thing I've defended and protected all these years? You've taken my life, dear wife, but you will never take my Faith.

He groped around for some weapon, some tool that he could use against the onslaught. His world was empty of all objects save the flag.

The flag! Rivard remembered that the flag had borne a message.

When he spoke, he took the words of the Oath out of context; his voice contained all the pious reverence of a priest: "I will not use the knife . . . but will withdraw in favor of such men as are engaged in this work."

"I wasn't thinking of a knife," the thing that was no longer his wife said. "That isn't civilized or human."

Rivard heard the words like some echo from a distant past. Civilized? Human? Weren't these words part of the moral code he had pledged his life to defend? Why would his enemy invoke words like Civilized and Human? She was now their opposite: uncivilized and monstrous.

"Euthanasia is not murder," the demon said, as if reading his thoughts. "I'm not asking you to commit a sin."

Not asking me to commit a sin? By taking life? You are asking me to violate every commandment of my religion!

"Now that you are gone, Constance, now that I know there really is nothing left of the woman I love, I'll remind you of something you seem to have forgotten: I took the Hippocratic Oath. My allegiance to the Oath is inviolable."

"I know it! That's why I'm asking this of you."

"You are asking me to violate the Oath in the name of the Oath?"

"Yes! No! All I'm asking is to hold on to my life!"

"By ending it?"

The face above the blanket was beautiful, completely incongruous with the attached body. She said, "This is what I've been trying to make you understand. I want my life. I want my life more than anything in the world. But it's got to be a *life*, not some sorry substitute for one."

"You sound like a deranged philosopher. Your life is still your life. Your organs are still pumping, still pushing blood and air." Constance's face turned white. Rivard did not notice and continued. "I hate all this talk splitting hairs over what's a life. The issue is completely black and white. You have a pulse, you are alive. Period. End of sentence."

"Thomas, I don't *feel alive*."

Rivard was suddenly in the water, positioned over the edge of a rock. The question rose up from his gut and filled his brain: Is a life stripped of *life*—of the things that make life worth living—not the same as death? Is death the cessation of life, or is it the cessation of feeling *alive*?

He dismissed the question with a snort and came back to the room. He wrote it off as crazy musing induced by desperation. The thoughts he had had the day Constance went into the falls had nothing to do with what was going on here.

She repeated herself, knowing she had struck him: “I don’t feel alive.” She watched his face contort into a tortured frown. She said, “You are a reality-oriented person, so let’s stick with the facts: I have Rivard’s disease.” Rivard’s face untwisted and went slack. “It’s a defect I was born with, which I’ve learned other people have been born with, and which was bound to catch up with me.” The muscles in Rivard’s face were loose and hanging like a dog’s. “I have done everything that was necessary. I have taken counsel with Professor Dunn, who knows more about these things than anybody. It stumped the best cardiologist in the world.”

The muscles of Rivard’s face tightened, then made a peculiar up-and-down, in-and-out motion. It was not quivering; the muscles did not shake. They seemed to be rolling over her words—taking them in, grinding them into dust.

“I have been in active treatment for four years—since the time I went to Dunn. The symptoms have grown progressively worse, in spite of our efforts. This was to be expected based on all known knowledge of the disease, which isn’t much. It officially began with me."

Constance looked exhausted. Rivard had never before seen his wife look so much as tired. The reality of her condition began to dawn on him.

"Keeping this from you was not a deceit. It was about my mental health. I wanted to live. I've had a life. You and I have had a life."

Rivard thought: Had? Had a life? We have a life and we still can!

"Let me be clear about something," Constance said. "If there were any hope at all, any chance, if recovery were possible—I would not ask you to do this thing. The fact that this is a shock to you, the fact that you had no idea—means that my plan was a success: I *didn't* let it beat me."

You didn't and you won't!—Rivard thought. You're resilient enough, buoyant enough, far too alive—

"I'm not going to succumb to disease." The demon had gone and Rivard heard an angel. "I'm not going to let it take me."

The demon returned: "I'm not going to let it take me—I'm taking myself first."

Everything went dark. Rivard was surrounded by darkness. Within the space of several hours he had lost the world, regained it, and had it wrenched away.

A voice came to him through the blackness. It was his wife's voice, but it was not his wife: "If you do not help me do this thing, I will find someone who will."

This is not happening, Rivard thought. I'm stuck in some bad dream. There is no way this is really happening. Everything is the opposite of what it should be.

"I want it done before Thursday. I'm going home, and I'm not returning to this hospital. I want you to help me do it at home."

Do what?—Rivard thought. You're asking the impossible. I could no more raise my hand against you, than I could raise my hand against myself—

His head was suspended over the rock. He knew that it would only take one swift, decisive blow. He wanted it. He had never wanted anything more than he now wanted to end his life.

He was surrounded by darkness. The darkness seemed to come from his heart. There was a stranger lying in a hospital bed, a serene expression on her face. There was a stranger in the room, and a foreigner in his heart.

This is not real, he thought, groping blindly for the chair. I am not awake, I am dreaming. I am in the middle of a nightmare.

His hands touched the cold metal of the chair and bounced back. The cold was shocking because he could feel it. People do not feel cold in dreams, he thought. He reached out for the chair again. The cold bit him like a snake. He jumped back and stared.

If this is not a dream, Rivard told himself, if this is not a dream, then what she wants is real. But what she said is impossible!

Rivard tried to piece together the shards that were gouging his brain. He had been pierced so deeply, the shards were lodged.

She's dying. She's got Rivard's disease. Rivard's disease! She's been to Professor Dunn. Professor Dunn used my name. She refused help. She made the most of it. She wouldn't give in. She's giving up. She never told me. She's spilled her guts. She wants her life. She wants to die.

She wants to die!

Rivard could not reconcile the words. They made no sense. They might as well have been gibberish in a foreign language. He no more had the power to decipher the words, than he had ability to act on them: the thought and the implication were inconceivable. His brain was made to process facts; it did not register the inconceivable.

Constance had asked him to do something he considered beyond the realm of possibility. Rivard had been shocked, then overcome with disbelief—outraged, and then confused. He had gone through every shade and wisp of emotion—he had been pulled from love to hate, compassion to despair—he had felt sympathy for his wife and broiling anger. What he did not feel—was, in fact, constitutionally incapable of feeling—was agreement with her wish.

Her wish violated the very center of his core.

Rivard was a doctor. He was a protector and defender of life. His essence was so entwined with his profession—his identity so linked with his trade—her wish that he violate the dictates of his profession was a wish that he violate himself. Rivard did not separate himself from his work—he and medicine were twins—his life and the protection of life were one and the same—and Constance wished them split in two.

What he felt was profound grief—grief, because the woman he loved—the woman who had been the symbol and embodiment of everything he fought to achieve—had pulled the pedestal from her own statue and threatened to dash the statue against the earth. In harming herself, Constance harmed the embodiment of his values. Rivard's greatest value—joyous life borne of health—was manifest in the life of Constance, one with it. Her destruction meant the destruction of everything he cherished, everything he held dear. To lose her would be to lose what made life worth living. There would be nothing after that.

In his agitation, Rivard was incapable of conceiving that the values he cherished were identical to those that Constance cherished—that it was precisely *joyous life borne of health* that Constance was asking him to protect and defend. That in the loss of that value—Rivard did not see that it had already gone—Constance had lost that which made life worth living. Life without her greatest value, which was his, could not go on.

Rivard did not see any of this. He had become confused and hurt and thus literal. All he saw was an affront to his profession that made him defensive and feel like lashing out. He was going to stand by the flagpole of his abandoned world, all alone, even if she shunned him. He would continue to wave the banner on which the Hippocratic Oath was written. He would carry the banner into war.

Rivard declared war.

Prompted by a sudden, murderous rage, Rivard picked up the cold metal chair and held it menacingly over the bed. "I could kill you right now," he said, "seeing that's what you want."

Her pupils did not dilate; her eyes did not flutter or blink. She looked at him with eyes that were wise and unaffected.

"That's true," she said. "And you will carry out my wish. But only after you realize it's your own."

"My own? My own? How is it possible that you don't know me? How could you possibly think that I would ever agree to kill the love of my life?"

The stoic look vanished from her face. All the strength and resolve she had mustered were gone. For a moment, she saw the other side.

She looked down at her frozen limbs. She looked up at his face. She saw that he looked at her the same way he always had: in spite of his anger, his glance was filled with unwitting love and admiration.

She wanted to give him a reason to be proud. She regained and held her ground. She said, "Who is this love of your life?"

He lowered the chair to the floor. "A woman who does not give up. A woman full of strength and energy and vigor. A woman who would never conceive of going out without a fight. A woman incapable of suffering."

"Incapable of suffering—but made to bear a cross? A woman who does not give up—fit for the role of martyr?"

"You are the opposite of a martyr. Life for you has never been a cross."

She chuckled softly. "And now? What would you call this?"

Rivard spoke in a rapid gush. "That would stop other people, I know. Other people wouldn't have the strength to take it—"

"But I do? I'm to 'take it'?"

"I didn't mean—"

"It's all right. I know what you meant. Nonetheless, I'm choosing not to."

"Not to what?" Rivard did not have to ask the question. He already knew what she was going to say.

"I'm not going to 'take' anything. I've made my choice. It's the right one."

Rivard could not contain his anguish. "No, it's not! I know you! You never give up!"

"Do you think what I'm doing is giving up?"

"Yes! Why don't you fight for your life?"

"I am."

Rivard stopped. He wondered what had come over Constance. Had she been reading dangerous material? Had she been suckered into a cult? What person had been feeding her evil ideas? The only person who had any knowledge of her condition was—

"Professor Dunn."

He pronounced the name like a verdict.

"Constance," Rivard's voice was hard and cold, without a hint of agitation. "You are to remain here, to do everything Dr. Singer tells you. You are to eat, to sleep, to breathe. Do not attempt to starve yourself. Do not attempt to asphyxiate yourself with that pillow. You would not withstand what I would do to you." He looked at her once, hand on the open door—"There are fates worse than death."

The sound of the shutting door enclosed her words in the room:

"I know."

When Rivard reached Professor Dunn's office, the first thing he noticed was the lack of surprise on Professor Dunn's face. Professor Dunn looked as though he had been expecting him.

Rivard's suspicions were confirmed when the first words out of Dunn's mouth were: "You are later than expected."

Rivard stood in the open doorway, his large figure filling the frame. "If you were expecting me, then you know you are guilty."

Dunn motioned for Rivard to come in. He pointed to a chair. "Can I offer you a seat?" He looked well-mannered and hospitable, as though he had not taken notice of their initial exchange.

Rivard took two steps that were lunges. "When I come closer, it will be to squeeze my hands around your neck."

There was no hint of surprise or shock in Professor Dunn's face. His bearing registered interest—his eyes were keenly alert, but he showed no signs of being afraid.

Dunn's hand moved in a swift, dismissive gesture. "You *would* feel that."

Rivard stepped forward with another lunge. "I *would* feel that? If you know that I feel like killing you, why do you stand there playing the part of gracious host?"

Dunn's face grew bright, as if touched by a strange illumination. "Within the scope of your present knowledge, at this point in your life, your feelings are justified."

"Do you realize what you're saying? You're saying that I have a right to kill you!"

Dunn's blue eyes looked at Rivard's eyes. "That's quite right."

Rivard swayed back before he took another step. "I have every intention of exercising my right."

The clear blue eyes did not leave Rivard's eyes. There was no trace of a tremor in his voice. "I have always encouraged you to act on your judgment."

Rivard took another step. He was halfway across the room, several yards from Dunn.

"I have always encouraged you to think clearly, dispassionately—to act on your convictions with the certainty of a rule."

Rivard's gigantic figure towered over the old scientist. Dunn's white hair stuck out from his head in wispy strands.

"When you have come to a decision and know it is the right one," Dunn said, "you are obligated to act. Any vacillation at that point is a straying from the truth."

The two men stood looking into each other's eyes. Though Dunn barely reached his chest, the men were pitted as equals.

A silence seemed to last forever. Rivard was the first to speak; his voice was bitter as an acid: "I'm going to kill you. It's the punishment you deserve for taking the life of my wife. You know I'm not talking about her body."

"Her soul?" Dunn said. "You think I took her soul?"

"I've never seen a more thorough case of manipulation. She's as altered as if she's fallen in with a cult."

Dunn laughed, and it sounded to Rivard like glee born of diabolical scheming. Dunn said: "Constance has crossed over to the other side?" He turned to the window and muttered something in the manner of an annotation: "I'd hoped he'd have lost that dogmatic streak by now. I see he's as fanatical as ever. I'm going to have to wrangle with a zealous preacher."

"Constance has uttered things that are unmistakably evil," Rivard said.

"And you believe that I corrupted her? You think I've tainted her virtue with suggestions of the dark?"

"Now I've heard it straight from the horse's mouth."

Dunn laughed again and sat down in his chair. "Let me ask you something, Thomas. Why do you think I anticipated you? Why do you think I knew how you'd react? Do you think it's because my role fits neatly in your scheme?"

"Of course it does!"

"Ah. You are certain of the part I played. You are convinced that I am twisting my moustache in the title role of villain. You think that is the reason why I knew you'd try to kill me. I was caught red-handed, as guilty as a rat."

"You are!"

"Oh? Suppose the tables are turned. Suppose the wife is the hero and the husband is the villain. Suppose the wife is fighting for a cause that is noble and just—"

"This talk convinces me that my suspicions were correct. You are definitely the harbinger of evil."

Dunn's hair floated around his head like a cloud. There was no darkening in the cloud, no hint of a storm. Dunn's hair circled a face that was peaceful and open.

"What if I told you that the person framing this issue in narrowly defined, out-of-context terms is the harbinger of evil?"

Rivard's face was a violent exclamation point. The exclamation point was illegible; it was jagged and kinked. "What has happened to you, Professor Dunn? Moral relativism? What happened to the stalwart man of principle?"

When Dunn laughed again, Rivard wanted to reach out and claw his face. He barely heard Dunn say, "I am more than ever a 'man of principle.' My allegiance to principle is steadfast and absolute."

Rivard was incredulous. How was it possible that Richard Dunn had strayed so far off the path? What had happened to the medical doctor for whom protecting life was a sacred absolute? Why would Professor Dunn advise a patient to give up and deliberately end his life?

Rivard's voice contained every bit of his confusion and rage: "You are talking through both sides of your mouth, Dunn. You either stand behind your profession—and stand behind my wife—or give up and cease to become a doctor. You have done the latter. Some perverse part of your mind convinces you that you still stand up for truth."

Dunn sat forward in his chair. His face was illuminated by a sudden bolt of light. "And what is the truth, Thomas? Tell me quick."

"The truth is you have forgotten the truth. You have given up your own principles—those that guided your practice. You have abandoned your own maxim: Life is good and worth saving. For you, life at any cost is no longer an absolute."

"What would you say, Thomas,"— Dunn had moved to the very edge his chair and was nearly falling off—"if I told you that 'life at any cost' is precisely what I'm—what she is defending?"

"I'd say you're full of air. You can't say that you promote life in one breath, and in another, advocate suicide. It's a glaring contradiction."

Dunn's body was an eager slant, ready to fall off the chair. "Wouldn't that depend on what you meant by life?"

Rivard had had enough. His patience was wearing thin. He said, "Get on with it, Dunn. I'm tired of your madness and ready to end it."

"Wait! Before you kill me, you have to know the truth. I have not strayed from my old principles, my convictions or my profession. My adherence to the practice of medicine has never been as strong."

The insanity coming from the Professor's mouth was more than he could bear. Rivard knew that silencing Dunn was the best thing that he could do for medicine. It was the best thing that he could do for his wife.

Dunn saw the seething wrath coming from Rivard's face. He said, "Goddamn it, Thomas! The profession of medicine is not a religion and the Hippocratic Oath is not the Ten Commandments!"

Rivard's face was untouched as stone. Both he and Dunn knew that Rivard was and always had been a fundamentalist. Rivard was ready to kill and die for the literal version of his sacred word.

"Medicine requires judgment, Thomas, judgment! It requires discrimination. There is no set of hard-and-fast, pat rules that you can always go by, in times of crisis. The fact that you are dealing with the most difficult area in the universe—medical ethics—is not the time to call on packaged answers, ready-made. It is the time to call on your judgment."

Dunn had not even noticed that he had slipped from the chair and fallen to his knees. He looked like a supplicant, begging for mercy. It was not his life Dunn was defending; the only thing that mattered was unyielding defense of the truth. He said, "You must lose that dogmatic streak. It has never served you well. A doctor is not a dogmatist and the issue's not an either-or."

"It is an either-or," Rivard said, looming over the kneeling man. "She's either alive or she's dead. She either has a pulse, or doesn't have a pulse. My job is to keep hearts beating, hers most of all."

"And what is the human heart, Thomas? Is it just a mass of muscle pumping blood and air—or is it more? When you say you want to protect life, what exactly is it you want to save—an anatomy and physiology, or a human being?"

"Both! They are inseparable; they are one in the same."

"Ha!" Dunn shouted and raised his hands. "You are beginning to see. Do you remember what else it was I said at that lecture?"

"I remember every single word."

"Do you remember what I said about life, and its relationship to health?"

A bit of the violent anger passed from Rivard's body. He said, in the quiet tone of a recollection,

"Health and life are inextricably linked."

"Yes, Thomas! Health and life are inextricably linked!"

Rivard no longer had the poise of a terrorist, bent on doing harm. His arms, which had been raised, were hanging at his sides. His body did not look menacing or threatening. His face had untwisted.

He looked down at the kneeling Professor and it was as if their roles were switched. Rivard was the begging supplicant, making an appeal. Dunn was in a position for granting mercy.

Dunn clasped his hands together. "I do not envy you," he said. "The truth is, I don't think I'd have the strength to make the decision you're going to have to make. It is going to hurt. It is going to kill you. You'll wish that you could die, and end the necessity of making the choice." Dunn dropped back and settled on his feet. "This is quite possibly the worst situation that could befall a man. You are faced with an unparalleled moral dilemma: honor to your profession or honor to your wife."

"I don't see that the two are distinct."

"Ah!" Dunn shot back to his knees. "You don't! You understand that there is no contradiction between your role as doctor and your role as husband."

"Everything I do is about a single goal."

"Which goal?"

"To fight for life."

The Professor had become frenzied, was in a state of agitation. "And I know you will never veer from that sacrosanct crusade. I knew it while you were in medical school, I knew it before, and I've known it since. Thomas, you were and are my very best pupil. You are fully a doctor: a man of dedication, courage and conviction. A man with unbending resolve, undaunted by a trial. Thomas!"—Dunn looked at Rivard with eyes that had already seen the plot elements, eyes that were long past the situation unfolding—"You are being put to a test. You will hate me when I say this." Dunn paused. His voice became grave. "Of all the men I know, you alone can handle it, you alone will do the right thing. I am not happy about your predicament. I am glad it is you. Lesser men would fail."

Dunn's head dropped to his chest. Rivard looked down at the white wisps floating away from the ancient head. He felt something that he had never felt before: a blinding wash of hate.

"Dunn," Rivard said. "Dunn, look up." The old scientist raised his head. Rivard looked down into clear blue eyes that were untroubled as silent pools. "I do not see any contradiction or conflict here. There is no difficult choice." Dunn's clear eyes told Rivard that he understood. He was prepared for the inevitable. "You suggest that I consider this choice. What choice? My allegiance to my profession and my allegiance to my wife are one. What is good for one is good for the other: her life *is* life. To lose her would be the loss of life itself."

Dunn's face was turned up to his pupil; it

looked young and serene. The deep lines around his eyes had softened and his brow was not furrowed. Dunn listened without interruption; the lesson was his; it was silently received.

"There is no such thing as a choice between honor to my profession and honor to my wife. Honoring my profession *is* honoring my wife. Honoring my wife is honoring my profession."

Dunn looked at Rivard as a young man might look at a beloved teacher. His gaze was filled with admiration—admiration borne of respect.

"I do not recognize a conflict that pits my wife against my profession. It's a completely false either-or. To lose one is to lose the other—to give one up is to give up on both. Professor Dunn: I'm not about to lose either."

The Professor's face grew calm; it was the most untroubled face Rivard had ever seen. It looked as if Professor Dunn had caught sight of something, something that transcended his words, and hovered in the air between them.

Rivard said, "My wife asks that I take her life. She has all but taken mine. My trusted mentor asks that I consider the merits of her proposition. He has assisted her in twisting the knife into my back. You, Professor Dunn, have initiated a war."

Dunn's face continued to register untroubled serenity. He appeared to be looking on something he had seen long before.

"The issue is not: me versus my wife or me

versus medicine. The issue is: me and medicine versus you and my wife."

The verbal blow had fallen. Dunn did not flinch. He did not stoop. He did not grovel. He did not cower. His eyes did not contract. His eyes were steady and open as the sky.

"You and my wife must be beaten, must be stopped," Rivard said. "I am going to put an end to your sick notions and deranged plans. *She will live.* I swear by my life she will live. If I have to cut the heart from my own chest and stuff it down her throat before I die, she will live. I no longer care what you think, Professor Dunn. Life *is* worth dying for. I am willing to surrender my own."

Dunn's face did not change; his voice seemed to come from a great distance: "She feels the same way, Thomas. Life *is* worth dying for."

Someday you will see, Dunn thought. Someday you will see that life is too good, too precious to settle for anything less. You will see that life and health are identical twins. Your name means Twin, Thomas. You were born to be a doctor—born to unite the twins, born to defend the motion of those binary stars. Do not become too narrow-sighted. Do not lose sight of the whole. To speak of health without life is a contradiction; to speak of life without health is to speak of living death. Do not think we have deserted you! We have not deserted you and we will not. We want the very same thing you do. And because of it—because we love our lives—life!—we are willing to die for it:

Today, this moment, in the name of my life and the Hippocratic Oath which is my creed, I am willing to surrender my own.

Rivard had been looking at Dunn for some time. He saw the smooth, untroubled forehead; he saw the relaxed mouth settled into a quiet line. He saw the unnatural calm that belonged to a convict—or a saint.

He ground his teeth when he thought of it. Richard Dunn was the opposite of a saint. What had made him think such a thing?

Rivard began to feel mistrustful. He began to doubt himself. He began to wonder whether he was not in fact committing sin.

A fierce tug of war divided his mind.

They are wrong—completely wrong! They are advocating the exact opposite of what you know is truth.

Truth! What the hell is that? You thought you knew your wife. You thought you knew her inside out. Turns out she was deceiving you and has been for years. Everything you were so sure of turned out to be a fraud.

Precisely. That's why you must stop them—cling to what you know is true! Don't surrender it to anybody. Never let anyone take away your profession or your pact. You are bound to your oath—you are sworn to protect life—that much is absolute.

But what is life? Do you really think you know? That question has baffled philosophers for centuries and you're arrogant enough to think you have the answers.

But there is a kernel of doubt. You yourself have looked upon fat people with contempt—and it wasn't because they were risking a heart attack. You questioned their quality of life.

Quality of life! Damn that! The whole notion is one big excuse.

One big excuse? The quality of your own life has just plummeted.

I don't want to hear that mushy, wishy-washy, philosophical mumbo gumbo! I am tired of it all. Without life, there is nothing left—there is nothing at all.

Correct, friend. Without *life*, there is nothing at all.

Then the issue is settled. She's got to live.

Without a life?

Rivard screamed. He stomped his foot and pulled his hair. He grabbed Richard Dunn and jerked him off the floor. The old man did not struggle or resist.

"Say something, you bastard!" Rivard shouted. "Struggle against me. Fight for something, instead of becoming passive and giving up!"

Rivard had Dunn's frail shoulders in a vice-grip. Dunn's voice seemed to come from some source other than his body: "It is not you I wish to fight. It is the thing that makes you so certain I am doing wrong. It is that literal way of looking at things. I had hoped to get you to see the entirety."

Rivard's voice was an icy gust. "I am on the opposite side. I will fight death with every last bit of breath in my body. That is what doctors do. So help me, I will never, ever give in to death. Never."

"If you keep her alive, Thomas, if you force her defective heart and breath, it is precisely death you are giving in to."

The outrage came out of his hands. It came out of his hands and passed to Richard Dunn's body. Rivard's hands left bruises around the old man's neck.

"I don't believe you! I don't believe you!" The rage continued to spurt from his hands. "You are lying! You are sick! I don't believe a word of it! I will never let it go! Never give up!"

He began to shake the old man. He shouted into Dunn's face, cursing and spitting. All the anger and disbelief at his wife's condition shot from his hands and mouth to the guilty object.

"You named it after me, you sick bastard! What would make you do it? It doesn't matter, because I'm going to wipe it out, I'm going to find a cure. I'm going to make her get better!"

Rivard placed two massive hands on Richard Dunn's shoulders. Dunn's body was jerked violently; his head snapped in the opposite direction of his frame. Every time Rivard pulled or pushed his body, Dunn's teeth rattled in his skull.

"You are sick! You are sick! I can't let this go on!"

Dunn's voice came out a broken chatter: "She—can't—either—Thomas—she—can't—live—with—it—she's—tried—I've—never—seen—such—

courage—or—strength."

Rivard heard the compliment and became enraged. He wound his fingers around Professor Dunn's arms. "And you want to kill it! You want her strength to die. I'm not going to stand for it. You're the one who's going to die."

They stood face to face: teacher and pupil. Richard Dunn and Thomas Rivard were locked together in a deadly grip.

Dunn looked at his son—he had always regarded Rivard as his son—he looked at the man who was the product of his life's work, his creation.

Rivard looked at Dunn. He saw a guilty traitor. He saw a man who had betrayed his principles, turned his back on his son. Rivard looked at his father—he had always regarded Dunn as his father—he looked at the man who had created a life, then abandoned his creation.

Dunn said, "I expect no less from you, Thomas. Stand behind your principles. I am proud."

For one moment, Rivard forgot what he was about to do. For one moment, he saw the untroubled face of the scientist, a face unclouded by lines of doubt, and nearly understood: he almost grasped that thing that had hovered in the air between them. He almost grasped that what was required of him was reasoned judgment—not blind adherence to a set of rules—but independent thought, an independent weighing of the facts. He almost grasped what Richard Dunn had wanted him to understand: adherence to the Hippocratic

Oath *is* an absolute: one must discover the correct interpretation.

It was roused from his subconscious—some ephemeral truth that had come to him from time to time—and was written on his mentor's face. It played on the periphery of his mind—and was ultimately lost. The reality of the last twelve hours came back into his conscious awareness like a flood, sweeping all delicate considerations out of reach. The floodwaters carried one image into his brain: the tiny hurting body of his wife.

The man before him had hurt his beloved.

The tone of Rivard's voice became murderous. "You have violated our Oath," he said. "You have, in one blow, struck at the two things that I hold dear." Rivard's body seemed to grow to twice its size. "I cannot allow such an outrage to continue."

Though Rivard's body was swollen with anger, bloated by rage, Dunn stood before him undaunted.

"I may be an outcast," Rivard said, "but it is your own doing. You have estranged me from my wife. I'm going to get her back. I'm going to reclaim what is mine. As a first step, I'm going to wipe out what took it."

Rivard raised his hand over the body of his mentor. It was not the hand of a doctor defending a patient; it was the hand of a husband defending his wife. With all the ferocity of a male lion protecting his pride, Rivard let his hand fall.

There was a crack—skin burst—and a bright

spout of blood.

Rivard saw the blood and horror struck his heart. Can this be real?—he thought. Am I capable of taking this man's life?

Rivard saw his hand fall again and he knew that he was. The principle mattered more than consequences.

Suddenly, there was no difference between Rivard and a zealot. He had forgotten himself, in a cause that was greater. The defense of human life—that to which he was sworn—required that he destroy its enemy. The defense of his wife's life meant more to Thomas Rivard than his own.

An outpouring of bitter violence issued from Rivard's hands. He felt nothing, when he saw the battered pulp which had been his beloved teacher, crumple to the floor. He did not think of what he would do or where he would go, when he calmly wiped his hands and walked out to the street. Rivard did not realize that in the name of life, he had just committed murder.

5

Bill Metcalf impatiently drummed his fingers on the table. He watched half-frozen raindrops hit the window and roll down in sluggish streams. He shivered and pulled his collar around his neck.

Come on, Burt! Where are you? I haven't got all day. I can't wait around while you gossip with the neighbors.

Burt's voice came from the front of the store.

"Why don't you join me and Billy for lunch, Cindy? There's always room for a fun gal such as yourself."

Bill heard Cindy giggle and ground his teeth. Now he's done it, Bill thought. How the hell are we going to accomplish anything with another person around?

Three baskets lined with greasy wax paper were set down on the table. The booth shook as Cindy's body crashed down on the seat. Bill looked at the basket of limp French fries and lost his appetite.

"I invited Cindy for lunch," Burt said, giving Bill a conspiratorial wink. "She's got some information I think you'll want to hear."

Bill pulled back his hamburger bun. He grimaced at the dried ketchup encrusting the lid of the jar.

I don't really care what she's got to say, he

thought. Not only will we get nothing accomplished, I no longer want my lunch.

Cindy's appetite was unaffected by Bill's morose face. She dunked her French fries in mayonnaise, smacking loudly.

Burt sat back, a confident, gloating expression on his face. He patiently waited for her to talk.

She did not speak until her food was gone. She gulped down several mouthfuls of soda and let out a belch, before saying, "Burt says you've got it out for Tom Rivard."

Bill's eyes shot to Burt. He said, "I don't have it out for Tom." He looked back at Cindy. "Dr. Rivard is my friend."

She snorted and reached for one of Bill's untouched French fries. "Kind of one-sided, isn't it?"

"What do you mean?" Bill asked.

"The fitness Nazi? He's not exactly the friendly type. That one can be downright mean."

Bill looked at Burt for some sign or a clue. He gave Burt a look that said: What's going on here? Burt's face registered nothing but confident amusement.

"We're here to talk about an intervention," Bill said flatly.

"He does need an anger management course," Cindy said, her voice just as bland.

"What do you mean?"

Bill wondered what kind of knowledge the woman could possibly have.

"I've been in his class," she said. It was a flat statement and she offered nothing more.

"And?"

"Tell Bill about the way Dr. Rivard runs his class," Burt prompted.

The flesh of Cindy's face went slack. A slight ripple of disgust ran through her cheek. "The place is a hate fest." She reached for her soda and sucked noisily through the straw. "Dr. Rivard is the biggest bigot I've ever seen."

Burt watched Bill's face expectantly. A look of triumph bloated his own. When he saw that Bill was not shocked or interested, he goaded Cindy on: "Tom said some mean things to you one day, didn't he Cindy?"

Righteous pride colored her voice: "No one's *ever* talked to me that way. My self-esteem coach said that it's criminal. He says that I don't have to take it. My self-esteem coach thinks that—"

"Cindy," Burt said, roping her in, "what specifically did Tom Rivard say?"

"Oh that," she said flatly, let down and deflated. "He said he wants to change us, the fat people. He made it out like there was something wrong."

Burt looked at Bill, eyes rolling like an excited dog. "What do you think of that, hey? Pretty damn bold, he is."

Bill shrugged his shoulders. He had completely lost interest. "Tom has always been strict. It gets results. I don't see that it's anything criminal."

Cindy started to pout. She wanted sympathy.

"He said we're never good enough. He was picking on me and the class. Tom Rivard was mean and he laughed at me and told me I couldn't move."

Bill looked at Cindy's body, swollen with gluttony. He watched the way her stomach spilled onto the table; it was huge and soft, like a yeasty dough. He thought: Tom may not have been far off the mark.

Cindy looked at Burt. Her expression was a question: Should I go on? Burt signaled for her to wait for the cue.

"I think what Cindy is trying to say," Burt said, following Bill's eyes to the frozen rain hitting the window, "is that Tom Rivard has a mean streak."

Bill did not look away from the rain. It interested him more than the conversation. He said, "I know Tom can be harsh. If you think he's hard on his classes, you should see how harsh he is on himself."

Burt was disappointed that Cindy had not disclosed something new. He encouraged her to tell it all.

"My self-esteem coach told me to watch out for people who don't accept me for who I am," she said, falling back on her favorite subject. "My self-esteem coach is convinced that Rivard's fitness program is damaging peoples' self-esteem. Self-esteem is about loving who you are, not trying to be somebody else. I don't care what Rivard says: I love myself."

As she spoke, Cindy stabbed fat fingers into a massive breast, as though she could not refer to herself without demonstrative gestures. Bill thought: I'm glad you do, honey, cause from where I'm sitting, Tommy boy was right.

Bill looked at Cindy's earnest face and chuckled. He said, "Well, if this was all the news . . . Burt, I've really got to get going. My shift starts in a couple of hours and I had really hoped to catch a nap."

Burt's face fell. He groped for something to say. He was not about to lose an opportunity to hurt Tom Rivard. He looked over at his failed weapon. She was consuming the last of Bill Metcalf's untouched food.

"Hey, Cindy—heh, heh—so glad you could join us for lunch. Just want you to know that we're on it—the case, I mean. We're not going to let that fitness maniac hurt a fine, upstanding member of the community, such as yourself."

She spoke to no one in particular. She spoke through mouthfuls of food. "Maniac is the right word. There's something crazy about that man's face. He's got some funny look that he gets in his eyes—"

Bill had been putting on his coat. He froze, and looked down at Cindy. Suddenly nothing mattered more to him than the chatter coming from the booth.

"—his eyes get all funny. It used to scare me, when I'd sit in his class and he'd be looking at me, like—" Cindy paused, and looked thoughtful as she chewed her food. "He'd be looking at me like he could *force* something. I don't think he looked all that different from one of those suicide bombers, who's doing it in the name of God. Tom Rivard sometimes looks like fitness is something on some tablet from

God."

Bill stood in the middle of the isle, one arm thrust in his coat. He had become so interested in Cindy, he had forgotten all about the coat; it was hanging near the floor.

"It gives me chills, just to think about it. How I'd feel like I was being accused of something by wanting to eat. I know fitness is important, I know that it's good to eat right. That's why I took the class in the first place. A second heart attack would have been very bad news." Cindy chewed slowly and swallowed. "I think there's a difference, though. A difference between wanting to be healthy and forcing it on others. I don't know. I don't know what I'm saying. Maybe it's not coming out right."

The coat had slipped from Bill's arm and fallen to the floor. Bill's eyes were glued to Cindy's face; Burt was watching Bill. The corners of Burt's mouth were raised in an unseemly grin.

"I guess what I'm trying to say is that he wasn't right. Something was off." Cindy dabbed at the corners of her mouth and shrugged. "It doesn't make people feel like being healthy when the teacher's got eyes like he's possessed."

Burt was about to say something, but Bill shot him a look that said: Don't you dare. The two men were quiet while Cindy struggled to her feet.

"Thanks for lunch, guys. I've gotta go. I'm running late for an appointment with my therapist."

The jars on the shelves rattled as Cindy waddled

through the store. Bill and Burt silently watched her go. As soon as they were alone, Burt said, "See? I told you. I thought you'd find that interesting."

Bill looked uncomfortable, as though he were in pain. "I hate this, Burt. Tom has always been my friend."

"Did she say something that wasn't true?"

"No."

"Does it square with any of your own personal experiences?"

Bill hesitated, reluctant to talk. He finally said, "Yes. I know what she means."

"Care to elaborate?"

Bill was loath to share information about Tom Rivard with the town gossip. He suddenly regretted involvement in an intervention.

Burt sensed Bill's anxiety. Determined to carry out his promise to Heloise, he thought of something he could do: he made an appeal to public safety.

"We have a duty as citizens of this town to watch out for the citizens of this town," Burt said. "The more I learn about Tom Rivard, the more I'm convinced he's a danger. Am I far off the mark?"

Bill Metcalf was not the type to tell a lie. Any loyalty he felt toward Tom was second to the facts—especially facts as dangerous as amphetamines. He looked straight at Burt. "You're not off the mark at all," he said.

Burt looked pleased, as though he had succeeded in getting another person to do something underhanded that he did not want to do himself. He was convinced that an alliance with Bill was the best way to get at Tom. He had to be careful, though. He knew Tom and Bill were old friends. He would have to move slowly, using every available caution and trick.

"I just want to make sure," Burt said. "I want to be absolutely certain of the facts. You know that I would hate for anyone to be wrongfully accused . . . ."

Bill was suspicious of Burt's sudden concern over Tom's welfare. He threw in a wrench of his own: "Tom will get what he deserves."

Burt perked up at Bill's sudden change of heart. It was clear that he had overestimated the extent of their friendship.

Feeling confident, Burt said, "I never did like that man, never did. Too arrogant for my taste. And now this business about a possessed look in his eyes. Gives me the creeps."

At the mention of Rivard's eyes, Bill fell into a somber reverie. He no longer looked eager to talk.

Hoping to snap him out of it, Burt said, "The best thing for you and me to do is make sure the public is safe. It's the public that matters. You know that a lot of the boys . . . don't like anyone running around insulting our ladies, disturbing the peace."

Bill did not appear to have heard Burt speak. He was focused on some private thought of his own.

Feeling left out, Burt said, "What are you thinking of, Billy?"

Bill looked up, as if he had been startled. "I . . .

what? Oh." He frowned at the frozen rain clinging to the window. "It's this weather. November weather always gives me the blues."

It was apparent that something was nagging at him, not simply the fate of his friend. Burt was not about to let Bill get off easy. "That's not it and you know it. Something else is going on here. What's on your mind?"

Lines gathered at the edges of Bill's eyes. He looked old; talking seemed to take great effort. In a tired voice, he said, "I sometimes think killing the demon is killing the saint."

Burt jumped back in his seat. He took a glance around the store. When he was satisfied that no one had heard, he whispered, "What the hell kind of statement is that?"

Bill looked at Burt with eyes that were tired and wise. "I'm committed to the witch-hunt, so don't you worry."

Burt looked aghast. "I don't know what you're trying to imply—"

"Oh Burt, cut the crap. You damn well know what I'm talking about."

Burt's face was hurt and offended. "I don't know, I don't know what you're getting at. If you think this is some kind of—"

"Railroading. I know exactly what this is."

"But you—but you said—you made it clear—"

"Let me be clear. I've lived in a small town long enough to know the ropes. You and a bunch of other jealous goons are capitalizing on an unfortunate situation in order to play hero. You will never have Tom Rivard's energy, dedication or endurance. You will never have his steadfast commitment to a goal. Because of it, you will never have his wealth. You are all too eager to tear down the celebrity coach."

Burt's mouth fell open. For the first time in his life he was speechless.

"But I don't care about any of that. That is a broken record repeated in every small town. All small men want to lash out at the strong, and will do so, given the chance. I don't care about envy-driven malice. What I do care about is Tom."

"So do I!" Burt rasped. "We are all thinking of his interests."

"No, you're not. You're not thinking of anybody's interests, not even your own."

"Yes, I am! Me—the boys—we're thinking of the public safety!"

Bill thrust his head back as he laughed. "Ah, yes. The public safety. Tell me something, Burt: Just how safe is the public going to be without Dr. Rivard around to save it?"

"What do you mean? He's a public menace!"

"A public menace—the man who single-handedly pulled Stanley Humphries back from the brink of the grave?"

"Stan Humphries survived in spite of Tom Rivard's interference!"

Bill laughed again, long and loud. "It's really

amazing how the truth gets distorted, isn't it? Tom Rivard has saved more hearts than God. If you count the people who've purchased his taped lectures and books, he's probably saved more lives than the world's greatest cardiologist—Professor Richard Dunn. What you all can't stand is that he's got no tolerance for anything weak. That leaves you out in the cold."

Burt started to talk, but stuttered over his words. He was not sure whether he was being insulted or praised.

"Again," Bill said, laughing, "none of that matters. Your motives are not important. The inevitable can't be changed by pondering reasons." His voice changed abruptly. It came out a snap. "I do, however, want you to be clear about the consequences."

Burt groped for some straw of his original intentions, something he could say. He had trouble remembering what it was he had intended to do.

Bill said, "Don't be deceived about what you will accomplish. About what I'm going to help you accomplish."

Burt stared at Bill like an obsequious dog, ready to take orders.

"I want the results of our actions to be perfectly plain." Burt was silent, indicating that he was listening. Bill spoke in a voice that was even and low: "By taking that crazed look out of Rivard's eye, you are forfeiting your life."

Burt could not contain a gasp: "What the hell are you saying, Metcalf?"

"Just what I said. Remove the monomania—remove your rescue. Remove the thing that keeps him going no matter what, the thing that makes him work twenty-four seven, moving in a race with the clock—shave off your remaining years, the years you won't have, because Rivard won't be there to give them to you. Make no mistake about what you are doing when you seek to dull the glint in that man's eye: you are cutting your retirement short."

Bill laughed at the horrified look on Burt's face. "As for me," he said, teeth flashing in a brilliant smile, "I don't care about any of that. I just want to see my friend get off drugs."

The jar of pills had fallen to the floor. The floor was covered in small white dots. Rivard reached down with a shaking hand and grabbed at several dots.

He did not use the glass of water on the table. He had forgotten it was there. He ground the pills with his molars, not tasting the bitterness or noticing the lesions on his tongue.

Coffee had stopped working a long time ago. He had switched to sugar for several hours, flooding his system with high fructose corn syrup. The energy was an intense rush that had sustained him for a while and ended with a crash. He had switched back to caffeine—pills this time—hoping that would do the trick.

The glare of the computer screen gave his eyes a bluish tinge. The tinge did not mask or cover the crazy metal glint: the two shades blended until his pupils looked like pools of mercury.

His body was still. The only indication of life was the rapid scanning motion of his dead-looking eyes. Once in a while his forefinger stabbed at the button on the mouse. His wrist spasmodically jerked the mouse around.

He was looking at letters which had been grouped into words, and organized into sentences. He was seeing hieroglyphics. Rivard tried to make sense of what he read, he knew that it must add up to some meaning, but he could not tell what it was.

The words were expelled from two lips like dried-out lines: "It is difficult to say with certainty, for so little is known about the disease. Nonetheless, all historical cases show that the prognosis is grim." Rivard's mercury-poisoned eyes blurred when he read the words. "The first part that seems to be affected is the hands. What begins as a periodic numbness induced by abnormal circulation, ends as a complete and utter quadriplegia."

He repeated the last word, soundlessly moving his lips in the order of syllables. He knew that the syllables meant something, that they referred to some thing he had just encountered. He had blocked the encounter from his mind; as a form of defense against the memory, he blocked the meaning of the word. If Rivard did not know what *quadriplegia* was, if he was ignorant of it, then it did not exist. If quadriplegia did not exist, Constance was normal and things would be fine.

Not able to believe his own lies, Rivard read the words through a transparent film of self-deception.

"It appears that there is an inherent tension between the body of the Rivard's disease victim and his heart: almost as if, speaking figuratively, his heart was designed for a different person. I say this because the 'defective' heart of the victim does not possess a real defect. The heart itself functions the way a heart should: it pumps blood received from the veins into the arteries, thereby supplying the entire circulatory system. It is not the heart *itself* that is the problem, but rather the rest of the body, or the physiological relationship between the two. If I may speak poetically, rather than scientifically: the victim's body cannot handle the overabundance of heart. It is not a question of the heart's literal size, but of its capacity. The Rivard's disease victim appears to have too much heart."

For one moment, the metal glint in Rivard's eyes softened to a luster. His eyes glowed when he read: "The heart, in fact, functions *too* well. It does its job like a champion and burns out the limbs. Too much, too rich of a blood flow overwhelms arms and legs that respond by shutting down. It's a phenomenon I've never seen in sixty years of cardiology: a heart so full it stuns the body."

Mercury swirled into the irises of Rivard's eyes when he read what came next: "But a cardiologist is not a poet, and medicine is not literature. Nearly four years ago, I set out to find a cure for this bizarre disease. I wanted to wipe it out." Rivard ground the caffeine pills stuck in his molars. You didn't!—he thought. You stumbled and failed. You never did come up with a cure—you killed my wife!

"My first attempt," the tract continued, "involved issuing a type of sedative, a tranquillizer for the heart. My goal was to slow down its excessive functioning, bring it back to normal capacity. My patient reported something very strange: any alteration of the heart's functioning altered her heart's disposition: that is, a change in the literal organ created a change in the metaphorical one. My patient did not experience the paralyzing numbness while she was on the medication, but something which she says was worse: a paralysis of the heart. Her joyful, energetic attitude had completely disappeared. She felt morose and sleepy. She could stand no more than a few weeks of this before she refused the medication. She told me that the numbness was preferable to losing her native zest."

Rivard looked at the words on the computer screen and was whisked back four years. He could remember the period like it was yesterday. He could remember Constance wanted to do nothing but sleep. He could remember that she had lost interest in all the things she loved, including him. He could remember a mysterious dullness in her eye, and an out-of-character slackening of the limbs. He had recommended that she see her doctor. She had brushed it aside as nothing, and he had been scared, but after several weeks the bizarre condition left abruptly as it came, and Rivard forgot it.

Things were starting to make sense, old puzzle pieces locked together. Rivard kept reading the screen, scrolling rapidly, hoping to find some information he could use to help his wife. The first place he had gone was Richard Dunn's journal. He continued to read.

"Because the malady is a defective relationship between the heart and the body that encases it, and I had already tried to 'reduce' the heart to the body, I then tried the reverse. I tried to 'increase' the body to the heart."

Before Rivard read another word, he knew what was coming. He instantly thought of the time, not too long after the depression, when Constance had run circles around him and not been able to stop.

"The effects of this attempt were just as bad. Central nervous system stimulates, amphetamines, caused the patient to become irritable, restless and unable to sleep. Her limbs were keeping up with her heart—she was, in fact, jogging like a marathon runner during the trial—her muscular endurance had never been higher—but neither had her recurrence of insomnia. She was so far from the paralyzing numbness, she could not get to sleep. This state was not bearable for long, and we had to once again accept the debilitating symptoms of Rivard's disease."

You accepted them, all right!—Rivard thought. You accepted them and let them take over. You let the symptoms get so bad the disease will do her in. But not if I can help it! You were feeble and uncommitted and not brave or strong. You caved. You were not worthy of your title. I'll show you—where you are peering out from hell! I'm going to cure Constance!

His eyes were fixed on Dunn's words with a glaze. He relished every sentence, because he knew that he would triumph and contradict them.

"I have performed dozens of heart transplants in my time," Dunn's article continued. "A heart transplant is a viable option for those who are strong. There was no question about the strength of the patient, mentally or physically, in this case. That wasn't an issue. The issue was that she's headstrong."

Rivard grimaced and unwrapped a chocolate bar. Sugar flooded his bloodstream and he processed the words with a feverish brain.

"It had to do with the experience of the patient under sedation—or rather, how she felt with a tranquilized heart. The patient could not stand the change of heart—I speak of the metaphorical one—which accompanied lessened activity of her arteries and veins.

"And this is where I depart from the realm of pure science and enter the realm of philosophical speculation. One thing that sixty years of experimental medicine has given me—if you'll kindly pardon the expression—is a healthy set of testicles. We in the physical sciences tend to look on questions of health as a matter of black and white: there is a human anatomy; these are the human body's systems. That is simply how it works. Well, not quite.

"My experience has taught me a very important

lesson, one which I think is of greater import to fellow physicians than any specifics about the disease: if a patient's heart is not in it, a clean bill of health doesn't matter. In other words, wellness is relative. Not in the sense that we can make no distinction between health and disease, but in the sense that quality of life is a highly personal matter.

"I did not baulk at my patient when she told me that the physical altering of her heart altered her person. The connection between physiology and psychology is too complex to make hasty dismissive claims. I think there is a whole branch of science here to be explored. And though it fascinates me, I am too old to do it. I leave such exploration to another generation of physicians.

"What I intend to spend the remainder of my life pondering is the degree to which wanting to live in fact constitutes a life. Is life the product of a conscious choice—a will to live, and all that implies—or is it simply granted (not by God, of course, but by virtue of having a pulse)?

"Let me return to the question at issue. A heart transplant would undoubtedly give my patient a chance. I honor her request not to speak of it—for her, 'If a medication altered who I am, just who would I be with a different heart?'—and will continue to serve as her physician in any way that I can. I am sworn—absolutely—to act for the good of my patients, after all; it is their well-being that I must protect and uphold. Is anyone in a better position to know their own well-being than the patient?"

With one explosive swipe of his arm, the computer monitor crashed to the floor. Rivard leaped up and let out a roar that shook the walls. "No! Goddamn you, no! A doctor knows best! A doctor spends his entire life researching health, aiding and promoting it. Well-being is a completely black-and-white, objective state. I will have none of this!"

He kicked the screen with all his might. He hurt his foot and liked the pain. He struck the monitor again. A shock bolted up his leg and stabbed his knee.

He laughed contemptuously, hatefully. He suddenly hated the world and everything in it. There was nothing beautiful about existence, nothing noble or grand. Life was a bloody fight, and Rivard was going to fight until the end.

His palm slammed down on a stack of papers and twisted, sending the papers flying. He dropped down to his knees and rifled through the mess.

His eyes darted across the sheets, snapping back and forth like a clock's pendulum. His voice was a string of muttering; the words came out of his mouth with the toneless monotony of a chant:

"In no known case of this baffling condition has the victim been cured. Once quadriplegia set in, the victim had permanently lost use of his arms and legs. Death followed, but in no case was this the result of vital organ failure. Of the eight or nine documented cases worldwide, all victims were possessed of abnormally strong hearts.

"One report involved a Maori warrior. Local legend tells of a man so strong and swift, he was venerated as a type of living god. His tribe believed that he possessed spiritual power, that he was Tapu, sacred and untouchable. When he suddenly became paralyzed, the tribe believed that he had violated Tapu—that someone of lower rank had touched and polluted him, draining his strength. The warrior did not live long after: he refused food and drink, and quickly perished.

"There is the case of the gold-medal-winning Olympic gymnast from Spain. Ricardo Catramado was an undefeated athlete, at the top of his profession for years. Judges called the man 'the greatest male gymnast the world has ever seen.' He died in obscurity after suffering from some acute and sudden paralysis.

"A Navy SEAL from Maryland, John Boon, met a similar fate. The man was highly esteemed as the fearless hero who single-handedly rescued seven of his comrades being held by Islamic radicals in Tehran. Nothing could stop this man, whose incredible intelligence matched his physical strength. He spoke six languages, and was one of the greatest long-range marksmen in the world. Suddenly forced to retire after a mysterious paralysis took his arms and legs, Boon left behind a wife and two little girls."

Rivard spat at the paper and tore it to shreds. It's taken the best and the brightest!—he thought. His pupils dilated and filled his eyes. It's taken the world's best—of course it would get my wife!

Tears oozed out of his dry, sleepless eyes. He

crumpled to the floor. All Rivard cared about was Constance. It was not some great principle he was fighting for; it was not some lofty goal—all the things he had said to Dunn ceased to matter. The only thing of importance was finding a cure. That meant he had to get to the bottom of it.

He shot up, propelled by a sudden, unwelcome thought: The common denominator is strength. They were all hit because they are strong.

He slammed his fist down on the floor. The injustice of the situation overwhelmed him. He wished that Richard Dunn were alive, so that he could kill him twice.

"Goddamn you, goddamn you," Rivard said, pounding his fist into the floor. "You should have conquered this, you should have beaten it."

He continued to beat at the floor, bruising and damaging his knuckles. He stopped when his eyes fell on a scrap of paper.

It was one of the documents he had collected. He had gone from Dunn's office to the hospital, dropped off his car and walked home. He had spent ten hours finding every available bit of information about the disease. He thought that he had read it all. There was something he had missed.

With shaking fingers, Rivard picked up the paper and began to read:

"I have just completed it. Several days ago. The great work of my life is finished. My magnum opus is done.

“I am not writing this by hand. I am dictating it. I have lost all ability to move.

“I had known that something was going to happen. I wasn’t sure when or how. The numbness had been coming and going for years”—Rivard’s face turned sickly green—“and my only hope was that I would finish my masterpiece before the sickness took my life.

“I succeeded. I pressed on, ignoring it, not allowing it to take me down. I willed it from my mind, and focused on my art. The thing that I wanted the world to have is done.

“My name is Sebastian Long.”

Rivard gasped aloud when he read the name. Sebastian Long was a world-class sculptor, creator of *Self-Actualization*, a male nude said to rival Michelangelo’s *David* in the perfection of its form.

“I have achieved what I set out to achieve. The great work of my life is done. It is fitting that my life would end with this.”

Rivard gulped, because he knew what was coming.

“This is my suicide note, my final message. There is nothing more that I can do without the use of my limbs. Do not despair for me, for this is as it should be. Everything I wished to say in life I said; it’s in my art. There is, however, one final thing I wish to communicate.”

Rivard squinted at the paper, as though he feared to look at it. Desperation and curiosity goaded him on.

"For those who take up the study of this ailment, know this: the numbness that began in my chest and spread out to my hands, always came on when I was at a creative peak. Whenever I had succeeded in actualizing some aspect of my vision, whenever I was on fire with a creative blaze, my heart felt full to bursting, and stunned my very limbs. I must wonder at something, and perhaps I will find out the answer when I die. Does great joy necessitate pain? For you see, this is a truth: it is the full heart, the strong and passionate heart—not the empty one—that breaks."

Rivard let the paper flutter from his hand. The paper fell and rested on the pile. The floor of his office was lined with a blanket of snowy sheets. Just outside, the frozen rain had turned to snow and the ground was covered with a thin layer of downy cotton.

Rivard suddenly felt drowsy. He was overwhelmed with a desire to sleep. His thumping bloodstream had slowed to a trickle; his eyelids could no longer fend off slumber.

He collapsed on the floor. His body was spread out over the scattered sheets. His anguished brain continued to process what he had been through.

Rivard began to dream.

He stood at the head of the classroom next to the gym. He looked out at his pupils: his pupils were pigs. Mindy Parker had gigantic mottled thighs and tiny cloven feet. Cindy Beale's ears, studded with a row of hooped earrings, were tattered around the edges and fraying like cloth—evidence that she had been in a fight.

Rivard asked his pig pupils a question. They responded with a set of high-pitched squeals, barks and grunts. Rivard did not understand "Pig," so he did not ask any more questions. He gave the class a lecture.

He stood before a black board, frantically scribbling with chalk. A thick white line divided the board into columns. One column was labeled Pro, the other was labeled Con. He ground the chalk to a stub between tightly-pinched fingers.

He read the list on the Pro side. The pigs grunted and squealed as he talked.

"These are the reasons for killing Constance, these are the reasons why I should take her life:

1. She asked me to do it.
2. I am a good husband, and husbands never disobey their wives.
3. I don't want to be married to a cripple.
4. I can't have sex with a torso."

"Ahem." One of the pigs rose up on its hind legs and peered at Rivard through a monocle. "My good sir, you are forgetting something."

Suddenly, Rivard could speak "Pig." He grunted, "What is it?"

"Point five: You do not like to watch people suffer."

"True," Rivard said, adding it to the list. "I do not like to watch people suffer. Thank you, Pig."

"You are quite welcome, sir."

Rivard tapped at the Con column with a forefinger that stretched to the length of a pointer. He said, "These are the reasons why I should not kill Constance. These are the reasons why I should keep her alive:

1. I want her alive.
2. I am a doctor, and doctors seek to further life, not end it.
3. I took the Hippocratic Oath.
4. I am not a murderer.
5. I love my wife."

Cindy Beale shot up from her chair. She hysterically squealed, "There's a mistake, there's a lie. Number four is false!"

Rivard looked at the place where she was pointing with a cloven hoof: 4. I am not a murderer.

"True," Rivard grunted, erasing the lie. "You have a point. I can't use that reason."

He drew a bar at the end of each column and made the calculation: five for the Pro side, four for the Con side.

"I guess the Pro side has it," he said. "I guess I've got to kill my wife."

He grabbed a piece of chalk and drew a large circle around one of the points on the Con side of the board. Rivard circled the point that said: I love my wife.

As he stood looking at it, the pig with the monocle got up and moved to the front of the class. He silently took the chalk from Rivard's hand, wedged it into his hoof, and drew an arrow to the corresponding point on the Pro side.

"*Because* you love your wife," the pig said, "you cannot watch her suffer."

Rivard picked up an eraser and silently removed everything on the lists except the connected points. He drew a double-headed arrow between the words Pro and Con.

"You are Pro-Con," the pig said, grunting and shaking with amusement. "You are Pro-Constance."

Rivard sat up with a jolt. He glanced around the room, trying to recollect where he was and what had happened. The room gave him an odd, creepy feeling, a sensation he did not like or trust. He stumbled to his feet and grabbed his coat without seeing the room. He wanted nothing to do with it. He thought that everything would be all right if he just got out of the room.

Bill Metcalf collided with Millie Collins in the hospital corridor. He was lost in thought, his mind was still in the general store with Burt Lancaster and Cindy Beale, and he did not see Millie coming with the tray.

He heard the rattle of plates on tile and saw the splatter of tomato soup. His eyes moved from splotched shoes to splotched shirt front, to a red-and-purple-splotched face.

"Oh God, Mill, I'm so sorry. Let me help you clean it up." Bill stooped to the floor to gather the bowl and plates. He motioned to the janitor at the end of the hall. "I'm such a clunk. I'm really sorry. My mind's not in the same place as my body."

Millie frowned at her soup-coated shoes. "Don't worry about it, Bill. None of us are doing too well lately."

"No?" Bill looked at Millie from his position on the floor. He took the paper towels from the janitor and said, "What do you mean?"

Millie watched the janitor wring out a mop. Her eyes darted nervously, as if she were reluctant to talk.

Bill stood up. "Let's take a walk, Mill. I think you could use a break."

They sat in the vacant employee lounge, huddled over steaming paper cups.

"I need to ask you something," Millie said.

"Shoot."

"What would you do if you heard something awful, really awful—something someone was going to do, and you weren't supposed to hear it?"

Bill reached for two sugar packets and sprinkled the contents into his cup. "It depends on what you mean by 'wasn't supposed to hear it.' Are we talking about patient confidentiality, or . . . ?"

"Eavesdropping. None of this was entrusted to me."

"Mill!" Bill feigned righteous surprise. "I'm shocked! I never took you for a snoop!"

Millie smiled weakly. She had always had a crush on Bill, she had always liked his good-natured flirtation, but she was not enjoying it now. Her mind was deeply troubled.

Bill noticed her uneasiness. He regretted making the joke. He had only put on the show of humor in order to get rid of his own anxiety. He made his voice light as a breeze, hoping to cheer them both: "I'm sure it was an accident."

"Not an accident—concern."

"Do you want to talk about it?"

"Yes and no." Millie poured a dash of milk into her cup and swirled a wooden stirrer. "I need to get this off my chest—but I can't put this burden on somebody else."

Bill saw the pain on Millie's face through forced cheerfulness. He began to feel concerned. He said, "Millie—what's going on?"

"I—I can't tell you." Her face crumpled. "I can't tell anybody!" Millie began to sob hysterically. She flung her body over the table, upsetting their cups.

Bill leaped up. A dark stain covered the crotch of his pants. He was grateful for another chance at comic relief. "Great, Millie. Now you've gone and done it. Everyone will think I wet my pants."

She looked at the blotch between his legs: it *did* look ridiculous. Her sobs turned into heaving laughter.

"That's better," Bill said, letting out a sigh. He could not stand to watch women in tears. "There's nothing worth getting upset about."

"That's where you're wrong," Millie said. Her face displayed fear. Bill saw her look of panic. His concern turned into alarm. "What is it, Millie? Tell me what's going on."

There was a visible moment of torture, as Bill saw Millie's face swing between, I have to tell!—and—I can't! Her face switched back and forth several times, registering an excruciating dilemma. When the struggle was over, when the conflict was done, the triumphant side was declared in a look of helpless regret: I have to tell.

She said, "I know I shouldn't do it, it's not my place to say anything, I wasn't supposed to see any of it."

"What weren't you supposed to see?"

"I didn't mean to see it, it wasn't my intention to spy on them—really!—I didn't want to see."

"What didn't you want to see?"

"I was just doing my job. I'm a good, competent nurse—no one can blame me! If I *hadn't* been doing my job, if I had been slacking and hanging around the room, then I could see someone blaming me. But I wasn't, I was doing what I was supposed to do, so it's not my fault. It isn't my fault I saw—"

"What the hell did you see?"

"Dr. Rivard almost killed his wife!"

She looked down at the table and wrung her hands. "I shouldn't have told! I shouldn't have told! Oh God, I wish I could take it back."

Bill did not hear Millie, or even realize she was there. The only thing in existence was the string of words: Dr. Rivard almost killed his wife.

When Bill spoke, his voice was toneless and bland: "Tell me about it."

She looked up at Bill; her anguished face was streaked with tears. "I—I can't tell. I shouldn't have—"

Bill let out an ugly laugh. "It's a little too late for that, isn't it Millie?"

She bowed her head and wrung her hands.

"Go on," Bill said. "I'll wait until you're ready."

She got up to make another cup of tea. Somehow, talking about it was not as bad when she could keep her hands busy.

She sat at the table where Bill had taken a seat. She did not know where to begin so she started where she had ended.

"He had the chair raised up over the bed. One of those folding metal chairs. He said, 'I could kill you right now.' That's all I heard. I shut the door as fast as I could."

Bill shook his head. "Millie, you'll have to back up. What were Tom and Connie doing in Intensive Care?"

"You don't know?"

Bill shook his head.

"I thought everybody knew. I thought you'd have been at the scene."

"What location?"

"Nightmare Mountain."

"Not my jurisdiction. Next town over." Bill's voice had taken on the inflectionless tone of a reporter after facts: "Who, what, when, where and why, Millie."

"Constance and Ethan. Corinne's boy?" He nodded. "They spun out of control on that sharp left-hand curve. Totaled the car. They were brought in yesterday evening. I've been here the whole time. Double shift."

"Injuries?"

"That's the strange part. The boy didn't get a scratch. Ethan came out untouched." Millie paused. Bill looked at her expectantly. Millie hesitated before she said, "Constance lost her arms and legs. They cut her from the car."

Bill's eyes dropped. He looked down at his hands. He balled them into fists and looked at Millie. "What about Dr. Rivard?"

She looked away quickly, not wanting to talk. Bill was not about to let her off. The question was a command: "What about Tom?"

"He—he couldn't handle the news." She stammered the response and offered nothing more.

Bill did not care whether he had to pull her teeth one by one. He was going to get the information.

"Millie, tell me about Dr. Rivard. What was his response?"

"I told you. He didn't handle it well."

Bill altered his approach. "You wouldn't want anything to happen to Connie, would you?"

"No!" The cry was involuntary. Bill knew he had struck a soft spot. He waited, knowing she would talk.

"That's why I had to say something," Millie

said. "I couldn't let anything happen to Connie. I thought of her small, helpless body, and that maniac threatening her, leering down at her over the bed."

"Maniac?"

"Crazy lunatic! At one point I heard him scream. A little later she was screaming for me; she was shrieking! I went in to find Dr. Rivard sprawled out on the floor."

"On the floor? What was Tom doing on the floor?"

"I don't know! None of it makes sense. When I went in, he was lying on the floor, staring up at the ceiling. He told me I was blocking his view. He told me he couldn't see Professor Dunn."

Hallucination, Bill thought. It's gotten so bad he's starting to have hallucinations.

"Connie didn't tell you why he was on the floor? Was that before or after he raised the chair?"

"Before. I told Connie I'd come by a little later to change her pan. When I opened the door, Rivard had the chair raised up over the bed."

"Did you hear any fighting?"

"No."

"Any commotion? Anything that sounded like a struggle?"

"Nothing. The room was quiet. I assumed that the two of them had fallen asleep. That's why I thought it was a good time to peek in."

"Did either of them notice you at the door?"

The tone of Millie's voice was definitive as her

answer: "No. I'm sure of it. He had his back to me, and she—she was looking straight at him."

Bill let out a breath that seemed to last forever. He blinked and ran his fingers through his hair.

Millie's question came out a sudden wail: "What are we going to do?"

"Nothing," Bill said, placing a hand on her arm. "Not just yet." He gave her arm a squeeze. "You're not to feel guilty about any of this, okay? You didn't do anything wrong." She smiled weakly, attempting to be brave. "You did the right thing by telling someone. Don't worry, Millie."

"It's not me I'm worried about," Millie said. "I'm worried about Connie and Tom. I'm worried he'll do something to her. Bill!"—Millie's face twisted like a bent screw—"She's supposed to go home for a few days before she comes back for surgery. What if he, what if he—Oh, God! He might do it at their house. Bill, I'm worried Tom will try to kill her at their house!"

Bill forcefully took hold of her arm. "Don't panic, Millie. I'm going to get to him and see that none of that happens. You have to understand something: Tom has not been well for quite some time. It has nothing to do with Constance." Bill paused and looked out the window where frozen rain had changed to snow. "The truth is, we've been planning an intervention. Dr. Rivard is addicted to speed."

Millie gasped. Her hand shot to her throat. "That would explain why he was—"

"Acting like a maniac. Tom's strung out on drugs."

Her hand collapsed onto her lap. "Oh, my God . . . Bill, you don't understand . . . this explains so much. And in a way, I'm glad of it."

He nodded.

"The worst part of the whole thing was being crushed. I mean, I had this vision, an idea of the way things were. Mr. and Mrs. Rivard were the perfect couple. They seemed completely in love with each other."

Bill's hands were lying open on the table.

"I've always been jealous of their marriage. I always thought: *this* is the way things are supposed to be. This is the ideal relationship between a man and a woman. They are both full of energy and vitality, always cheerful and excited about their work. It seemed like they were completely in sync. Like they cherished and valued the exact same things. In a way, I kind of thought they were one person."

Bill closed his hands into fists. He slowly opened them.

"When I saw him lashing out at her, it was like a dream being shattered. You hear so much about domestic abuse. I didn't want it to be true. I couldn't believe it. Not them! Anyone but them!"

Millie reached out and grabbed Bill's hands. "I'm so glad you told me what you did. I'm so glad to know the truth about Endurance." She laughed softly. Bill's hands were warm and she gave them a squeeze.

"I couldn't have lived with the idea that their great romance was all a fantasy. I knew it had to be true." She looked at Bill with questioning eyes. "And you'll help him, right? You'll help Endurance get well, so he can continue to be a good husband to Connie?" Millie sat back in her seat, satisfied with Bill's affirmative nod. Her voice was thoughtful and unself-conscious. "That name . . . Endurance. I guess there are things that even the strongest people are not made to endure."

He thought of it the next morning, when he stood on Rivard's doorstep, ringing the bell.

What's come over you, Endurance? What caused you to turn to drugs? What would make you throw away a perfect marriage and a brilliant career?

He pressed the doorbell again and stamped his feet to warm his toes.

I know you are a perfectionist. I know your standards are high. But goddamn it man, your wife doesn't deserve it! Connie's a total babe. Can't you see what you have?

Something flickered across his brain, something so horrible he blotted it out before it became conscious thought. It rose up again, against his will, and he banged on the door with his fist, hoping to drown the hateful words in the noise: what he's got now is not a babe, it's a torso.

He slammed his fist against the door until it rattled. He did not like the thoughts that were filling his brain: Constance was hurt, she was injured beyond repair. Can you blame Tom Rivard? Could you live with it?

His hands had become numb and it was more than just the cold. Bill Metcalf was terrified of what Rivard would do. He was even more terrified of his own response: that what Rivard would do might be justified.

He shuddered and wondered what would make him think such things. He instantly thought of stress and lack of sleep. Stress does funny things to the body, he thought. Stress makes people edgy and rattled, just like they're on—

"Drugs."

The door had not been locked. Bill had not intended to let himself into the house, he had intended to look for Rivard at the gymnasium if he was not home, but something had impelled him to put his hand on the doorknob. When he found that the house was open, he let himself in.

Bill Metcalf entered the room Rivard used as an office. His jaw dropped open and stuck to the floor. He was not prepared for the sight. Nothing could have prepared him for what he saw.

Every drawer and file chest was open, the contents removed and flung onto the floor. All of Rivard's books, normally arranged on shelves according to subject, were scattered about, many with pages missing, whole sections cut out or torn. The scraps and sheets were covered with thick black lines and illegible scrawl, evidence of frenzied note taking.

The computer monitor, speakers and keyboard had been pushed off Rivard's desk and were lying in a broken heap on the floor. Someone had stamped upon the keyboard.

Bill's eyes darted around the room and honed in on one spot. The office chair had been pushed away from the desk. The floor space surrounding the desk was covered with candy bar wrappers and soda cans. A collection of coffee mugs, empty but obviously used, overlapped brown rings left on the desk and scattered sheets. Small white pills beside an empty unmarked jar specked the carpet.

Bill scowled as he stooped down to examine the pills. He thought: Goddamn it, Tom! Goddamn this! I hate being right! He picked up a half-eaten candy bar.

Drug addicts can never get enough to eat, he thought. Speed fiends are rabid about sugar.

He did not know where to begin. He cringed, because he suddenly realized Tom could be in the house. He did not want to get caught snooping. He left the room, intending to look through the papers when he returned.

"You home, Tom?"

He pushed open the swinging door that led into the kitchen. He smelled something burning.

Bill removed a crusty coffee pot from the burner. He swished the clouded liquid around the glass bowl of the pot. "Mud," he muttered under his breath, pouring the liquid down the drain. "That coffee was made hours ago."

He snapped off the switch. He looked around the room. Dirty dishes that had not been rinsed or scraped covered the counter and filled the sink. A gallon of milk had been left out on the counter. Empty egg shells and tomato seeds surrounded a yolk-encrusted glass.

Bill frowned when he realized the lights had been on when he entered the room. Tom must be home, he thought.

"Tom! You home? It's Bill!" Bill walked into the living room. He glanced out the picture window to the feeder in the yard. Cold weather had set in and bird feeders were swinging from leafless branches, packed full of seeds and corn. Bill watched a blue jay frighten off some chickadees and take possession of the feeder.

"Where are you, Tom? Thought I'd come by for a visit!" Bill tore his eyes from the feeder and glanced around the room. It looked as if no one had been there for days.

The pillows on the corners of the couch were stiff and untouched: stuffing bulged in the middle of each pillow and spread out evenly to the seams. Someone had placed them at neat diagonal angles and draped a decorative blanket over the side, as if the space were designed for show and not for lounging. A stack of glossy men's fitness magazines was spread in a perfect fan over a coffee table next to the couch. The mantle was lined with a row of medical encyclopedias, their bindings completely flush. The fibers of the carpet were whisked into orderly swathes—someone had vacuumed the rug, and it was unmarred by specks or sets of prints.

Bill shuddered in the grey light streaming through the window. The contrast between the living room and the two other rooms gave him a strange feeling: he felt like he had walked from one deranged world to another, moved between two antithetical worlds that constituted one diseased universe: he had left a drug addict's den, a world where hours of frantic scrambling had turned the office upside down and inside out, a world of anguished uncleanliness, chaos and disorder—and entered a world marked by obsessive compulsion, a space of whip-wielding discipline and certainty: he saw the world of a consciousness so obsessed with order that not even one fiber of carpet was in the wrong place. Bill shuddered, and wondered whether the world he was in was responsible for the world he had left. Did Rivard's militant perfectionism cause him to break? Was Rivard's addiction to speed the result of his addiction to health?

Bill could not decide. He did not know and he did not care. All Bill cared about was saving his friend. All he wanted was to help his friend get better.

He was certain Rivard was not home. A sense of duty prevented him from leaving. He thought that the snooping was justified, because he cared about Rivard.

He won't mind when he finds out, Bill thought, because I'm thinking of his interests. Tom will thank me for this later. He will realize it was necessary.

He was on the second floor, in their bedroom.

He did not reach for the switch, but stood in the morning light coming through the window. The branches of a dead maple were stretched like bars across the glass. The tree formed a cage locked against the window. Rays of pale light squeezed through the rigid bars and Bill suddenly felt like he was trapped.

He took giant strides across the room, trying to get away from the tree. The tree over the window made him feel like a prisoner. The half-light made him think of death. Desperate to escape, he opened the bathroom door adjacent to their bedroom.

Jars, bottles and tubes stood in lines behind the sink like tiny soldiers. A stack of towels, folded into perfect squares, sat unused on the side of the tub. Chrome fixtures glistened with the violent sterility of an institution.

Bill jerked a shaking hand toward a drawer beneath the sink. He clutched at vitamin jars and various salves in metal tins. "I know it's got to be in here," he rasped, feeling frightened and out of breath. "I know there's got to be uppers."

Bill dropped a lipstick. It clattered onto the bottom of the drawer. Heart pounding, he stiffened and listened.

I just heard a creak on the steps, he thought. I know I heard a creak.

His hand was motionless in the air, fingers slanting downward where he let the lipstick drop. He strained his ears; he fought to keep his body still; all he could hear was blood coursing through his ears in a violent rush.

He spoke out loud to interrupt the silence: "Get a grip, Metcalf. No one is home. Relax and keep looking."

He opened an aspirin bottle and spilled the pills onto the counter. He looked at each one before flicking it back in the jar. He froze, when the sound of a pill hitting the jar came out a creak.

"Tom?" Bill poked his head around the bathroom door. "Tom, is that you?" Bill's heart raced as he waited for a response. "It's just me—Bill!—I'm up in your bedroom!"

There was no reply and Bill cursed himself for being foolish. What's gotten into you?—he asked himself. Old houses always creak in the winter. Are you worried about that stupid tree?

He knew that his fear had nothing to do with the tree. He had been rash, going to Tom Rivard's house by himself. He had been foolish to enter when no one answered the door. The memory of Millie Collins's frightened voice sent hair-raising pricks up his spine.

He had the chair raised up over the bed. One of those folding metal chairs. He said, I could kill you right now.

Goddamn it!—Bill shouted internally, jerking open another drawer. Why did I come here? What was I thinking? If Tom is capable of killing Constance, if he is willing to do it—just what the hell is to stop him from killing me?

He jumped and looked up, when he caught a

flash in the mirror. He looked into the bedroom without adjusting his stance or turning around. His heart was in his throat, it was thumping wildly, as if it wanted to escape his frightened body through his mouth, and he froze, his brain sending mixed signals between a desperate choice of fight or flight.

"I'm in here!"—Bill shouted, preparing himself for the sight of Tom's drug-crazed face. "I'm in the master."

He looked around for something he could use in case of an attack. He would have to find something to use as a weapon. He was smaller than Tom, much less muscular and not as tall. His only hope would be an agile move with something sharp.

His eyes flashed around the room like darts. They moved quickly back and forth between the bathroom and the bedroom in the mirror. He did not want to take his eyes from the place where Tom would enter.

His eyes fell on something he could use. With a motion that resembled a stab, his hand shot forth and picked it up. He formed a fist around the metal nail file, holding the pointed tip away from his thumb.

He thought better about letting himself get cornered in the bathroom. With cautious, hesitating steps, he slowly made his way toward the door.

He strained so hard to hear he thought he went deaf. What had happened to the creak? Had Tom already made it to the top of the stairs? He walked through the dim bedroom, hand lowered, tapping the metal file against his hip.

He saw the dead tree out of the corner of his eye. The branches looked like bars closing him in. Bill's heart sank, even while it beat like a crazy drum within his chest, for he suddenly felt that he had walked into a trap.

Tom is not home, he told himself, trying to stifle a rising scream. And even if he is home, he is your friend, he would never hurt you. Bill took several steps to where the bedroom opened to the hall. You are being crazy—ridiculous! Tom may be a fitness maniac, he may be addicted to speed, but one thing he is *not* is a murderer.

This thought comforted him. Bill chided himself for letting irrational fear take hold of his brain. He laughed at himself and loosened his grip around the file.

You are just nervous because you don't want to get caught, that's all. You don't want your friend to know you are snooping. You were rattled by the sight of that office—it proves your suspicions are correct, Tom is battling an addiction—and you are worried about what you will do.

Bill took the first step down the flight of stairs. He smiled when the weight of his body caused a groaning creak. It made him certain that the earlier creaks had been products of an addled brain. They sounded nothing like the real one.

He whistled loudly and bounded down the flight of stairs. He had come here on a mission. He had come here to help his friend get better, to comfort him and make him understand that drugs were not the answer. He had come to counsel him and console him about Constance.

Bill headed back through the kitchen to Rivard's office. He had come for information about his friend; he had come to learn more about his mental state. Bill thought that before he left he should look over the scattered papers.

The office did not look nearly as disturbing as when he had first entered. Daylight was increasing every moment, the snow and rain mix of the previous day had given way to clear skies that promised sun, and the changed morning light made the office look more like a disheveled mess than a schizophrenic's den.

Bill pitched the nail file on top of a stack of papers. He knelt on the floor and took a quick glance around, trying to decide where to begin. He could not discover any system or method to the arrangement of papers; it looked as if they had been haphazardly tossed aside when Tom was done. Bill attempted to collect articles by matching type font and page numbers.

The job was not a quick one. The entire floor of Rivard's office was littered with heavily marked sheets, and Bill had trouble piecing them together. He became absorbed in the work, and forgot about the fact that he was spying.

His eyes skimmed over repeated words as he organized the papers: disease, arms and legs, quadriplegia. Defect, paralysis, abnormal heart.

Bill took little notice of the words that flashed

before his eyes. He was not prepared to read until the pages were organized. He could barely make out the notes in the margins; they all blended into one squiggly line of illegible scrawl.

The minutes passed. Bill felt a sharp crimp in his neck. He threw his head back and let it hang over his shoulders. He rolled it in a slow circle before holding it straight.

That is when he saw it.

The papers fell out of his hand. They slid along the floor and blended into the white layer. Bill rose to his feet slowly, not taking his eyes from the wall. He rose slowly and with wooden limbs, pulled upright by some invisible string attached to his neck. Several quick jerks of his wrist groping for the file looked like the motions of a marionette. He did not find the file; the tug that pricked at the back of his neck was the tug of some malicious puppeteer.

Breath escaped between his parted lips: "Oh, my God."

His pupils dilated and filled his eyes. His eyes expanded to the size of the sight.

The wall behind the door was marked with huge block letters, massive black lines that stuck out like criminal evidence on the clean white paint. A solid black bar divided the white space into columns. The words "Pro" and "Con" stood at the top. In the Pro column, the words "Reasons for killing Constance" were followed by, "I do not like to watch people suffer." An arrow connected it to the message on the

Con side: "I love my wife."

Bill felt the pricking tug of the marionette strings at his neck. His limbs were wooden rods, his body had become stiff and immobile, and he did not know which was worse: the fact that he was looking upon a rationale for murder, or the fact that the rationale referenced love for his wife. For Bill, the two concepts—matrimony and murder—were irreconcilable and did not compute. He was more frightened by the reason Rivard had given than the actual crime itself. There was something deeply troubling about a person who believes that his crime is motivated and justified by love.

Bill shuddered, because he knew he was looking upon insanity. He began to quake, for he realized he had placed himself in peril.

There was a sudden sound. Bill jumped, and feverishly looked around the room. The sound had come from just outside the door.

His heart stopped. He tore his eyes from the office door and, without thinking whether he should do it, stooped down to retrieve the metal file on the floor. It was buried beneath the layer of white sheets. His fingers shot out like misdirected probes; he fumbled for the slim file beneath the litter of paper, barely able to breathe or see what he was doing.

The blow came down on his head. He cried out as he was knocked to the floor. A knee stabbed into his back, forcing his stomach against the floor. His arms were wrenched behind his back. Metal cuffs sliced his wrists.

"Tom! Tom, don't do it! It's me!"

"Shut up! We know who you are!"

"Tom!" Bill had not heard the voice. Certain he was going to die, he continued to wail and scream: "Tom! Tom! Don't do it! Don't kill me!"

"If you don't shut up"—there was a blow to the back of his head that broke his face against the floor—"we *will* kill you. Keep quiet!"

Bill tried to speak. Blood gushed from split lips and poured from busted gums. "I won't—go out without—fighting Tom—I'm not gonna—let you get—me or her."

A club was raised up over his head. Bill said, "I won't let you get her." The club was poised to fall. Suddenly, a hand shot out and held it back. "Wait! Don't hit him. Something's wrong." Bill noticed a slackening of the pressure on his back and he struggled like an animal. A large hand slammed down on his neck and the club was swung into the air. "Wait! Ray, don't do it!"

"Tom Rivard?" The question was barked like a command.

A reply came out of Bill's battered mouth like the mewling nonsense of an infant: "Tom, please don't . . . it isn't worth it . . . to kill . . . ."

The commanding voice let out another bark: "Dr. Thomas Rivard!"

"Don't hurt Constance . . . you've got me now . . . leave her alone."

Bill heard a set of voices speaking back and forth.

"Do you think he's faking?"

"Of course he's faking!"

"Do we have the right place?"

"White, middle-aged male. Hospital attire. Rural Route One, number four."

"The guy was larger than average. This guy doesn't fit the profile. This guy's kind of small."

Bill was confused and delirious from shock at the sight of his blood. He continued to speak to the person on his back. "Tom, please let her go. It's your wife. She doesn't deserve it."

"Who doesn't deserve what?"

"I know you love her, Tom. Please let Connie live. It isn't me, it's her."

"Ray," the voice hovering above the two men on the floor said, "Ray, get up. That's not our guy."

Bill felt an absence where there had been a painful pressure. It seemed that every bone in his body cracked when they rolled him over.

"Are you Thomas Rivard?" one of the voices asked.

Bill opened two black and blue slits that had been his eyes. He knew that his head had been hit hard because he was experiencing double vision. "Tom, it's me, I'm so glad you changed your mind."

"Are you Thomas Rivard?" the other man asked.

Bill wondered what Tom was doing in a state

police uniform. He said, "Just me, Tom. I'm sorry about snooping. It's just your old pal Billy."

Within ten minutes the state police officers had Bill propped up, cleaned off, and fully informed.

"What you're telling me is impossible. It just can't be true. Tom would never do that. He isn't capable of killing."

"No?" The officer's name was Joe McBride. "You were pretty certain Rivard was going to kill you. Do I need to remind you what you said when you were down?"

"No." Bill frowned, because he knew the officer was right. He did not want to believe it, but Rivard was fully capable of killing. He threw his head back against the couch and pressed a cold cloth to his face. He thought: An old man? Why would Tom kill an old professor? Bill scowled; the situation had gone from terrible to horrific.

"Car's not in the garage." Officer Ray Durham stood in the doorway.

"We've lost a lot of time with Mr. Metcalf." Joe McBride turned to Bill, from where he was sorting papers on the floor. "Sir, you say you've known Rivard for years. Any idea where the man would flee?"

Bill shook his head. "I used to know Tom. I can't say that I know the man who took the life of Professor Richard Dunn." An afterthought painfully bludgeoned his skull.

With his bare hands. Tom killed Dunn with his fists.

Bill grew angry. A jagged bolt of rage coursed through his body and forced him to sit up. “Under normal circumstances,” Bill said, “I would tell you to look for Tom at the gym.” The officers looked at one another before focusing on Bill. “He lives at the hospital gymnasium. At least he used to.” Bill frowned as he said, “But Tom never takes his car anywhere. If he were at the gym, he would have walked. You didn’t find any prints, and after last night’s snow you wouldn’t anyway. If the car is gone, he’s probably made it to another State.” Bill’s face lightened slightly; it was an imperceptible change, something that happened more to his heart than to his face. “That’s where I’d go, if I were you. I’d go straight to Rivard’s office at the gym. There may be some clue to where he’s gone. If you don’t mind, I’d like to catch a ride there with you. I’d like to go to the hospital and check up on Connie.”

He had walked through the night and into the morning. He had placed his feet at the head of the trail system that snaked through the wooded acreage behind his house, and continued to lift one foot from the ground and place it in front of the other. He had no destination in mind; there was no place he had set out for or to which he wanted to go. There was no fixed purpose—never had been and never would be. The only thing was the motion of two feet carrying his body over the trail.

Snow had fallen through the night. At first he had brushed it from his shoulders and sleeves; he had tried to stay dry, or at least avoid getting drenched. After awhile, the wet flakes began to clump and run from his hair and clothing in tiny, half-frozen streams. He decided that it did not matter—nothing much mattered—so he stopped brushing it off.

He had not outfitted himself with the right pair of shoes. Each time his body weight pressed into the sole of his shoe, he felt a cold puddle ooze out around his sock. The sensation had been uncomfortable at first, but it had ceased to matter hours ago. It began to matter less when his toes went numb.

His toes had numbed long before his fingers. He had noticed that his feet were moving over the ground, the snow was heavy and wet on ground that was not yet frozen, and it was only a heel and arch that met the earth.

He had removed his shoes and, sitting on a boulder in the white snowy light—trail posts lit up a thousand tiny bulbs that were snowflakes glistening—he had checked to see whether his toes were attached to his feet.

"They're still there," he said, clutching bare toes with icy fingers. "They are little pink prunes, they look like they've been pickled, but they're still on my feet."

He had pulled wet socks back up over his feet and laced his shoes. He sat on the boulder, wiggling his hidden toes in the shower of sparkling flakes. "What an awful thing to have no toes," he said. "And even worse: to have toes but not be able to feel them." He leaped from the boulder onto what felt like imaginary feet and kept walking down the trail.

His body did not matter anymore, he could not feel half of it anyway, and so he let his thoughts wander to things that mattered: how beautiful the old woods looked at night.

When he spoke, his breath formed an ephemeral cloud that rose like steam: "I've hiked these trails for years, and never really noticed how lovely they are. Why does everything look so fragile and perfect at night? Is it because the objects themselves have changed—or is it a change of vision?" He looked at the leafless branches of an old sugar maple, raised in solemn offering to the sky. It seemed that if he just stood up on his toes, if he stretched a little and extended his arm, he could reach and pluck a branch from the tree. One branch looked delicate as a flower's stem—both delicate and powerful, like a wand. He pretended that he held the branch in his hand, a wand with which to make his troubles disappear, a wand with which to wipe the last seventy-two hours out of existence.

"I have no such wand," he said, passing the old tree. "I can't make any of it go away or take it back."

He knew that he could keep walking. He thought, perhaps, it was the only thing left to him. His life was gone—it had been taken away in a nightmare span of seventy-two hours—but his body remained, his stubborn organs continued to pump and beat, to support a person who was no longer there.

He wondered where he had gone. He wondered why the loss of his soul had not resulted in the loss of his body. How was it possible that the two had been severed? How was it possible that the muscles and veins, the bones and marrow of his body had not died the moment he committed treason?

He did not know what he had committed treason against. At times he thought he had harmed his wife by killing Dunn—but that did not make sense—it was *her* life the act defended. At other times he wondered whether he had committed treason to a memory, memory of the man who had taught him all he knew about the human heart. But that man had ceased to exist, the noble scientist had died, had vanished, and the death of his body was a necessary completion. No, he was not sorry about Dunn. The horrible thing had had to happen. Had he committed treason against himself? Was it himself that he had violated? That could not be the case, for it was precisely *his* values and convictions he had defended all along. He had protected and fought for that which was true.

The problem was: the truth did not seem true anymore.

He had walked along the trails for hours, through the falling snow, trying to find the pieces of his lost convictions. Where had they gone? If his actions were justified—if they were the right ones, why had he died upon committing them? Or—if his actions were wrong—why was he still alive? Why was he made to wander through the woods aimlessly, like some homeless nomad in search of his soul? If his soul had vanished, why did his body refuse to know it?

What good is my body without its soul?—he thought. If the spirit that once animated my limbs has ceased to exist, what do I want with a collection of atrophied muscles and joints?

He did not know and he did not care. The questions seemed unanswerable. He was tired of thinking about questions that had no answers—questions which used to have answers, but now did not. The very notion that there *were* any answers seemed like an impossible dream. The world of black-and-white, yes-and-no answers had vanished.

He thought of these things as night began it fade. Night slipped into the coming dawn, and he passed through a black space to a space of midnight blue. The blue hovered between snow-coated branches before it turned to sunless grey.

In the waxing light, he saw the state of his body: frozen fingers bent into hooks, dark clothes streaked with water, formless like a drowning bird. He had never seen his body look pitiable—his figure had always been bronzed with proud strength, shoulders held back and head lifted, posture straight and muscles firm—his figure had always matched the poised confidence of his spirit. Now that the confidence had drained from that spirit, the strength was seeping from his limbs. Now that doubt had entered his intransigent mind, emaciation was wasting the body in which it lived.

He looked down at his hands. He could no longer feel his fingers. The cold damp night had worked its way into his bones. His hands had never looked like they belonged to a physician—he had never had the long, slender, overly protected hands of a doctor—he had hands that properly belonged to a carpenter—or an inmate: short, powerful fingers; a thick, muscular wrist; blue veins that formed a map on the back of his hand. He laughed out loud when he saw that his hands looked like they belonged to a broken criminal. He laughed, for that was exactly what he had become. His moral convictions had led him straight to blood-drenched crime. Was there something wrong with him—or something wrong with his convictions?

Suddenly, a gunshot broke the air. He jumped, completely startled by the crack. He looked down at his chest, expecting to see a red trickle. He glanced up and scanned the woods, expecting to see a posse approaching through the trees. There was no red trickle; there was no posse. He checked his coat and the woods again, thinking the threats had been missed. His eyes had not deceived him: nothing threatened.

He curled his frozen fingers into fists. I may be a criminal, he thought, I may have lost my soul—I have been walking through the night to find it!—but that doesn't mean that I'll give up. It isn't over yet.

He braced himself for what he knew was coming. They've probably followed me into the woods, he thought. They've probably got dogs. Even if the snow has covered my tracks, their canines will smell me.

There was another shot. He huddled over like an animal. His chest had sunken and a hunch had grown up on his back. The heart health and fitness expert who had posed for glossy men's magazines—the most influential medical doctor in the region—the man who had been militantly certain of his commitment to life—was now frightened for his own.

He crouched down into the wet snow and cursed the morning light. He would have had a chance if it were dark. Dawn was quickly becoming early morning—pale grey was tinged with a faint rose that prefaced sun—and he knew that there was not a single place to which he could flee.

What is more—he did not want to flee. The animal part of him that felt fear and wished to avoid a cage at any cost—the self-preservation instinct that generations of ancestors had passed down through their genes—the pointed canine teeth and quick reflexes that survived the unforgiving process of evolution—none of it beat out his desire to live like a man: he was not going to cower, shirk or run.

As soon as he thought this, his body straightened. As soon as he realized that survival at any cost did not matter more to him than his dignity, the vertebrae of his spine resumed their skyward thrust. The tiny bones of his neck moved back into their proper place: they held up his chin.

He stood in the pink and yellow light of early morning, the fibers of his clothes were so wet they were separating and falling off his frame, his frost-nipped skin had already gone from red to blue, but he paused, and he stood tall, and he smiled. He would not succumb to an animal existence; he would not hunch and spit at a threat, or frantically run from it. There was a difference between the way an animal faced adversity and the way a human being faced it: a human being, unlike an animal, places his life above his mere survival.

He knew that he wanted to take the path of a human being. Calmly, and without a trace of fear, he set off in the direction of the gunshots.

He heard the hunting party long before he saw it.

"Hey, Todd, get over here. Get over here and fry us up some eggs."

"Cook up your own damn eggs. While you're at it, put on a pot of coffee."

"I'm not your slave!"

"But I'm yours?"

"Hell, yes! Camp cook has to feed us all. We're sleepy-eyed and hungry. You don't think we can get our seven-pointer on granola bars, do ya? Fry up some bacon, hash and eggs."

"Goddamn it, Byron, it's cold! Why did I let myself get talked into hunting?"

"Because we're gonna have a freezer full of deer—that's why! Get out of your sleeping bag and lace up your boots. If you don't, I'll shoot ya."

"Don't matter. I already feel like I've been shot in the head."

He had veered off of the main trail and walked in the direction of the voices. He heard a sizzling sound, and smelled a griddle slathered with bacon. Through the leafless bramble, he saw the stove pipe of a hunting shack belching wood smoke.

Hunting season, he thought. I completely forgot about hunting season. The gunshots were not a posse after all. The authorities haven't found me.

These thoughts came into his mind, and were blasted away by the explosion of another shot.

"Got it! Got that old damn crow. That'll teach you to buzz around our camp, now won't it? I goddamn hate those old damn crows."

"Little Byron, what have I told you? Don't go shooting at birds before breakfast. It isn't right." There was a pause. "Todd won't have time to plunk out the feathers."

"Don't matter. If you want to waste shells killing pests, go right ahead. Me, I'm saving up for the county's biggest deer."

"It's your own hide you better worry about saving, never mind no deer. If you burn that bacon, I'll kill ya."

"Don't matter. My head hurts and I'm cold. Only thing that'll warm me up is another drink."

He watched through the brambles as the man they called Todd cracked open a beer can and drank the contents without stopping. He threw the empty can onto a massive pile.

"Goddamn drunk cook," the one named Byron said. "If you weren't my cousin, I'd kick you out of this camp. Can't even make a edible plate of eggs."

"Here are your eggs, Cousin, cooked just the

way you like em': raw. Little Byron, you ready for some eggs?"

"You don't want me to run fetch that bird? We can burn it."

"Hell, no. Come and get your food."

The members of the hunting party sat around a smoldering fire, rear ends planted on plastic ice chests. They did not talk while they ate. They bent their heads over their plates and gulped mouthfuls of barely-chewed food.

He did not like to look at it. He felt like he was watching a ravenous pack of dogs. He did not know whether it was hunger or ignorance that caused them to bypass any attempt at manners. By the camp's appearance, he was certain it was ignorance.

The little shack was in complete disrepair: front steps rotting into the ground, door hanging crazily off one broken hinge. The stove pipe jutted straight out from the wall between two plastic-coated windows and then rose in a diagonal line, forming a tilting L. Creosote ran down the sides of the pipe in thick black globs, inviting a chimney fire. The ground surrounding the shack was muddy and bare of snow: the outdoor fire had melted it. The mud was littered with rifle shells, beer cans and dog droppings. Bits of rusted old metal—everything from saw blades to automobile parts—formed a giant heap along the tree line. An old hound that had not moved once the entire time he had looked on, lay in a loose pile next to the smoldering fire.

Todd stood up and flicked the remainder of his

food onto the ground next to the dog. “Eat up, Bess. You’ve got to help us get a deer.”

The men chuckled. Little Byron stood up and gave the dog a kick in the ribs. “Worthless old sack of bones. You ain’t worth the cost of feeding. We ought to clean you and use your old hide for a rug.”

There was another round of chuckling. The old dog did not raise its head or flinch. “You dead?”—Little Byron said to the dog. “Good. We won’t have to deal with you losing your bowels all the time, stinking up the place.”

“Here, here!” Todd said, raising a beer can. “I won’t have to deal with a beggar while I’m trying to cook.”

“What do you mean?” Byron asked, looking sorrowful. “I like my old Bess. She’s a good girl. Damn sight better company than you.”

Todd sniffed. “What company? The old thing’s half dead. It’d be better off that way, too.”

Little Byron leaped for his gun. “Want me to shoot her? I could take care of it good.”

“Don’t you dare touch my dog,” Byron said, glaring at his son. “I want that old beast.”

“But you heard Todd. Bess’s better off dead. We should put her out of her misery.”

“No.”

“You don’t want her to suffer, do you Pop?”

“Course I do. What else good is a bitch?”

The three men laughed themselves into silence. They stared into the fire, making no effort to rise.

One of them said: "I suppose . . . ."

He barely had time to take in what happened next. There was a shout, chaotic scrambling and flailing of arms. Dishes were pitched to the ground and a beer can flew as all men scurried for their guns.

"It went that way, beneath that birch! Shoot it son, kill it!"

A loud crack cut the morning air. There was a crash of something heavy falling on leaves. The three men trudged through the snow to look at it.

"Goddamn doe," Little Byron said. "Goddamn illegal deer."

"Not for eating, it ain't." Todd greedily rubbed his hands together. "That illegal deer will be damn fine eating. Fish and Game don't need to know about it. Don't matter."

"No, it don't," Byron said. "That's one for the freezer. But how about a trophy? Let's go get one for the mantle. We can dress that old bitch when we get back. You two can take care of it while"—Byron glanced quickly at Todd—"I go tend to some *separate* business."

"Damn right," Todd said. "We have bigger bucks to blast. This one's just an appetizer. Let's go kill her daddy." Todd slapped Byron on the back. "Best of luck with your big kill, Cousin."

He watched the men pull on layers of wool and bright orange vests. When the orange vests had disappeared into the woods, he walked over to the fire.

He almost stepped on the dog. "Oh! Sorry girl."

He reached down to pat it. His hand recoiled when he saw that the skin of its belly was blotched with some disease. The dog looked at him with drooping, lifeless eyes. It did not thump its tail or raise its head. It was completely indifferent to the presence of a strange human.

"Maybe they were right," he said. "Maybe it would be better if you died."

The dog did not respond to the sound of his gentle voice and he began to get angry. Those ignorant rednecks!—he thought. How dare they treat this animal so poorly. It's almost as if they feed the thing just to sustain its misery, almost as if they—he shuddered, because he knew it was true, yet unbelievable—they keep it going just so they can watch it suffer.

He took several steps back from the dog. He looked at it with horror. He thought of the time one of his schoolmates had waved him over to a tree. The boy was proud of what he was doing and wanted to show it off. He remembered the sick feeling he got in his stomach when he saw the collection of live toads, their legs deliberately severed. The boy had laughed when they rolled around for a long time before they died. "I think it's funny," the boy had said. He never played with that boy again.

The man who owned the dog suddenly seemed like the most twisted person in the world. He could not fathom that kind of perversion. He thought: What kind of person delights in the agony of another creature? Or worse—what kind of person deliberately keeps a creature on the brink of death, perpetuating its agony, encouraging an existence of suffering?

A monster, that's what. His heart bled for the dog and he knew he had to leave. He knew he could not stand the sight of the hunting camp for one more second.

He was about to turn back in the direction he had come when he heard what sounded like rustling. What's that?—he thought. It's coming from beneath that birch. He remembered the deer. Something must have found it, he thought. There's probably a skunk or weasel on the carcass.

He made his way to the carcass of the deer. He was horrified when he saw that it was not a carcass. The deer was very much alive.

He saw one huge eye rolling like a marble. The black marble shined like it was wet. There was a body laid out on the ground, there was a head and there were legs. The only thing he saw was the rolling of the marble.

The deer's body was concentrated in its eye. In one instant, its life had drained from its limbs and filled the black marble. The marble was full to bursting and looked like it would pop.

The eye barely remained in its socket. The eye that now held the deer's entire body looked as if it wanted to leap from the body, leave the old dead part of it—the superfluous limbs—behind.

He thought that at any moment the eye would jump out and go rolling away, rolling off through the woods over the snow and leaves in search of a new body, like a wandering vagrant in search of a home. He thought that if he pressed a finger to the side of the deer's face, the eye would pop. He was terrified of the trapped eye and of the thought that he could free it.

He almost leaped from his own skin when the head that held the eye rose up off the ground. Neck muscles twisted in a tortured rise—each fiber and strand strained to pull itself up and away from the rest of the immobile body—and the sickening motion made the head look severed.

He saw that the head was all that was left of the body. He saw that the small dark hole hit the very spot that divided head and limbs. The thrashing head that contained the rolling eye was all of it: the rest of the body had been paralyzed by the shot.

No ripple, no wave of muscle raised its coat. The tight chest, back and rump of the doe were still. Each of its four legs shot out like a poker: they were stiff and hardened—not by death—but quadriplegia.

The frost-eaten leaves made scratching sounds as they were crushed beneath the head. The head rose, the wild eye rolled, and the leaves were ground into particles of dust. Each time the head rose he could see an arc-shaped furrow, a semi-circle in the dirt marking its frenzied sweep.

The body and the head were incongruous—two things attached which should not be attached: a corpse and a living animal. It suddenly seemed like the neck of the deer was an outrage, something that should not be allowed, something that should not be at all—yet was: a thick set of cords binding the corpse and the animal together.

He watched the hysterical rise and fall of the animal's head, he saw the eye rolling with an acute terror that made it pop—and then he saw the stiff rails of deadened limbs. It was not the wild head that bothered him—it was not even the corpse-like body. What disturbed him was their joining by the neck.

His cold, exhausted body could not take it anymore. He turned away from the deer and retched into a bush. The sugar that had flooded his bloodstream came back out as sickening bile, watery thin and very sweet. The sweet taste was exactly like the smell of Pine Manor. He had the smell of the Alzheimer's ward in his mouth: he tasted the scent of living death.

He coughed and choked on his own fluids. The taste made him sick—the taste like the smell of a morgue. He wiped his mouth with the back of his hand and spat into snow-covered twigs. He felt like he was in some kind of horrific nightmare; the nightmare had gone on for seventy-two hours and was quickly getting worse. He wondered whether the deer's head would snap off and go floating through the frozen forest right before his eyes.

He could not bear to look at it. He could not stand the sight of the dead limbs attached to the living head. The worst part was the deer's reaction: it did not understand what had happened to it. It fought to rise; it kept trying to leap from its position. It did not realize it was permanently pinned. He watched the deer fight a losing battle; he watched it struggle to rise up on disobeying limbs, and what he felt was pity.

Why couldn't those redneck fools take better aim?—he thought. Why didn't that bullet strike a little higher?

He looked at the tiny black hole that had done so much damage. It seemed inconceivable that one little hole could destroy so much. He saw the perfect body of the fallen deer—a tawny coat hugging tight muscle, not one bit of superfluous flesh, not one wasted cell. He frowned when he looked down at the still, perfect form: they had hit it just right: all the cells were wasted now.

Feelings of pity turned into jolts of stabbing rage. He gnashed his teeth and curled his fingers into fists. Every cell of his body cried out in protest to the injustice of what the hunters had done.

They knew they hadn't killed the deer, he thought, grinding his teeth. They knew they were leaving this poor animal here to suffer. Those drunken hunters—ignorant bastards!—they deliberately left this animal alive. Couldn't they have used one more bullet and mercifully finished it off?

He thought of the long, agonizing stretch that awaited the deer. He thought of the excruciating ten or twelve hour period before the hunters returned—if they even came back to it.

They might not even remember where it was, he thought. Or that they'd even shot it. Those beer-drinking fools might get lost in the woods and forget about their own hunting camp.

He cringed, because he knew that the doe on the ground was facing an unending period of misery. It was very much alive—not even close to dying—and there would be an indefinite number of hours before it starved to death or froze. If the weather warmed up—November could go either way—the body of the living deer would fester and rot into the ground.

The situation seemed unconscionable. It was beyond his ability to contend with or deal. His body and his brain were starved and half-frozen, he had been on a swooping pendulum carried between love and hate, fear and rage, and he had been able to handle all of it. He could not handle the twitching head over the lifeless body of the deer.

He locked eyes with the eye of the deer. He knew that his presence aggrieved the animal. He knew that the animal had no ability to comprehend what had become of it—that it did not understand its present state. He knew that the fear that popped its eye was not borne of the knowledge of an indeterminate period in that state. It was not reasoning about its condition. Every instinct it possessed told it that the condition was one to fear.

Feelings of rage turned into nauseating waves of revulsion. He detested the animal, because of the way it feared and mistrusted him.

"I'm the only hope you've got!" he shouted to the animal. "Without my help, you'll lay there like that forever. You'd better be glad that I'm here!"

He felt sick at the stomach when the deer tried to move away from him. Its head flopped up and down in one convulsive twitch. The eye rolled around in the socket and fear gave it a brilliant gloss.

He shuddered—not at the ugly motion—but at the fact that the animal feared the only thing that could help. Its instincts told it to run from its savior.

It isn't me, he thought, bitterness filling his mouth. That deer would try to run from a coyote or a bear. It wouldn't understand that the only way out of its condition is a quick and violent strike. It wouldn't understand that the alternative to an instant death is a long and painful, drawn-out one. It doesn't know the difference between its life and its survival. It hasn't the ability to know—the thought tore through his sick and tired brain—that life depends on survival, but survival does not depend on life.

He looked down at the flashing eye of the deer. Suddenly, he saw the flashing violet eyes of his wife. All at once it came to him.

He understood.

A long time ago, he had asked himself a question, and then pushed it from his mind: Is a life without health worth living—is it really even life at all? Now, the question came back into his mind; it rose back up from that dark crevice into which he had pushed it. This time, it was coupled with the answer: life without health is mere survival. Mere survival is an animal's goal, not a human being's.

He fell to his knees.

His body lay crumpled on the ground. All the will to fight was gone. All the will to resist, to struggle, to take up arms against the thing was gone. He no longer wanted to fight. He had fallen to the frozen ground, his face was pressed to the cold dirt next to the fallen deer, and it was as if he had given his body in an act of surrender. He was not surrendering to some great opponent, some powerful rival who had beaten him. He was surrendering to the essential unity of their vision. He was just beginning to know it.

I wanted you to be the deer, he thought, speaking to Constance. I wanted you to live without your life. I was wrong. I was wrong! That wasn't and isn't the goal. What you want is a human life, not an animal's existence. And it is human life—not animal existence—that I am sworn to uphold.

He suddenly remembered Dunn. He realized that was the very thing Dunn had been trying to teach him. And he had rejected it. He had failed to grasp the final lesson his mentor had given: adherence to the Hippocratic Oath *is* an absolute. Human life is too good, too precious to be left unaided.

His limbs were unmoving, as lifeless as those of the deer on the ground. He opened one eye to look at it. The deer flung its head backward; it arched its head toward its spine in a single thrust, as though it were trying to snap its own neck. He closed his eyes and felt nothing for the deer.

The deer did not matter. Nothing mattered but the thing he had to do. He was going to do it, even if it took his life.

It will kill me, he thought. This thing will kill me. In a way, it already has. But it isn't her wish, it's mine. I'm the one who has to choose. Even if it's my final act, even if it's all that I can do before they catch me, I have to do it. There's nothing left to be done.

With slow, deliberate movements, he rose to his feet. He took unhurried, even steps toward the cabin. The door was unlocked, and he let himself inside. The single room was a storage space for guns and ammunition.

Without uncertainty, without emotion or hesitation, he picked up a rifle and carried it outside. He walked to the spot beneath the birch.

The blast of a report broke the stillness.

Thomas Rivard walked away from the animal. He did not look back.

6

When the search party arrived at the hospital, the police officers went straight to Rivard's office next to the gymnasium. Bill Metcalf headed for the recovery ward, adjacent to Intensive Care.

His hand hesitated on the doorknob before he entered the room. He leaned on the cold metal, bracing himself for what was coming. He took a deep breath and opened the door.

"Hi Con—" he started and did not finish. He thought he was in the wrong room. He did not recognize the person in the wheelchair.

"Hi Bill," the person said. "Come in and shut the door."

"Connie?"

"It's me." She smiled. "What's left of me. Don't feel like you have to put on an act. I know it's a shock."

He had known that she had lost her arms and legs in the accident; he had prepared himself for the worst possible scenario. All of his experience on a rescue squad had made him impervious to the most horrific sights. None of it was enough to insulate him against the appearance of Constance.

Her arms and legs looked as if they had shrunken to half their size. The full, tight muscles that he remembered were gone; they had withdrawn, leaving little more than strips of bone. Her hands, which had always been lovely, curled limply on her lap, like the feet of a fallen bird. Her head was propped up around the shoulders with an ugly metal brace.

Bill suppressed a shudder. He could not stand the sight of the living head propped on a dead body. Her head and body were incongruous; they did not go together. Her face was there—it was the same lovely face that he remembered seeing—but it was unnatural now that it did not have its body. There was something profoundly wrong with it—with her—and he cursed himself for wondering why God could not have been merciful.

She saw the guilt on his face and knew what he was thinking. "It's okay, Bill. I've thought the same thing myself a thousand times."

He started, stunned that she had been so perceptive—and so honest. He stuttered a reply, not knowing what to say. "I—I didn't mean—"

"Why couldn't I have died? Why couldn't God have been merciful and taken all of me, rather than three-quarters?"

His jaw dropped.

"Why do people fear and resist death, when there's a fate that's ten times worse: a state of living decomposition?"

His mouth hung open like a startled child.

"Why is it so hard to tell the truth, or utter the unthinkable? That taboo thought—I'd be better off dead?"

He took a step back. He did not mean to. He had intended to comfort Constance. He had intended to lend her a shoulder and sympathetic ear. He had wanted to be a good friend, and break the news about her husband gently, even while he was procuring data about his location.

He realized that in her presence, he was the one in need of comfort.

"Don't be shocked, Bill," she said gently. "There is nothing you could possibly think that I've not told myself before."

"You—don't think those things Connie. It isn't right."

"Why? Because it's true? Since when is it wrong to tell the truth?"

He did not answer. He looked at her flashing eyes and thought: They are exactly like his. There's that crazy metal glint.

"I mean it, Bill. Why is it so hard for people to just come out and say it? *You* know, you see it all the time: fortunate people do not survive trauma."

He shook his head. The motion was involuntary and it was not merely a response to her words. He said, "We don't think that way, none of us. You shouldn't either. You were very fortunate to survive that accident. We're all glad you're alive, Connie. The only thing that matters is that you're *alive*."

"Am I?" The words came out a contemptuous snap. She saw the hurt look on his face and her voice softened. "I'm sorry, Bill. That was cold. Thank you for thinking of me."

He looked into her eyes and retreated another

step. Her eyes said something very different than her voice: If you really cared about me, you'd kill me this instant.

He gasped. He was appalled by her ruthless honesty. He felt like she had jumped inside his mind, had viewed the horrible contents, had seen the thoughts that had troubled him since that morning on their porch: he had been terrified of what Rivard would do, and even more terrified that what Rivard would do might be justified.

But none of that was true anymore. Rivard had killed a man, one of his old professors, for no apparent reason. He had placed himself outside the bounds of sanity or morality. His wanting to lash out at his wife in her helpless condition was an outrage, a crime, a monstrous gesture. There was absolutely no justification for such action, and it had to be stopped.

Bill would never allow his thoughts to align with the heinous desires of a monster. The fact that his secret thoughts had mirrored those of the monster was an added incentive to root the monster out. He could project his guilty feelings into a hunt for the one who had articulated the unthinkable.

The fact that Constance herself had spoken the unthinkable had been a surprise, but he dismissed it as the inevitable offshoot of grief and depression.

Who wouldn't lose heart after going through that accident?—he thought. She has no idea what she's saying. It's just because she's sad and angry.

The metal glint in her eye had been a shock,

much harder to ascribe to grief or depression. It frightened him because it was the very same glint that took over Rivard's eyes, when he was saying something bold. It seemed as if Rivard had taken possession of her body; he was coming out of her eyes, from her mouth. It was him speaking, feeding Constance evil ideas.

No matter what, Rivard and his evil ideas had to be stopped.

Bill took several steps forward, regaining sense of his original purpose.

"I'm surprised Tom is not here with you," he said.

Her voice was clear and emotionless. She said, "I'm not."

"No? Where is he?"

"I have no idea."

Bill saw two unclouded eyes that corresponded with the unclouded tone of her voice. He knew she was not lying. An imperceptible shade of edginess colored his voice as he said, "You have no clue, no idea where he might be?"

Constance detected the masked uneasiness. "No Bill, I have no idea where Tom is." Obvious desperation began to crack the mask and she said something that was the equivalent of tearing the mask from his face: "For all I know, he's left the country."

Bill jumped. He thought: How does Constance know about Dunn? Did Tom tell her? He couldn't have. Tom killed the Professor after he left the hospital. There is no way Constance could know about Dunn . . .

unless—he pushed the thought out of his mind. It was unthinkable. He cursed himself for thinking that she could have had anything to do with it.

She could see a struggle. Some tortured thought deepened the lines on his face. She wanted to know what gave him that kind of visible anxiety. She asked, "Are you that concerned for my welfare?"

Her voice startled him. He looked at her as though he had momentarily forgotten she was there. Something he had not considered earlier raced into his brain: She knows that she's in danger. She knows that Tom has definite intentions to carry out his threat.

When Bill did not respond, but merely looked at her, Constance said, "It's very good of you to be concerned for my welfare, but really, the situation is very different from what it seems."

Does she mean that Tom is not going to hurt her?—he thought. Or is she speaking about Dunn? How does she know that I know her life is in jeopardy?

"You are a dear, Bill, to think of me, but it isn't me you should be thinking about."

Is it Tom? Should I be thinking about him? She wouldn't tell me this if she didn't know that he was one to fear.

"There are far more important matters at stake. Your focus should be elsewhere."

Ha! She knows that her husband is a criminal. This is her offhand way of telling me that I should watch out.

"My well-being is the last thing you should be

concerned about."

She doesn't know! She must not know! She wouldn't think her well-being was secure if she knew her husband wanted to kill her.

"I don't need company, Bill. Don't feel like you have to stick around."

He was convinced she had no idea of the truth about her husband. She felt secure, she felt that she was not in need of looking after, and this meant she really didn't believe Rivard when he had told her he wanted to kill her. She didn't take the threat of the raised chair seriously. Bill was certain of this, and because of it, he was determined to stay by her side. With Rivard on the loose, there was no telling what his drug-crazed, murderous mind would goad him to do. The police were at a loss, and that meant that Constance needed protection. He was going to serve as her personal bodyguard. If Rivard did show up, if that maniac tried to carry out his deranged wish, he would stop it. He would defend Constance and shield her from harm.

He said, "I think it would be better if I stayed."

"You really don't have to, Bill. I know you're terribly busy. Millie is here to look after me—until she takes me home."

All the color drained from his face. "You can't go home!"

She chuckled in amusement, like an adult chuckling at the silliness of a child. "I'll be all right. Honest! Millie's going to pop in every few hours to see that I'm okay. I need to go home before—before I—

before I come back for surgery."

Bill spoke through tightly clenched teeth: "You really shouldn't go home, Connie."

"Good grief! What in the world's gotten into you? I am perfectly all right. I'll be fine. Nothing will happen."

His teeth clenched tighter. "There are a lot of things that could happen to you, Connie."

"Like what?"

He almost said: Your husband could kill you. He thought better of it and said, "You wouldn't be able to alert someone if—if something were to happen."

"What's going to happen?"

He wanted to shout: Tom will come home and kill you! He checked himself and said, "There are lots of things that could go wrong. Any number of things. You never know what might go on."

She smiled impatiently, for she had had enough. "It is really sweet that you want to look after me. I know that you're doing it out of loyalty to Tom." Bill shuddered. Constance did not notice and continued. "I know that your good friendship with him makes you feel obligated to help. I know that you feel like you have to look after me in his absence—almost like you're carrying out his wish. I'm telling you there's no such obligation."

If you knew the truth, Bill thought, if you knew that your husband wanted to kill you, you would not talk about high things such as loyalty. If you knew what his hideous wish really was, you would know that any talk of values was a monstrous perversion. You'd better be glad he isn't here.

Bill did not wish to trouble her already troubled heart with even more bad news. He thought that the worst possible thing he could do would be to tell her of her husband's wish.

That would be cruel, he thought. There is too much going on to let that out here. I've got to protect Connie from Tom, without letting her know about his evil plan.

He said, "If you insist on going home, I'd like to take you."

"Don't trouble yourself with that. Millie's going to take me."

"I really think it would be better if I gave you a ride—and stayed there with you until—"

Her patience broke and she snapped: "Bill, I'm fine! I don't need your help!"

Her outburst came as a complete surprise. Bill could not figure out why she was resisting. He thought that she would have been glad to have the company and the extra assistance. After a brief reflection, he changed his mind.

Connie might think my gesture is charity. She probably feels as though she's being treated like a beggar. Nonetheless, she's not going to get rid of me.

In his most authoritative voice, Bill said, "You can't function by yourself. I'm going to take you home, stay with you, and bring you back here for surgery on Thursday. Don't argue." He felt like adding: If you knew the reason why I won't leave your side, you'd be glad of it.

Her face crumpled. She wanted to shout; she wanted to argue and contradict him. There was no way she could have Bill hanging over her, watching her every second. She was not going to be placed in the sickening position of fawning dependence. That was the very thing she was trying to avoid.

She opened her mouth. She was about to say: Leave me alone! The words did not come out. There were two police officers suddenly standing in the room.

"Mr. Metcalf? Sorry to interrupt." The officer nodded at Constance. "We'd like you to come with us."

Bill looked anxiously at Constance. Her body was tiny in the wheelchair; it looked fragile and vulnerable. There was nothing delicate about her face: it was set like steel. She did not look at all surprised at the presence of the officers.

"I—I think it's important for me to stay with Mrs. Rivard," Bill said.

"Mrs.—Mrs. Thomas Rivard?" Bill and Constance both gave the questioning officer a nod.

There was a moment of hesitation. The officer looked about to unleash a volley of questions. His partner touched his arm, as if to say: Not now, there will be plenty of time for that later.

They looked at her before turning back to Bill. Their expressions registered both compassion and pity. They saw a victim in the tiny body in the wheelchair: a potential murder victim. They could think of nothing more dishonorable than a man who would harm his wife. When they saw how pretty and tiny Rivard's wife was, their chests swelled with rage: they were not about to let someone who would kill this woman get away.

"Mr. Metcalf, come with us." There was an unmistakable tone in the officer's voice that said: Don't disobey.

Bill looked desperately from the officers to Constance, and back at the officers. "I can't leave her. What if he comes back for—"

"He won't be coming this way, you can be sure. He wouldn't be that bold or stupid. And even if he does, this entire facility has been given the alert. Any sighting is to be reported immediately. We need you to come to the gym."

Constance followed the conversation, her curiosity piqued. She finally blurted, "Who and what are you talking about?"

The three men glanced at each other, before turning to Constance. The senior officer said, "It's your husband, Ma'm. Thomas Rivard is wanted for murder. There is a warrant out for his arrest."

Constance thought: But I'm still alive. He hasn't done it yet. How can he be wanted for murder without a victim?

"We're sorry to break the news to you here, like this. We wouldn't have done it but for"—the officer looked at Bill—"extenuating circumstances."

He refused to do it!—Constance thought. He refused to so much as consider the idea! How can

Thomas be wanted for a murder he did not commit—would not even dream of committing?

"The details will have to be filled in later, when we have learned more. For now, that is all we can tell you."

"All you can tell me? But it's impossible!"

"We know this comes as a shock. We know you have gone through a great deal already"—the officer's eyes shot from her face to her body and back to her face—"and we don't mean to burden you with more. We're terribly sorry."

"Sorry about the impossible?!"

The senior officer looked at his younger partner. His unhappy eyes seemed to say: I've seen it a thousand times. They can never believe it. Wives can never believe their husbands are capable of murder.

The junior officer turned to Constance. He saw her pretty face twisted into a disbelieving scowl. He thought: Joe's right. She can't believe it. That poor woman refuses to accept that her husband's a killer.

Constance saw the three men looking on her with pity. If there was one thing she could not tolerate, it was being pitied. She knew they thought she was a hysterical wreck—that she was distraught and emotional—incapable of grasping an ugly truth. The irony of the whole matter was that Constance desperately wanted to believe them.

In her confused frustration, she let out a shout: "You don't understand, it's not that I'm in denial: there is simply no way what you are telling me is true!"

The men remained quiet, and looked down at their shoes. This was the kind of reaction they had anticipated.

"It's not that I don't believe you! There's been a mistake! My husband can't be wanted for a murder he didn't commit: *I'm still alive*."

She does know, Bill thought, shaking his head. Poor Constance knows that her husband intended to kill her. She's thinking of her own murder. She's not aware of Dunn.

"How can there be a murder charge without a victim?!"

The officers cleared their throats, communicating two things: embarrassment and a desire to leave.

Bill said, "You both have a job to do. Time's pressing. I'll meet you at the gym after—after I finish up here."

The sound of the shutting door was a signal for Bill to talk. He said, "Constance, there's a lot more going on here than you realize. It has nothing to do with you. Tom is wanted for the murder"—he saw the expectant look on her face—"he's wanted for the murder of Professor Richard Dunn. Dunn was found dead in his office."

A faint ripple passed over her face. Bill did not know what it was that made her skin tighten and then go slack. Was it shock? Was it horror? He did not think that it was either. When she did not reply, he said, "No one has questioned you because you were here the whole time, under supervision. They've been to the house. The whole county's on alert. The whole region knows of it. If he resists arrest in any way, they've—they've been given the orders to shoot."

Another ripple passed over her face. Bill did not like her reaction: there was no hint of surprise, nothing in her expression that indicated shock. He could not figure out why she was not stunned. There was only a strange limpness, as though the life had gone from her face; her face and her limbs now looked like they belonged together.

He said, "Connie, are you all right?" There was no answer—only two violet eyes staring into space. "Do I need to get the doctor?"

A burst of violence tightened the muscles of her face. She shouted, "Don't you dare!"

He felt his body sway back on his heels; the force of her words nearly knocked him over. The burst sounded as if it had come from a body three times her size.

"All right," Bill said, "I won't call the doctor. This is not when or how I wanted to deliver the news."

What news?—she thought. You're telling me something I should have already known. I should have seen this coming. I should have known that *that* would have been his answer. I'm as guilty of Dunn's murder as he is . . . .

Constance pressed her lips into a rigid line. Yes, she thought, I'm as guilty of Dunn's murder as he is. I should have known the extent of his loyalty to his oath.

And goddamn it! I knew he wouldn't take it well—not any of it! I brought this down upon us. And because of it, I'm going to help him out. I'm going to absolve my husband.

She deliberately softened her voice: "I—I'm sorry, Bill. I'm acting like a monster. Forgive me. You have to understand—this is really just too much."

He nodded slowly.

"Tom and I—we've had our differences, the usual marital squabbles, nothing serious. You've given me quite a blow. I never saw it coming."

Bill bowed his head respectfully.

"I told you this was a complete misunderstanding. I told you that there had been a horrible mistake. It's much, much worse than I had thought."

Bill's head jerked up from his chest. His eyes shot to her face.

She knew she had him in the right place. She continued: "I'm afraid I have to confess to something." Bill's eyes turned into two dark lines, slashed across his face. She said calmly, "I am responsible for Dunn's murder."

Bill swayed back and took two staggering steps, like a drunk. I knew it!—he thought. Didn't I tell myself that she had had something to do with it? He looked at her crippled body and the words that finished his thought were: But how in the hell—

"You see why I'm stunned," Constance said. "My husband has been blamed for it—and I'm responsible. That's why I couldn't believe it when you said that he was wanted for murder: it's me they should be after."

Bill's eyes moved over her lifeless arms and legs. He began to say, "How could you possibly—" but she cut him off.

"No. I did not accomplish the deed by myself. It was a hired thug."

Bill was incredulous—and growing suspicious. He said, "Tom was the last person to leave Dunn's office. There was a witness."

"Tom went there to intervene, to stop it from happening. I told him about my plan—when he came to visit me. He grew angry and said that I couldn't go through with it. He said it was unthinkable. He was furious, he grew violent."

That would explain the chair, Bill thought. That would explain why he threatened her. That would also explain why he was muttering something about the Professor when Millie came in.

Something nagged at him. Bill looked at her with narrowed eyes and asked, "What possible motivation could you have had for killing Dunn?"

She looked back at him and said in a clear, calm voice, knowing her husband's life depended on it, "That poor excuse for a cardiologist couldn't cure me."

"What do you mean? Cure you of what?"

"Rivard's disease."

Bill's hand shot to the nearest chair. He used it as a brace. He said, "This is too much. What the hell is

Rivard's disease?"

"Do you want the long answer or the short one?"

"The true one."

Constance paused, carefully considering her next words. She said, "I have a rare heart defect. I've been seeing Dunn about it for years. It's grown progressively worse, and Dunn did nothing to help me. He's the one who gave it the official name: Rivard's disease." She took a deep breath before she said: "I think Dunn was deliberately keeping me ill—keeping the proper treatment a secret—so that he could procure funding for research. A stubborn disease receives perpetual funds."

Bill tried to sort through the jumbled mess of facts he had been given. So much had happened, so many strange and horrible things had occurred during the last seventy-two hours, he was no longer certain of what was true and what was false. All he knew was that his original intention had been a simple one: to help his friend get off drugs.

The things that had happened since—discovering that Tom was a wife beater and a murderer, and being mistaken for Tom by the police—all of it was being contradicted by his wife. Constance was now telling him that she had been responsible for all of it. If her story was true, Rivard was innocent and the police were after the wrong person. If what she said was a lie, Rivard was still a threat, his whereabouts unknown.

Bill was caught in a desperate situation. He did

not want to believe any of it—not the original story, not the story Constance had given. Either version of the events was abhorrent and unbelievable. Did he have any reason to think that Constance was lying? Only the obvious one: she wanted to protect her husband. But why would Constance protect a murderer? What reason would she have for shielding him, and personally taking the blame? He decided to find out.

In his most impartial and unaffected voice, Bill said, "You are accepting full responsibility for the murder of Richard Dunn?"

"I am." She wanted to scream: This story I've concocted doesn't matter—it really is my fault!

"You say that you orchestrated the whole thing—and carried it out by hiring a thug?"

"I did." Her mind screamed the rest of it: I'm the thug! I'm the thug who asked my husband to do something barbaric! I asked him to take a life! I implicated Dunn! He killed Dunn in my defense—in defense of my life!

"You provided the assassin with all the necessary information—detailed maps of the interior of Dunn's house?"

"Yes! I provided everything." She looked at his narrowed eyes and thought: Just do what you will with me. I am a criminal. I am a brute. I tried to get my husband to do something that violated the very center of his conscience. I have no defense.

"You directed the assassin to perform the deed at Richard Dunn's house?"

"Yes, I did. I did all that. I sent the thug to his house and had Richard Dunn killed."

"At his house?"

"At his house."

"Ah ha!" Bill shouted. "The body of Richard Dunn was discovered in his office!"

Constance's eyes grew large, then quickly narrowed. She knew that Bill did not believe her; he was certain she was pinned. With a brief statement, casually rolled off her tongue, she made him doubt her innocence: "Both locations were mapped out and marked. I told the thug to use his judgment. If Dunn was not at home, he was to do it at the office."

The doubt did not last long. Something was off—Bill could sense something desperate in her story: she was trying to maintain a firm grip on it, but appeared to be grasping at straws. Was it the tone of her voice? Was it the tortured look on her face? Bill did not know. Could the horror of what she had learned about her husband drive her to do something foolish? There was no easy answer to the question, but an enormous amount riding on it. He had mere minutes to discover the truth, before—

"Tom dies, Constance, if he resists arrest in any way. He was the only person to enter Dunn's office—he signed in with the secretary. He left, walked out through the front door, and Dunn's secretary found the Professor dead on the floor. He was the only person at the scene."

Bill saw the muscles of her face cave into her

mouth. He did not know whether to hate himself or keep pushing. The urgency of the situation drove him on: he had to get to the bottom of it, before—

"You'll be taken into custody, Constance, if you give your story to the authorities. Are you prepared to go through that just to—feed them an implausible tale?"

"I know it sounds impossible," she said, her voice broken and hoarse. "I know you don't believe me. But Bill you have to! There's been a mix-up! Tom went there because he was trying to stop it! The real murderer crawled in through the window. Tom was horrified by my plan and went to warn Dunn. He—he did not succeed." With all the conviction she could muster, she twisted her face into an unseemly, insidious smile. "But I did."

Bill felt a series of pricks run up and down his spine. A shiver took over his body when Constance said, "I accomplished what I intended to do: the old man is dead. I'm happy that I killed him."

This was too much—far too hideous to be acting. It was not the words; it was the look on her face: her lips were curved in an obscene, spreading smile; her pupils were dilated and took over her eyes. It was a face waxing at the mention of something perverse. Bill was stunned silent—he just stood and looked at her.

"I know you're finding it impossible to believe," Constance said, pointing her massive pupils at his face. "You're too good and noble to conceive of such behavior. But listen to this: Richard Dunn crippled me. This paralysis is not a result of the crash but a result of

Richard Dunn's incompetence." She saw the stricken look on his face, she knew that she had surprised him, and she used it to her advantage. "I'm in this condition for no other reason than the incompetence of Dunn. The incompetence—deliberately manufactured. That money-grubbing scientist used me as a tool: an incurable disease requires lots of funding."

It was starting to make sense. If Constance would never walk again, what did she care if she was guilty of committing murder? What did she have left to live for—except revenge against the one who couldn't help? Bill thought that he had it figured out—until he realized the same chain of reasoning justified the other side. If she would never walk again, what would stop her from sacrificing herself for her husband—who did have a reason to live? He knew that battered women often clung to their husbands, defended them no matter what, even at the price of their own lives. He thought that this must be the case with Constance. What he needed to discover was Tom's level of knowledge about her condition. That would tell him what he needed to know regarding his innocence or guilt.

He said: "Connie, Rivard's disease made you lose your arms and legs?"

"Yes."

"It had nothing to do with the crash?"

"Nothing."

"Does Tom know that?"

Her eyes pierced his face, trying to detect a visible reason or motive underlying the question. She was not certain of the direction in which he was headed.

If I say yes, she thought, will that make Bill think that Tom wanted to kill Dunn, or that he wanted to defend him?

She was not sure, and so she gambled on the latter: “Yes. Tom does know that the crash had nothing to do with it.”

“He knows that you are suffering from a rare, incurable disease? That you will never get better? That your condition is completely helpless?” His eyes asked: Would Tom want you to carry on that way?

All of a sudden his motive was plain. She cursed herself for not realizing what he was after. She could not take back her statement now, and so she stuck to it in the way that a suspected liar clings to a lie. She said calmly and with no emotion, in her most unaffected voice, “Yes. Tom knows that I have Rivard’s disease, and that there is no available cure.”

Damn it!—she thought. I know exactly what he’s thinking.

Of course!—Bill thought. What else would make Rivard want to kill the both of them—both Constance and Dunn? Of course he would want to strike out at the person he believed was responsible for his wife’s condition—before he alleviated her suffering by putting her out of her misery. That Rivard had killed Dunn—that had never made sense. But the police don’t even know of the connection between Dunn and his wife, and that’s the missing piece. That explains why Tom would murder Dunn—and then his wife. The first is an act of revenge, the second—an act of mercy.

As if she knew what he was thinking, Constance said: "Tom would never dream of putting me out of my misery, don't you worry."

Caught off guard, surprised at her clear-eyed perception, Bill stammered, "He's capable of more than you think." He was remembering the words written in black marker on the wall: Reasons for killing Constance: I do not like to watch people suffer.

"Tom doesn't love me that much," she said. It was followed by the thought: Or does he love me that much?

Bill heard it all, even the part she did not say, for he remembered the last words written on the wall, like a final, culminating thought: I love my wife.

He said, "I think you're mistaken about your husband, which makes his situation all the more insane: what he's done, what he's going to do—he's doing it out of love."

She drew in her breath; it was a sharp, cutting noise that sounded like a gasp. She thought: Why did he use that tense?—Why did he say, *what he's going to do*—as if it can't be stopped?

"It's clear what we're both thinking about," Bill said. "So there's no use in speaking in riddles. There is no use in your putting on an act." He looked at Constance with an expression of great sadness, before his face became set like a mask. It was the dramatic player's mask of tragedy. "Don't try to save him. Don't sacrifice yourself in some heroic measure. He needs to be held accountable for the unthinkable thing that he's done."

But it's what I've done!—she screamed inside her head. I did it! It's really me you should blame. I asked—I demanded that my husband do something impossible. What other action could you expect from a man who's lost his sense of moral grounding?

The mask of tragedy continued to speak: "I know what you're doing, Constance. I know you're giving up your life in order to save his. I know that you feel you have nothing to live for, but that he does. You feel that if you are convicted of the crime he committed, he can have the rest of his life."

No! That isn't it at all. I did commit a crime! I committed the ugliest, most horrific crime imaginable. I took my husband's life! What kind of monster forces a man to choose between two forms of evil?

"You wouldn't be sparing him anything, Constance. He would still have to live with it. It would beat against his conscience every day of his life. He would tell himself: I did it. I killed a man. I am guilty of murder, and my wife sacrificed herself to free me. I killed two—no three people: Dunn, Constance and myself."

It was I who killed three people—not him!

"Giving yourself is not the answer, Constance. Don't give up your life. Don't waste what's left of it on a lost cause."

Constance was about to say something, she opened her mouth to speak, she was going to scream a protest, but she heard him and paused. It was the words he had used. He had said: lost cause.

That's it, she thought. Those were the words that I had used to describe myself, and didn't even know it. I had thought that it was hopeless: I had thought that any attempt at living was a lost cause, a dead end, an already-decided battle.

Bill looked at her eyes, grown into disks. He looked at two eyes widening to encompass a vision. He did not think that it was him she was seeing, though she was looking right at him.

He did not know that she was seeing the germ of a new thought, sprouted from his words. He did not know that that new thought broke the packed soil around all her previous decisions.

Lost cause—yes! I had lost it. And I was correct in wanting to end a life without purpose or meaning. But now there is a purpose. There is a reason. That reason is—

She saw the tall, unbending figure of her husband, as if he were suddenly standing before her in the room. She saw his body as she had seen it for the first time, all those years ago, in the hallway of Pine Manor, and all the times that she had seen it since: skin bronze and smooth as stone, muscles broken into slabs of solid rock, the tight cords of his neck lifting an arrogant head, which contained a proudly, defiantly arrogant face. She realized—with all the immediacy of a blinding flash—that he was the symbol and embodiment of everything she had ever valued, and because of it—her very greatest value, something equivalent to her life—the life that she had nearly died to uphold.

All at once it came to her.

She understood.

Constance saw, in her mind's eye, a man whose every nerve and tendon, every fiber and cell projected joyous life borne of health, the very thing that she had worshipped and would never surrender—not even at the cost of her life. She saw a man who used his body to further his ideal, which was hers—a man who literally used his life to perpetuate life—to inspire and create in others the very greatest life that others could achieve. She saw a man who tirelessly promoted health—that thing that was inextricably linked with life: Thomas Rivard was a champion of life with quality.

How could she abandon that man—and his courageous vision? If she did not act to save him now, if she let him get torn apart and trampled by others, she would be sacrificing the very thing she held dearest to her heart: she would be sacrificing life to death, she would be sacrificing ecstatic joy to pain and suffering. If she did not save her husband's life, she would be failing life itself.

She was not going to let that happen.

She looked directly at the face of her husband, as she held his image in her mind. She said to that image: You were right. My darling, you were right. I was the one who was wrong. I was so very, very wrong. Can you ever forgive me? Can you forgive my shortsightedness and ugly, improper decision? I see it all now. I see that I left you no choice. I take the blame for your actions. It is my fault. You were acting to defend me.

She nearly began to cry, when the vision of her husband smiled at her. She felt that he was telling her not to worry, that everything would be fine—now that they had the same view of things. Now that they shared one goal—one reason and motive—now that their aim was identical—everything would work out for the best. There was no need to despair. An unobstructed future lay before them. All she had to do was tell the truth. Their salvation was possible as long as she was honest.

Constance knew that Bill wanted to help. She felt confident that he would assist her once he learned the truth about her husband. She looked at him with sparkling eyes, the kind of dancing eyes that communicated such a limitless energy and vitality as to render her inactive body irrelevant.

She said, "Bill, you are absolutely right. That entire story was invented—it was an attempted deception, a fraud. I had nothing to do with Dunn's murder, in the physical sense. I did not plot to kill him, and I did not hire a thug."

A look that was part satisfaction, part anxious concern, took over Bill's face. He knew she had something to tell and he waited for her to tell it all. He was glad she had decided to be honest; he was terrified of what he would learn about Tom.

Constance continued: "You were right. The

police are right—as far as implicating Tom. But it's not the whole truth—and the part you don't know is critical."

He wondered what Constance could possibly tell him about the murder of Richard Dunn that would make any difference. If Tom killed Dunn—which was almost certainly the case—he would be arrested, tried and convicted. The introduction of certain motives might result in a reduced sentence, once presented in court, but was irrelevant as far as his being taken into custody at the point of loaded guns. Did Constance know something that could change that?

"You have to understand something," she said to Bill. "Tom was acting on my behalf. He was acting in my defense."

Your defense?—Bill thought. The man wants to kill you. He's going to kill you, unless the police can find him in time to prevent it.

"Tom was acting to protect me. He was acting to save my life."

Acting to save your life? Tom killed Dunn as a preface—as a prelude to your murder. His intention is not to save, but to end your life.

"Tom could not stand the idea of assisted suicide. He thought that Dunn planted the idea in my head. When I asked him to help me die, he thought that Dunn had encouraged it."

Suicide?! Where does this fit into the scheme? We're not talking about suicide, we're talking about murder!

"I'm not suggesting that Tom's action was right. It wasn't. But the truth is, he didn't have the facts. Tom thought that Dunn was an accessory to my murder. He was acting to prevent a crime."

Acting—to prevent a crime? Because Dunn was an accessory to murder? This has been twisted into something impossible!

"Connie," Bill said, looking into her hopeful eyes, "I don't know where you are getting this information. It just doesn't square with the facts."

"Doesn't square with the facts? I'm trying to give you the facts!"

Poor woman, he thought. He felt a stab of pity, before he said, "There are things you just don't know, and I'm afraid I've got to tell them."

She was silent. Her eyes said: Say what you wish; there is nothing I don't already know.

"You have not been home in a while. I stopped by your house, hoping to speak with Tom. He wasn't there, and I found some things that were very disturbing." He thought he caught a slight change in her eyes, as if some light had dimmed. He knew that he was being cruel, but there was no way around it: her life was on the line. He continued. "Drugs, Constance, small white pills all over the floor. I couldn't be certain what they were, but his office was a wreck, like a cyclone had blown through. He had the whole place turned upside down. There were papers scattered everywhere, scribbled on; it looked like he was frantically searching for some type of information."

Of course, Constance thought. He wanted to learn about the disease. Tom was looking for any available information about my condition.

Bill swallowed, before he said: “That was not the only thing. It seems that Tom had a second target. After he killed Dunn it—he was—there was evidence that—he would be moving on”—her face was lifted in a giant question mark, waiting for him to come out with it—“it seems that his next goal was to kill you.”

Bill was stunned by what came next: Constance burst out laughing. It was an ugly, unnatural sound, a mixture of snorting and cackling. She laughed and then she said, “That is impossible—trust me. The reason he killed Dunn is the very same reason why he would never lay a hand on me. Or, more precisely, it was for my protection—an act to save my life—that Dunn was killed.”

“You wouldn’t say that, Constance, if you knew what I saw on the wall.”

“And what was that?” There was still a hint of ugly mirth in her voice.

“Reasons for killing Constance.”

“Written on the wall? What were they?”

Bill let out a breath that sounded like a sigh. He paused, then said, “I do not like to watch people suffer. I love my wife.”

The humor drained from her face. It was replaced by something that resembled rage. “You’re lying,” she said with a voice of steel.

“Connie—I’m not. Tom is not well. He’s been

in trouble for quite some time. He's drug-crazed and dangerous. You need protection."

"It's against you I need protection! Tom would never lay a hand on me—no force on Earth could make him!"

The urgency of the situation came back to him as a sudden rush that swept away her words. She had confirmed the fact that Tom had killed Dunn—that was all he needed to know. He was loose, the murderer was somewhere, no one knew, and Bill did not have time to pacify his disbelieving wife.

"Listen to me," he said. "I have to meet the officers at the gym. You are to stay here. Do not go home, or anywhere else with Millie. Do not leave this room. I will come back for you as soon as I'm done with the officers. Connie, stay here and wait for me. Your life depends on it."

The door was shut and she was alone. It suddenly felt as if she were the last human being left in the universe. It seemed as if every human presence and influence was gone. The feeling bothered her for one moment, then disappeared. None of it was relevant: she had a job to do.

Her first impulse was to jump up from her chair. She bit her lip and cursed when she remembered she could not stand. She ground her teeth and struggled—by a sheer act of will—to rise from the seat. Her dead arms and legs would not move. Several minutes passed in this manner and she began to feel desperate.

I've got to get out of here before Bill comes

back, she thought. I've got to get away from him, so that I can get to Tom.

Tom!

The full reality of her husband's position suddenly came to her. He was a fugitive, wanted by the law. If he was found, and tried to get away, the police would shoot to kill. He was considered highly dangerous.

The irony of the situation was appalling. Thomas Rivard had spent his entire life struggling to keep hearts beating, instructing others about proper nutrition and health. His every waking moment had been utilized in a crusade against cardiovascular disease. Now, it was *his* heart that others intended to stop. If they did not kill the literal organ—by shooting him—they would kill the heart that animated his spirit, by locking him in jail. Constance feared the second alternative, more than she feared the first: it was the best within him—the part that would never give up—that would slowly perish under a fate of that kind. She could not allow it to happen.

The problem was—she did not know what to do. She did not know where Thomas was—and even if she did know, she had no way to get to him. She was incapable of moving herself from the room. She certainly could not drive a car in search of him.

Think, Constance, think!—she told herself. There's got to be something you can do. There has got to be a way that you can help. You have always hated passivity, you have never in your life given up. Don't fail now. Your life means more than ever now—and it's your brain that cannot fail you.

She strained as hard as she could, struggling to come up with a solution. Each moment that passed by filled her with a fresh wave of dread: each passing second was one second closer to the time when Bill would come back for her. She was not going to let him take control of her—she could not afford to let the situation fall out of her control. She knew that much of it was already out of her control—and she was determined to maintain some level of autonomy over her condition.

Her eyes moved like darts around the room, looking for something she could use.

There's got to be a way, she thought. There's got to be a way that I can get myself out of here. There has to be! I can't let Bill come back and get me. I've got to get myself out of here so that I can rescue—

Her eyes suddenly fell on the phone. It was sitting on a table on the other side of the room. Her plan fell into place. She was going to dial the police department, and give them some anonymous tip, say something to get them out of town, throw them in a false direction: it would at least give her some more time to think.

If she sent them several towns over, the focus of the hunt would head there, and she could use the extra time to devise some way to get to Tom. At the very least, she could have Millie take her home and, once there, she could search around—perhaps there was some clue to where he had gone.

Yes, she thought, that's exactly what I'll do. The police won't know it's me calling. I can say that some janitor or nurse came into my room and picked up the phone, if anybody gets suspicious. I'll tell them that I saw a man on foot, headed west along the highway. I'll describe Tom's exact appearance, and the type of clothes he always wears. I'll make it sound as if the man was hiding in the tree line, turning his face away from traffic, hunched over like a criminal. I'll tell them that he was headed west, toward New York. I'll tell them he was trying to get out of New England.

Her mind raced, as the pieces of her plan fell together. It was perfect: the very thing that would buy her the time she needed to find out where Tom had gone. As long as the police were headed in another direction, she could conduct her own search. She would find Tom, and the two of them would plan an escape. Perhaps they could flee to Canada. She did not know—there were many possibilities—she just needed to get to her husband before the authorities discovered where he was.

She decided upon the tone of voice that she would use: she would have to sound concerned, but not hysterical. She would have to give the impression of a concerned citizen, doing her duty by alerting the authorities of a public danger. She would have to use her most convincing voice to make it sound as though she wanted the police to succeed in catching the violent criminal, to see that the cause of justice was served. She would have to pretend that she wanted Tom to be punished.

I can do it—she thought. I can put on an act. The rest of Thomas's life depends on it.

She was certain that the plan would work—and confident that she could do it. Constance was prepared to carry it out—until she realized she could not get to the phone.

In her excitement, overcome by a sense of desperate urgency, Constance had forgotten she was paralyzed. When the fact of her condition came back into her conscious awareness, when she realized that she could not get to the telephone—much less pick up the receiver and dial a number—she felt her heart drop. There was absolutely nothing she could do. She was helpless.

She felt a sob rise up and constrict her throat. It can't be!—a voice of protest screamed inside her skull. This can't be real, this can't be happening!

She looked at the tan plastic of the telephone, several yards away from her. There it was—the means of saving Thomas. It was mere feet from her body, and there was nothing she could do to get to it. The telephone was excruciatingly close, because it might as well have been millions of miles away from her. She no more had the power to travel a few yards, than the power to travel a million of them.

She clenched her teeth in a burst of rage that had quickly followed disbelief. Anger reddened her cheeks and flooded her eyeballs, momentarily blinding her.

She could not see—now she could not even see the telephone or the rest of the room—and the self-induced loss of vision only increased her feeling of impotence.

Her violent emotion did not last. She realized that it was doing no good, that it was only frustrating any attempt to help her husband. She relaxed the muscles of her face, and told herself to breathe. She closed her eyes and took a series of carefully controlled breaths.

She opened her eyes. They fell on the telephone. She looked at it with an expression of helpless longing, as a poison victim might look upon an inaccessible vial of antidote. It was so close—her solution was right there—if she could only get to it.

It's not a matter of if, but how—she told herself, regaining a feeling of confidence. I'm going to get to it. There's nothing I can't do, if I just put my mind to it.

She closed her eyes, inhaled deeply, and told her body to rise.

It did not move.

She took another breath and, summoning all her powers of concentration, commanded her body to rise.

It did not move.

Undaunted, determined to make her body obey her mind, she gave orders to her arms and legs. She told them: It's easy. You've done it before. There's nothing to it. Just act together and—stand.

At the end of it, she found that she was still sitting.

Discouraged but not without hope, she tried

again. She tried to trick her body into standing up.

There's nothing wrong with you. Nothing wrong at all. You're completely healthy and normal. All this talk about a crippling disease is a myth. None of it is real. You have no disease and *you will move*.

It did not work.

Resolute, she tried it again: *you will move*.

And again: *you will move*.

And again: *you will move*.

Her muscles did not obey her mind. Her body did not obey her soul. Crushed with despair, certain that all was lost, seeing nothing but the vision of her husband she had held as inspiration, she lowered her eyelashes and let the tears drop.

Bill Metcalf stood in the middle of the room and stared. The police officers had admitted him into the hospital gymnasium, though the facility had been shut down and was closed off to the public. He stood and looked with an open mouth, no sound coming from between his parted lips, only a great gaping hole formed by a disconnected jaw.

"Any idea who might have done this?" It was the senior officer who spoke, Officer Joe McBride. His junior partner, Ray Durham, was picking up empty spray paint cans. He wore a pair of latex rubber gloves.

"I—I have absolutely no idea," Bill said, licking dried-out lips, running shaking fingers through his hair. "I—I'm sorry. I can't believe what I'm seeing. None of this—the last time I was in this place none of this was here."

"I know it. Hey Ray, you mind opening up those double doors? The fumes in this place are enough to knock me out."

Bill heard the click of the metal bars, as Ray opened the doors. Large round magnets affixed to the brick wall outside held the doors in place. A stream of pale, early-winter sunlight flooded the room, lighting up what had become of the inside.

It was no longer a gymnasium, but a chamber of horrors.

Every square inch of the wall and floor was covered with spray paint. Layer upon layer of foul-smelling paint blotched the cement blocks and snaked along the floor. A gallon of bright red paint had been flung at the wall. It ran down in thick streams that looked like blood. Someone had sprayed a demonic-looking face in one corner, and the entire gymnasium was marked with hateful messages: We'll get you, fitness Nazi!—Tom Hitler Rivard wants to rid the world of fat, we'll rid the world of him!—We don't trust doctors on speed!—Fat people get back at killers!

Bill shuddered when he saw it hanging from a set of gymnast's rings: a life-size, stuffed doll dressed in fitness clothes, strung up by its neck. There was a stick thrust in its back. Someone had labeled it: Endurance.

"Ugly, isn't it?" Joe McBride said, standing next to Bill, looking at the effigy. "That kind of thing gives me the creeps. I'd take a real killing over that witchy stuff, any day." He shook his head. "This situation just gets worse and worse. Looks like the one we're after is going to need protecting."

Bill's eyes shot from the effigy to McBride, and back to the effigy. He said, "You don't think—I mean, this is all a joke, right? Some silly prank pulled by some kids." He did not have to hear the answer. He already knew it: Tom Rivard was in trouble.

Officer McBride made the point explicit: "I hope we can get Rivard before they do . . . man, this is ugly. I hate that—hey Ray, you mind cutting that thing down? It's giving me the willies." He turned to Bill: "Any clue who they are? Local cops hadn't the faintest. Either that, or—"

They heard a sound. It came from the hallway just outside the door. They turned to look.

When they saw that it was the hospital security officer, all three men let out their breath. None of the men knew they had been holding it.

Bill waved to the man standing just outside the door. "Hi Grady, how are things with you?"

The security officer gave a brief reply that was nothing more than an upward thrust of his chin. He stepped out of the doorway and disappeared.

Bill turned to McBride: "You were saying?"

McBride's eyes lingered on the door. He looked at Bill and shook his head, as if to say: Not yet—don't talk.

Bill studied McBride's face, looking for a reason or a clue. He started to say: "Oh, that's just"—

but did not finish. Something in the officer's manner told him not to talk.

McBride touched Bill's arm and then walked over to the door. His head protruded into the hallway as he flicked it quickly in either direction. He kept his gaze focused on the corridor that led to the wing housing ER and Intensive Care.

Bill did not know that the security guard looked over his shoulder several times, as he walked down the corridor—that he looked back at McBride with narrowed, shifting eyes—that the expression on his face caused McBride to think: There's something off about that man. He resents our presence here. He definitely doesn't like the police. Is it jealousy—that we're invading his turf? Or is it something else?

McBride walked back through the gymnasium slowly, looking over the vandalism. Bill could almost see the cogwheels turning in his head: he was on to something.

Bill said: "What is it? Did you see something?"

McBride did not answer, but walked over to the huge black trash bag filled with spray paint cans. The cans rattled together as he reached in and pulled one out. He spun the can around with his fingers until he found what he was looking for. He glanced up from the price sticker and said, "Where is The Village Grocery?"

"It's on Main Street in town," Bill said.

"You can buy paint supplies, rope and hardware there?"

"Everything. There's all that stuff at the general

store attached to the market, and a restaurant where everyone hangs out."

"Who owns The Village Grocery?"

"Burt Lancaster."

All at once it came to him. Bill thought: I should have known! Goddamn it, I should have known!

His breath came out a rapid gush: "I think I know exactly what happened here. I should have known it. They call themselves the Males for Public Defense. It's a fraternity, a good old boys club. It's a bunch of guys who think they've got to protect the town, a combination of amateurish vigilantism and neighborhood watch. They've been after Rivard for some time, thinking he's a public menace. It started when Heloise Humphries raised a stink about her husband. They usually just gossip a lot, and try to get outsiders to move. I've never known them to do anything like this."

"What's all the stuff about fat people?"

"That's just it," Bill said breathlessly, trying to include everything. "They feel they have some obligation to protect women who've been wronged. There is this fat woman—one of Rivard's former clients—her name is Cindy Beale. She complained that Rivard hates fat people, that he discriminated against her. She called him a fitness Nazi."

Their eyes fell on the vandals' message: We'll get you, fitness Nazi! They all looked at the effigy, face down on the floor, a stick thrust in its back.

Bill suddenly felt responsible for all of it. He

said, "I know all this because several of the guys and I had been planning an intervention, about Tom's addiction to speed. I never dreamed—"

"Who are the members of this fraternity?"

Bill hesitated, and the officer barked, "Are you a member?"

"God, no!"

"Who are the members of this Males for Public Defense?"

"Just about every blue collar man in this town."

McBride frowned, looked down at his watch and said to Durham: "Radio dispatch. Tell Gale we've left the hospital, and she's going to have to send someone else to watch for Rivard on this end. We've got to have a conversation with Mr. Lancaster."

The tears had stopped falling from eyes too upset, too frustrated to cry any longer. There was nothing left that she could give: her soul had rolled down her cheeks and dripped from her chin, leaving small salty patches on the front of her shirt.

She was not resigned—she refused to accept the position she was in—she rebelled against it with every band of her fiery heart—only, a sense of rebellion was all there was: she had a desire, but no means to implement it; she had a wish, but no ability to make it come true. She wanted desperately to move; she wanted it with a passion greater than any she had ever known—and the degree to which she wanted it was the degree to which she loved her husband's life.

It was Thomas she felt she had failed: it was her greatest value she felt she had abandoned.

I'm sorry!—she internally cried. I'm sorry that I can't rush to help. I'm trapped in this hideous, unmoving body! I'm stuck in a body that has chained my soul, a body that is imprisoning my soul. If only—if only I could make my soul defy my body! If only I could make my body serve my soul, make it act in unison with it, place the two in harmony. If only I were a whole person . . . I could help . . . if only I were whole . . . .

Her thoughts were broken by the sound of a voice in the hall. Though her door was closed, she could clearly make out what the man was saying: "Yes. Yes, I know. I was surprised and disgusted to find them already here. I know! . . . You—*what?!* They've been there, too? . . . Oh, oh I see. They're just pulling up. I don't know—tell them anything. Anything to keep them away from here . . . Keep them there—stall them!"

Who is that man?—Constance wondered. Who is to be kept away from here? Why does he sound so frantic? Does it have something to do with Tom?

She strained her ears, in order to hear the rest: "I know for a fact he'll come back by here. That is—if he wants to make a quick get-away . . . Because his car is parked outside the gym, that's why! No fool would try to flee on foot . . . Yes. Yes, his car has been here the entire time, we've been watching it. Don't you worry: we've got a better eye on this place than the cops."

If he's not a police officer, Constance thought, who is he? Whose car is parked outside the gym? It must be—could it be Tom's car? That means he's still here! That means he hasn't fled. Oh God, that means there's still a chance for me to get to him. There's still a chance! Let me keep listening.

"Don't be a fool—we can't turn back now! It's got to be done, as soon as possible . . . I know the stakes are high. I know things are getting hot—hotter by the minute! But don't you see? Those incompetent fools haven't been able to get him. It's up to us, now it's all up to us . . . Yes. Good. I'm glad you're starting to see. We have a duty. We can't turn our backs and let him get away, just because we're scared. We have to stand up for justice . . . Yes. It's all been arranged. I'm standing outside the room right now. What number? 406."

That's my room number—Constance thought, feeling a prick at the back of her neck. Why is that man talking about my room?

"I told you I don't know! I don't know whether he'll come by for her or not. But there's the car. If he's aware that they're on to him, he'll avoid this place like the plague. If he doesn't know—well, *we'll* take care of it . . . Yes. Yes, he's there. He's been in his position since dawn. Best deer hunter in the frat. Took the county record last year. No—heh, heh!—it's not a seven-pointer he's after."

Constance did not know what the man in the hallway was talking about. Her conscious mind was so overwhelmed with anguish—she was so distracted by the fact she could not move, the fact she was helpless—she could not make sense of the partial conversation. Just when she had been certain the man was talking about Thomas, he had changed the subject to something totally unrelated: deer hunting. She cursed herself for thinking that the stranger's conversation had anything to do with Thomas.

She fell back into despair. Fresh tears began to fill her eyes: small pricks of anger, anguish and exhaustion transformed into drops of liquid misery, blurring her vision. Her eyes brimmed, were about to spill over, when she heard the click of the latch: the person was entering her room.

Instinctively, she shut her eyes. She remained still, pretending she was sleeping. She peered at the unknown person through tiny slits disguised by dark veils of lowered lashes.

The man was wearing some type of uniform. She thought she saw two shades of blue: navy slacks and a sky-colored shirt. Through the thick screen of eyelashes, she could not be certain. Was it blue that she was seeing, or two shades of green? She knew that hospital security wore blue; janitorial staff wore a muddy shade of olive.

Her heart nearly stopped, when the man—it was definitely a man—stood and peered at her closely. She could see his eyes, carefully watching her face. With mounting panic, she thought: Can he see my eyes? Does he know that I'm watching?

The man looked at her with narrowed eyes, as if he were trying to discover something. After a time, it appeared that he had his answer, because he turned and walked to the window.

When his back was turned, Constance opened her eyes a little wider.

I was right, she thought. Blue uniform is hospital security. He's got the belt, the radio, a cell phone. I wonder what hospital security wants with me.

She saw the man clutch the windowsill and train his eyes on some object.

What is he looking at?—she thought. There's nothing out there but a town park, and behind that, the edge of the forest. Why did he come to my room to look at a line of old trees?

The man had something in mind, when he pulled a pair of tiny binoculars from a case on his belt.

Does he see a deer?—Constance thought. He said something about hunting, and bagging a seven-pointer. Maybe there's a deer feeding along the trees.

She changed her mind, when she saw the man raise his arm and give a signal. The hairs on her head began to rise, and she slammed her lids shut—not against the sight, but against a sudden thought: People don't give signals to animals. He's communicating with somebody. *Somebody is watching my room from the trees.*

She opened her eyes slightly, and looked at the man through the cracks beneath her lids. She felt one eye twitch, wanting to fully open. The twitch turned into a spasm, her eyelashes felt like the vertical bars of a cage, imprisoning her vision, but she kept them lowered. A stab of fear told her to keep up the pretense. She did not want the man to know she was awake. She could not let him discover that she had seen his gesture.

The next several minutes were torture. The man raised his arm, and again gave the signal. Constance wanted to shout: What are you doing? Get away from that window!—but did not say a word; she did not let out an audible breath; she did not exhale at all. She was caught in an excruciating form of torture: the task of keeping her facial muscles perfectly still. She had never missed her unimpeded vision more.

The man lowered his arm and slipped the binoculars back in the case on his belt. Without so much as glancing at Constance, he turned and marched from the room. The door slammed shut with one decisive snap.

Her eyes popped, as if jolted by the door. Some invisible string passed between her eyelids and the doorknob. As soon as the door closed, her eyes were open.

They instantly passed to the window. Fortunately, her wheelchair was positioned in a place where she could look through the glass. Her eyes became scanners, as they moved back and forth along the line of trees.

What was he looking at?—she thought. Who is hiding in the woods? What the hell do they want with my room?

A cold suspicion drove through her skull like an icicle: They want to kill me. They've staked out my room and they are plotting to kill me. There's a man outside, waiting for the time to strike.

Her certainty of the man's intention was second only to her certainty that she would not allow him to succeed. They might think my life is worthless, she thought, they may think that they are doing me a favor by plotting to end it—but they are totally wrong! My life has never been as valuable to me as it is this minute: I've got to rescue Thomas, and I have every intention of doing it: nothing in the world—not even a bullet in my chest—will stop me now.

Her eyes flicked over each tree with violent defiance; her pupils dilated into black wells of bitter scorn. She said: "Where are you, hidden sniper? Which tree is disguising your frame? Are you a coward, hiding behind a sprawling maple?—Or are you fairly bold, standing up against a slender spruce?"

She saw a flash between two trees. Certain it was the glint of a gun barrel, she said to the marksman: "You are a fool. You are a fool to think that I'd let you take me now. Yesterday, I would have told you to shoot. Yesterday, I would have leaped up from this chair to place myself directly in the path of your bullet. Yesterday, I would have looked upon you as my savior, and thought of that gun as a righteous tool.

"Today, I won't let you have it. I'm not going to die, and let my husband follow. I'm not going to give up, and send Thomas to his grave. I won't let you finish me, and finish the thing that my death was going to make possible: Thomas's life, in the truest and only sense of the word: his life free of guilt and marked by joy. Because I love it—life unburdened and unimpeded—I'm going to place my burdened, impeded body in service to it. You're not going to take that from me now."

The flashing gun barrel moved further down the line. She wondered whether the marksman was adjusting his position to better hit the target. Though her vision was keen, she could not see all that the security guard had seen with his binoculars.

Some security guard!—Constance thought. What gave him the right to decide that my life isn't worth a damn? How dare anyone think they can make that choice for me! I'm the only one who has the right to make that choice!

She pressed her lips into an inflexible line. Her mind was as straight and inflexible as her lips. She had come to a conclusion, and nothing would stop her—not even the marksman's bullet. She was going to live, to save her husband's life.

A man stepped out onto the street, and began to walk up the road. His pace was even and unhurried. There was no sign of distress or agitation in the smooth planes of his face. He was, perhaps, the only person in the entire town who was not frightened or uneasy.

He had no cause for uneasiness. There was, for him, nothing to fear. Because he was certain—because his mind had discovered truth and was intransigent—all trace of prior fear and uneasiness had vanished, like the previous night's frost on a sunny autumn day. He knew, beyond any shadow of doubt, that the action he intended was the right one: he knew that he had to save Constance from the fate of the deer; he had to act for her welfare. Even if it killed him—and he knew the act would take his life—he had to grant her request. It mattered more than his life.

He placed one foot down on the road; he lifted one foot up, out and ahead of the other, then repeated the process, alternating sides. He did not pitch or hurl his body through space, moving with a sense of urgency or desperation; he did not cringe when an automobile passed him by. Because there was no trace of urgency, desperation or cowardice in his soul, there was no trace of these things in his bearing. There was only that which is the result of their absence: an almost tangible—but wholly untouchable—sense of calm. Because there was no struggle—physical, mental, spiritual—there was serenity; because there was serenity, there was its highest form: a state of perfect Grace.

Thomas Rivard walked along the road that he had traveled hundreds of times, over many years. It was his body following the familiar path—the very same organs and limbs that had always carried him along—but a wholly different person animating that body, a gentle and unexpected stranger.

He watched his foot rise from the pavement and

come back down on it—he felt his leg muscles tighten and stretch—he saw his breath departing his mouth, a pearly, evanescent cloud—and all he could think was: It's so simple—what freedom when we do not struggle!

He had always relished the sensation of his organs and muscles, his tendons and veins operating at their optimal capacity—he had always lived for the exhilarating rush of making his body work. Now, when his body was working harder than it ever had—when his body was carrying him toward a purpose that was the hardest and most important, the crucial and definitive moment of his life—he marveled that the steps he took were easy—not in the sense of being carefree, but in the sense of being certain. Certain steps are the opposite of forced ones.

That was the quality that had defined his character, up until now: all his life he had been insistent—insistent that his clients live the way he thought they should live, insistent that their failure to do so was nothing but his own disastrous incompetence. He had tried to make people, shape people, *force* people: he had been convinced that their lives were something he could manage and control—and it was nothing other than the very best intentions that had made him insistent about it.

But now, now as he walked along the road, headed toward the hospital and Constance, certainty had replaced insistence, and he felt no desire to fight or struggle against reality any longer. Clear-eyed judgment had replaced dogma, and the words of

Richard Dunn reverberated in fully receptive ears: What is the human heart, Thomas? Is it a mass of muscle pumping blood and air—or is it more? When you say you want to protect life, what exactly is it you want to save—an anatomy and physiology, or a human being?

Rivard knew that the heart he was going to protect was the most precious and noble heart on earth: the unlimited heart of his incredible wife. He knew that she had asked him to defend—not an anatomy and physiology—but a human being. No life was more precious to him than hers. No matter what the consequences to himself—and he knew there would be dire consequences—he had to avoid the law just long enough to carry out her wish, which was his.

He was going to live, to save his wife's life.

He made the long trek from his house to the hospital without drawing attention. The town was empty—everyone had been warned that there was a killer on the loose—and most people had gone home, locked their doors and closed their curtains. There was no activity. No one stirred. If Rivard had not known better, he would have thought that it was a holiday. The town looked like it had settled into the sedentary lull of a nap. He knew that the appearance was deceptive, and the abnormal quiet was just a preface to the tumult that would occur when the authorities discovered where he was.

He thought of this in a detached, impersonal way, as if it were of no especial significance, neither to himself nor to his future. The fact was, he knew he did not have a future; he knew that his actions in Richard Dunn's office had eliminated the possibility of retaining his former life. What is more: he did not resent the fact or wish to challenge it. He was fully prepared to accept responsibility for his action: it was wrong, and he had to pay the price. His only hope was that he could defer payment until the time he had completed his final, professional obligation as a medical doctor. If he could just complete his one last medical duty, he would accept what came next without a struggle. If it looked like he would be arrested first—if it looked like the authorities would get to him, before he got to Constance—he would put up the fight of his life. There was no force on earth—not even a police officer's bullet—that would stop him from saving his wife.

He thought of these things in an abstract, dreamy way, as if none of it was fully real, as he calmly rose up the front steps of the hospital entrance. It did not occur to him to sneak or hide—the serenity that had entered his soul had made him incapable of covering his actions, acting as though they were wrong—so he did what any man of self-esteem would do: he walked through the front door.

There was a brilliant flash as he placed his hand on the metal bar, depressed it and walked into the lobby: the large glass doors had been freshly polished, and Rivard caught his sun-flooded reflection for one brief second, before he set foot on the carpet.

Two people thought the same thing

simultaneously: He looks like hell.

The person behind the front desk shared Rivard's thought, and added the following: Must be here for the pre-holiday community meal in the cafeteria.

Rivard gave the receptionist no reason to think otherwise: he looked exactly like what he had been all through the previous night and into the morning: a wandering vagrant without direction.

But now he did have a direction. Without a second's hesitation, with no hint of reluctance or uncertainty, Rivard walked over to the sign-in clipboard on the counter and wrote: Thomas Rivard, M.D. Pick up wife.

The receptionist did not glance at the clipboard, or even give the man a second thought. Free turkeys and oranges were being distributed to the needy, on account of the coming holiday, and she had no reason to think that the man was at the hospital for any other reason than free food. He certainly looked hungry enough, and his clothes were typical of the types that took advantage of the hospital's charitable functions: sopping wet and hanging like rags.

No, there was nothing peculiar or alarming about this man: he was just another one of the down-and-out, poor souls who was looking for a hot meal and a handout, prior to the holidays. The only difference between this vagrant and the others was that he had come through the front door, rather than using the loading-dock entrance. The homeless people usually gathered at the back of the building, near the kitchen, so they could examine the contents of the dumpster before shuffling inside.

The receptionist looked up once, giving nothing but a fleeting, perfunctory glance at the man as he walked through the lobby. She observed his appearance and made an instantaneous judgment about his circumstances, motivations and character. She did not question the accuracy of her judgment: there was simply no reason to do so. She was just glad the beggar had not attempted to hang around the front desk and talk. She could not stand speaking to people like that, answering their mumbled questions. Thankfully, this one had displayed no interest in conversation, and she continued to clack away at her keyboard, preparing the latest hospital memorandum.

Rivard left the lobby and headed to the wing of the hospital housing ER and Intensive Care. He took the shortest route—the direct path—knowing that he would make his exit near the gymnasium, after he had gone to Constance. His car was parked near his office, and he would carry his wife the short distance from his office to the car. There was, however, quite a distance between his wife's recovery room—which he had found listed on a special clipboard—and his office next to the gymnasium. He would have to wheel her through the entire facility to get to his office. He was bound to run into people; there was no avoiding it. His only hope was that the people he did encounter were not aware of the latest news. The chances were slim—his status as a criminal was probably common knowledge—but he had to take the risk. There was no question of changing his mind; it was set: he was going to get Constance and they would make it out of the hospital. He would bring her home, as she wished.

Rivard's presence did not cause a single raised eyebrow as he walked through the corridors of the hospital, toward Constance's room.

Has my appearance changed that much?—he thought. I've seen all the regular staff members and none of them recognized me. They didn't even glance in my direction! I've seen orderlies and janitors, nurses and—oh! There's Dr. Singer!

Rivard turned to the wall, and pretended to be studying some document while the emergency room surgeon approached. Rivard heard the sound of distinct, confident footsteps—he knew his long-time colleague by the sound of his steps—and prepared himself for the equally familiar sound of Dr. Singer's voice.

The footsteps grew louder; they were coming close—Rivard felt beads of cold sweat spring to his forehead. Each step seemed to echo, each step stood out like the measured fall of a hammer on an anvil, and Rivard felt the unbearable pounding as a series of blows on his brain. The pounding intensified—Rivard held his breath as Dr. Singer came closer—was directly beside him—stood on the very same row of tiles—Rivard felt about to burst from lack of freedom and oxygen—he felt that he would surely die, deprived of breath and identity, forced to become a hallway fixture—until suddenly freedom and oxygen became possible—the steps did not slow down or change, but miraculously continued their even, pounding rhythm on the hallway floor, growing faint, and then inaudible when the surgeon rounded the corner.

I must look like a completely different person, Rivard thought, knowing it was true. He expelled another breath held by tension. I must look nothing like myself—no one has greeted or stopped me. He frowned and thought: This is all for the best. An altered appearance will help me rescue Constance.

He felt a stab of anguish, as soon as he thought of his wife. What will Constance think, when she sees me like this? Instead of the proud, masculine figure she married, she'll see a run-down criminal. Instead of a rescuer, she'll see someone who needs rescuing. I won't even need to tell her about any of what's happened. It will be written all over my face.

It was this thought that pained him, more than any other. More than the threat of trial and imprisonment, Rivard dreaded watching his wife's face perk up, when she saw him—then fall, when she saw what a mess he was in. He dreaded going to her in a questionable state. He was coming to her aid, he was going to grant her request, and instead of looking like a man in control of his actions and thus destiny, he looked like a person who had been trampled by fate.

But I won't let that happen!—he thought, rejecting any notion of helplessness. I am in control, I have possession of my faculties, and even if I can't turn back the hands of the clock to undo my actions, I can make up for them now. I was wrong, Constance was right, and I'm going to help her, even if it kills me.

He was standing in front of her door. His eyes fell on the number: 406. He placed his hand on the doorknob and gave it a turn.

The car doors slammed shut. Joe McBride and Ray Durham exchanged glances before McBride turned the key in the ignition.

"What the hell kind of cockamamie story was that?"

"Good question," Durham said, adjusting his visor against the sun. "That man was full of it. Five empty shelves—not one spray paint can in the entire store—and he's 'on back order.' Can't remember who came in and cleaned him out. Right."

"And not one gallon of red paint—but a full row of everything else. Again—no clue who came in for it."

"Said it was probably tourists, someone passing through—that's why he can't remember."

McBride cleared his throat. "Tell me something, Durham: When was the last time you ever heard of tourists stocking up on paint?"

"And gallons of Barn Red—exactly what skiers and leaf peepers need."

The men broke out laughing. McBride said, "You never know: maybe a group of snowboarders will want to stop and touch up a farm on their way to the mountain." They laughed again.

"You know what the worst part was? That bit about the scarecrow. Telling us to drive around to all the cornfields and see if one is missing. Right. Someone had a voodoo doll of Tom Rivard standing in their field."

McBride's face became grave, at the mention of the effigy. More than any other part of the scene at the gymnasium, he hated the effigy. It filled him with a sense of cosmic dread, as if it signified far more than mere hatred of a man. He could not put his finger on it, he was not certain why the sight of the stick thrust in the doll's back made the hairs on the back of his neck stiffen and rise—he had investigated many crime scenes involving real people and never had a reaction like that—but there was something about it that filled him with terror—not for himself, not for his own safety—but for the world in general, for the world and anything good. A nameless instinct of warning told McBride that the effigy portended something evil.

He was stewing over these thoughts, he and Durham had lapsed into a somber silence, when several whining beeps and radio static were followed by the dispatcher's voice: "Thirteen-hundred to thirteen-twenty. Thirteen-twenty, do you copy?"

McBride pressed the button to his speaker: "Yes, I copy. Go ahead, Gale."

"Tom Rivard's location is confirmed."

The police officers glanced at one another, before looking away to gather their thoughts. Both Joe McBride and Ray Durham had become so wound up with the situation at the gymnasium, they had forgotten all about their initial search. They had forgotten the killer, in a quest for those who wanted him dead.

The full reality of their original purpose came back by way of the dispatcher's voice: "Did you copy that, thirteen-twenty? Tom Rivard's location is confirmed."

"Ten-four. What is the confirmed location?"

"Memorial Hospital. Receptionist said he passed through the main doors. She did not recognize him: he's disguised like a bum. When she was printing off the wanted posters for hospital distribution—the photo issued by the barracks—she realized it was him. Said he headed into the ER / Intensive Care wing of the facility. Receptionist states that suspect's wife is in critical care, room 406. Over."

Silence followed, as both McBride and Durham realized what was happening: Rivard was making good on his threat: he was headed to the hospital to slay his wife.

"Did you copy that, thirteen-twenty? Rivard is at Memorial, headed for Intensive Care, recovery room 406. Over."

"Ten-four. Fifteen-hundred and I are on our way. Over and out."

With a renewed sense of urgency, the two officers sped down the road in the direction of the hospital. Flashing blue lights and a piercing wail alerted the sky that they were coming, and that they had been given the strictest of orders: any sign of resistance—

shoot to kill.

Bill Metcalf had not moved. He was incapable of moving. A combination of bewilderment, fright, anger and exhaustion had left him immobilized. He wanted to collapse—his body would not let him. He felt an overwhelming desire to fall to sleep—or unconsciousness—his body would not obey. Everything that had occurred over the past several days came down like an oppressive weight, paralyzing his body, preventing him from either moving on with it, or giving up. All that he could do was stare—stare at the horrific sight in the gymnasium.

If he had had the mental strength to formulate coherent thoughts, or put them into words—he was long past the point of having the energy to think—these would have been the thoughts: It's all my fault. Every single bit of it. I have no one to blame for this nightmare but myself. I alone am responsible. Why am I responsible? Because I didn't get to Tom in time. I didn't help him get off drugs . . . .

Bill stared at the twisted, demonic-looking face that had been spray-painted in the corner of the room. It was hideously ugly and, as such, perfectly matched his mood, and the way he felt about himself: There you are, Metcalf. You dragged your feet and this is the result. None of this would have happened if you had gotten him into rehab when you first learned about his drug problem. If you had just recognized how serious the problem was . . . .

The demonic face winked. Bill did not know whether he was delirious from exhaustion, or whether the face had come to life. Either way, the demon-face began to talk.

"Oh, come on, Metcalf—stop deluding yourself. You absolutely knew how serious the problem was. That's just an excuse: lack of knowledge is a good cover-up for something you don't want to admit: fear. You don't want to admit that you were scared to talk to Tom."

Though Bill did not speak out loud, he replied to the demon in his head.

But I did talk to Tom!

"The conversation you had the morning after Stanley Humphries collapsed in his yard doesn't count. Tom was so high—he didn't know what was going on. He wasn't prepared to listen to a word you said."

That's not true! I mean—I know Tom wasn't listening—but it wasn't because of any failure on my part. I let him know just where things stood. I let him know that the boys were on to him, and that there was help for his condition—right here in this hospital! I did what I could!

"Oh really? Take a look around. Your assistance did a world of good. Your help went over so well that—not only is Tom still on drugs—he also managed to kill his old professor. You didn't just fail to help, Metcalf: you let things get worse."

I couldn't help it! Tom is arrogant and stubborn and—beyond help! His type doesn't admit defeat—not ever!

The demon-face began to laugh. Its lips curled upward in a malicious grin. It said, “Whether he admits it or not, friend, he’s headed in that direction. The people who created me weren’t kidding.”

Bill shuddered as the face winked at him before it grew still. He did not know whether he had imagined the conversation, or whether his exhausted brain had produced a hallucination. Either way, it was completely unsettling.

He took another survey of the gymnasium. Each time his eyes fell on some new form of ugliness his body shrank, as if receding against signs of an acute disease. The degree of malice displayed in the vandalism was disturbing, and Bill had trouble understanding how a group formed to protect the community could wind up sabotaging it.

How did it ever come to this?—Bill thought. Why this outpouring of ugliness and hate? I know they’re jealous of Tom—but enough to wish him dead? Enough to destroy the building?

Bill looked at the dark red globs of paint running down the wall. There was no question that the color had been chosen because it resembled blood. He closed his eyes against one of the most disturbing sights he had ever seen. Being an emergency responder, he routinely encountered sights of running blood. None of those sights had affected him like this: with an automobile accident or sudden crisis, everyone works tirelessly to halt the flow of blood; here, they intended to spill it. They had made an exhibit out of death.

He did not know what to do, what steps to take. Another emotion had been added to the combination of bewilderment, fright, anger and exhaustion: horror. He was horrified that his neighbors—the men he had lived with and worked with, the men whose children all attended the same school—had done something so totally vicious. He was stunned that they could have carried out—

Bill's eyes paused on the effigy the same moment his mind raised the question: How *did* they carry this out?

There was nothing equivocal about it: the vandalism was a giant, concerted effort—not some quick, spur-of-the-moment job—and would have taken many hands, over a sustained period of time. How did the group avoid attracting attention? How did the vandals not get caught? Where was hospital security the entire time this was going on?

Suddenly it all fell into place. Bill thought: Grady Bullock is a member of Males for Public Defense. Hospital security was in on it.

The pricks that ran up the center of his back had less to do with the effigy lying on the floor than the memory of Grady Bullock's face, when he had walked up on the state police. Bill had not noticed it at the time, but now it was perfectly clear: there was a reason the normally gregarious Grady Bullock had not opened his mouth to chat—there was a reason his usually friendly face had been pinched into a set of closed, horizontal lines—there was a reason the man had disappeared as quickly as he had come: Grady Bullock had been part of it—not in the sense of stringing up the effigy or flinging globs of paint at the wall—though that, too, was possible—but in the sense of letting it happen, pretending it was not happening—turning a blind eye while the destruction was carried out, under the pretense of attending to some other section of the hospital. A crime of this magnitude could only have occurred with the aid of an accomplice—in this case, the very person entrusted to patrol the grounds.

Bill thought of McBride and Durham, and that they had gone to Burt Lancaster for information. He wished desperately that he had some way to alert them that the man they wanted was here, right in the building, that in order to prevent the threats in spray paint from becoming reality, the police officers had to get back here.

Bill paced back and forth over the blotched floor of the gymnasium. His mind and his body were in a state of frenzied agitation. What if they don't discover Grady in time?—he thought. What if Burt sends them off in a false direction, and they don't get to Rivard before Grady does? What if Grady and his gang already know where Tom is, and they are plotting his murder? What if someone is lying in wait for Tom this very second, ready to take aim, to pull back the trigger and—

Bill nearly tripped, when he saw the message on the floor. He regained his balance, blinked, and squinted down at the letters scribbled in dark red paint:

Fitness Nazi and his bimbo wife are dead meat.

A cold flood of panic washed away everything but the words. Bill froze, and cursed the very marrow in his bones. He had become so wound up in the fresh turn of events, he had forgotten to go back for her; Bill had forgotten to go back for Constance.

Terrified that he might be too late—terrified that Constance had gone home with Millie—gone home to where she was a sitting duck, an easy target for both her husband and the murderous mob—Bill fled the gymnasium and headed for her room. Determined to save her from an awful fate, rushing as if life itself depended on it—Bill tore through the hospital to where he had left Constance: Room 406.

Grady Bullock sat in his small, dimly-lit office, two fists pressed to the table, and thought: I did it. I did what I needed to do. The worst part is over. Now I can relax.

He thought these things and knew they were lies. There would be no relaxation—none was possible. He was the furthest thing from relaxed: his heart was racing, beating frantically, like a rabbit's heart; his breath was quick and shallow—labored, as though he were wheezing; cold sweat oozed from the pores on his forehead, even though the day—and he—was cold; he had to keep mopping his hairline.

He was nervous, anxious, rattled: distress vibrated every cell of his body until he shook. He could not be certain whether he had carried it out in secret, or whether she had noticed. He had thought that she had been asleep. He had been totally certain at the time, but now—

What if she wasn't?—he thought. What is she was only pretending to be sleeping? What if she was awake the entire time, with her eyes open just wide enough to see it all? What if she is a good actress and, suspecting something right away, put on a convincing act? What if her lowered eyelashes were functioning as a screen, to hide the motion of her watchful eyes?

He grabbed a dirty towel, to wipe the slick of sweat from the palms of his hands. He had been confident, completely self-assured at the time. While he had been in her room, it had seemed so . . . easy. But now . . . now he was certain of nothing, and nothing was easy. The police were around, that boob Bill Metcalf was meddling in it all, and he could not be certain that she had been sleeping.

If she saw any of it—his paranoid mind thought—if she saw me gesture to Byron, the whole thing is over. She would have called for the nurse as soon as I left the room. They would have studied the tree line, to find what I was looking at. They would have seen Byron, standing up against the spruce. They would have called the police.

Grady Bullock grimaced. At the very same moment he thought of the police, the voice of the dispatcher came over his scanner.

"Thirteen-hundred to thirteen-twenty. Thirteen-twenty, do you copy?"

"Yes, I copy. Go ahead, Gale."

"Tom Rivard's location is confirmed."

Every fiber of Grady Bullock's body leaped, separated and unraveled, until he was nothing but a loose skein, heaped upon the floor. The strands lay in a giant coil that quickly became a snarl, tangled and twisted. His face took on the disorganized look of squiggly yarn.

"Did you copy that, thirteen-twenty? Tom Rivard's location is confirmed."

"Ten-four. What is the confirmed location?"

"Memorial Hospital."

At the sound of these words, Grady's face went rigid. The loose strands of his skein body wound into a tight coil, which became a snake. The fibers of Grady's body condensed into one long serpent, caught in a corner and ready to strike.

He did not have to hear the rest of it. When the dispatcher said "Room 406," he sprung from the floor. Each step he took as he raced down the hall was a venomous leap. Two thoughts animated his reptilian body: I've got to give Byron the signal to abort. The action's going to happen inside.

When he opened the door, when he stood inside her room, when he saw her sitting in a chair, looking back at him, he thought: Yes, they are connected. They always have been and always will be: my wife and my profession, Constance and my life.

When he opened the door, when he entered the

room, when she saw him standing, looking back at her, she thought: Yes, they are connected. They always have been and always will be: my husband and my values, Thomas and my life.

The thing that he dreaded did not happen. Constance did not look at him, seeing what he appeared to be; she looked at him, seeing what he was.

She had no reason to doubt or fear. Thomas did not look at her, seeing what she appeared to be; he looked at her, seeing what she was.

They looked at each other, saying nothing. They looked at each other—through all appearances, past the outer shells, bruised and beaten. There was no shell, costume or mask. There was no veil, where things were hidden. They were naked before each other, though clothed to the rest of the world: no matter what state their bodies had descended to, no matter what nature had caused them to bear—their souls were untouched—their souls rose, met and merged within the air. It was achieved with the meeting of their eyes.

There was suddenly no distance between them. It dissolved—was overcome, transcended, surpassed. Though he stood at one end of the room, though he was several yards away from her, he was next to her, touching her, inside her. His eyes both penetrated and enveloped her, as her eyes both penetrated and enveloped him.

He hesitated to take a step forward. It seemed like a superfluous act, as if there was no need. Their souls had melded with the meeting of their eyes, their souls had broken through that one part of their bodies left untouched by pain or disaster, and it seemed that any sudden movement would sever the connection.

He hesitated, resented to move—but lost. Time with its unerring steady tick goaded him on, like a beat he could not ignore. The physical reality of distance could be transcended—the merging of two separate souls had been achieved with the convergence of sight—but time could not be conquered. Time alone necessitated action. The urgency of the situation pressed upon him; each passing moment was a summons calling, home.

He took a step forward.

She was suddenly uncertain of her part. Any intention of rescuing Thomas was forgotten in her desire to be rescued. Here he was, a man of unlimited strength—masculinity personified. She did not know what it was she had been thinking. All of her former plans and motives dissolved into a single emotion: the desire to surrender. It was largely unconscious, a feeling that she wanted to relinquish control, to let him do what he would with her. She felt a weakness that was not lack of strength, but worship for one who is strong.

But even this came to a sudden halt. Two things occurred simultaneously which restored her former plan: a voice from the far end of the corridor shouted, "Get ready! We're going in armed!" The same instant, a black shadow passed in front of the window, obscuring daylight, darkening the room. The ominous bird and the voice merged in her mind as the sudden recollection of the forgotten threat: the sniper in the woods, with his gun trained on the window.

Thomas heard the voice in the corridor and knew in an instant he was caught. Every muscle in his body tensed, as his mind shifted back and forth between the crucial choice of fight or flight.

Her pupils dilated as she, too, considered a course of action. Her mind was a frantic whirl of questions: Where can he go? Is he trapped? If he steps into the hallway, the police will have him. If he ducks into another room when they tell him to freeze, they'll shoot. If he tries to exit through the window, that gunman will mistake him for me, and—

Rivard stepped forward and she suddenly understood. That bullet's not for me!—she thought. That bullet's meant for him!

There was no time for speech. Rivard had made the decision to seize his wife and run. In order to get to her, he had to pass before the window.

There was only one thing she could do. There was no question, reluctance or vacillation about it. It was not a miracle; the thing occurred because she willed it.

Constance rose.

She rose up on her feet, one smooth motion that began with the muscles of her abdomen and spread out like a glorious wave. Her mind sent a message to her stomach muscles, which sent a command to the flesh of her buttocks and hips; her hips gave simultaneous orders to her back and thighs, which demanded obedience from her arms and lower legs. The motion that began in her core reached completion with the tendons of her neck and feet.

But that did not end it.

Constance told herself to rise from the chair—and she rose. She told herself to stand—and she stood. She told herself that she could move—and she did.

There was no gulf separating the function of her soul and the function of her body; her soul and her body were unified. Her arms and legs had become infused with life born of a purpose, a life-saving purpose, and nothing on earth could keep them down under a goal of that kind: no matter what, she had to keep Thomas from the window.

She hurled her body through space, flying to meet him. The force of her self-propelled motion created a gust of wind.

He rushed forward to meet her, startled and overcome by joy, not knowing why she held out her hands and screamed, "Get back!" Confused, both happy and desperate, thinking that they could now flee together, he continued forward. He was ecstatic when she flung herself into his arms.

There was a sudden violent pop, and a crashing cascade of shattered glass, as the marksman's bullet broke the window. He felt her body tighten, cling to him with a rigid tension that he thought was fear. He was about to say: Don't worry!—but his open mouth would produce no sound. Her body softened, quickly melting.

He looked down at her back, his chin thrust over her shoulder. There was a small round puncture mark, and a red-black stream of blood. In the cold daylight freely passing through the window, the indentation was unmistakable.

He clutched her shaking body, and plunged his finger into the hole to halt the stream of blood. He felt her distressed body spasm.

The police officers entered the room in time to see Rivard fall to his knees, cradling Constance's body. Joe McBride was about to shout: Put her down! Hands behind your head!—but saw Rivard's face and lowered his gun. He put his hand on Durham's arm, silently sending a signal to his partner. The police officers bowed their heads and were gone.

Rivard moved large, tear-filled eyes from the empty doorway to his wife's face. Several drops spilled over and formed a tiny pool in the hollow at the base of her neck. He looked into her eyes, which were the clearest, brightest eyes that he had ever seen. It almost looked as though they were sparkling.

She smiled at him, and he choked on a sob.

She said in a voice barely audible, "I did it because I want it, Thomas: want more than anything for you to live."

He felt her body quake, and knew that the vibrations came from him.

"I made it happen. I beat it. I didn't let it get me"—there was a pause—"or you."

His body shook. He could not control the quivering of his chest and arms.

"Isn't that what you wanted me to do? Does that make you proud?"

His hands clutched her body. His voice was broken and strained. "I am more proud of you than I can say." Her eyes glistened and he gasped. He spoke through a sob that wracked his body. "You are a hero, Constance." He cradled her neck with the palm of his hand; with the other hand he touched her cheek.

He said, "My wife."

Her body quivered, then stiffened. With a great deal of concentration, eyes glowing as she looked at him, she said, "My husband." Her eyes contained the peaceful light of eternity.

It was several moments before she spoke again. When her voice came out, it was changed, growing weaker. She said, "I didn't give up. I fought for my world. I achieved it."

She closed her eyes. He wanted to speak, but his throat constricted his voice. She opened her eyes; there was no trace of sadness or fear in them, only joy, as she said: "I love you, Thomas."

His voice was faint and breathless, nearly a whisper. He steadied it, and said: "I love you, Constance."

She smiled at him with her eyes. She could no longer use her voice. She sent him a wordless message: *Do not fear for me, Thomas. Do not be afraid. You have your life to live, unburdened and untroubled. There will be no suffering. The suffering has ended. A clear path of happiness and joy awaits you. Go to it. Begin.*

She looked at him. Then she did not see him anymore. She saw Peace. She closed her eyes. Her body grew still. She went to it.

He held Constance in his arms. He placed her head against his chest and did not move until ER personnel entered the room and gently lifted her.

It was some time before he rose from the floor.

Bill Metcalf hesitated in the doorway. There were no words—nothing he could say. He did not try.

Rivard spoke first. His voice was toneless and unemotional. “Where are the police?”

“They’re coming back. They apprehended Grady. They saw him run when the sniper hit the window. Both he and the gunman are in custody.”

As Bill said this, the police officers stepped into the room. Before they could say anything, without hesitation or pause, Rivard walked across the room toward them. He silently placed himself into their hands.

He sat at a desk, head bent over papers. A large stack of books formed a tower looming over his head. He shook his head and reached for a pen. He drew thick black marks through several lines on the sheet. He reached for a book and, raising his head, glanced out the window.

The apple tree was dotted with chickadees. The small black and white birds were bouncing between the feeder and the branches, scattering sunflower seeds over a frosty bank of snow.

He smiled. For ten years he had watched the birds, and he had never tired of it. He had moved his office materials into the living room, and placed his desk beside the picture window, just so that he could watch the birds.

The birds had been there when he had returned to his home; the birds had been there during his ten years of research and rehabilitation: research—to find a cure for Rivard's disease; rehabilitation—to repair his heart. The birds were with him now, as he continued his work. The birds were there, singing their joyous song to a sun-flooded earth.

He bent his head over his papers, to continue his life's work—the purpose that had never wavered or changed—the purpose that had grown stronger over the years, reinforced with maturation—the purpose that was his beginning and end, his very reason for being: dedication to the furtherance of life: uncompromised commitment to keep hearts beating.

He felt the beating of his heart within his chest, he heard the glorious singing of Constance's chickadees, and both of these things were a song proclaiming fealty to existence.

THE END

Made in the USA
Lexington, KY
13 March 2010